THE NONSERIAL MURDERS

ANGO SAKAGUCHI

Translated by
SHELLEY MARSHALL

ISBN: 978-1-7349644-1-7

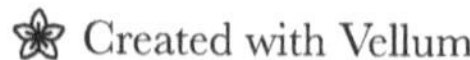 Created with Vellum

CONTENTS

1

TEN MILLION VULGAR HUMAN RELATIONSHIPS

At the end of June, Showa year 22 (1947), Utagawa Kazuma called to ask me to meet him at a small restaurant called Tsubohei in Nihonbashi. The proprietor of Tsubohei, Tsubota Heikichi, used to work as a cook for the Utagawa family. His wife, Teruyo, was a maid at the Utagawa residence. Kazuma's father, Utagawa Tamon, was a selfish lecher who was well-acquainted with mistresses, the company of geisha, and the seduction of maids. Teruyo, an attractive woman with charming features, was no exception. Tamon had her marry Tsubota Heikichi as his replacement and gave them money to open a small restaurant. During the war, Kazuma's Tokyo home suffered damage, so he stayed at Tsubohei on visits to Tokyo.

"The truth is I have an unusual request for you. I'd like you to spend the summer at my home?"

The journey to Kazuma's house deep in the mountains was an ordeal. After I got off the train, I faced a bus ride for about fifteen miles up mountain roads, followed by a walk close to two and a half miles. That's why many in our literary circle evacuated to his home during the war. Most importantly, his family brewed sake, and drinking sake was our other motivation.

"You probably won't understand my reason, but that fellow Mochizuki Wani unexpectedly showed up at the beginning of this month. Tango Yumihiko and Utsumi Akira appeared soon after. They said they received invitations to spend the summer from my younger sister, Tamao. I will reveal my shame only to you. This spring, Tamao had an abortion. She never said who the father was, and I still don't know. For about half a month, she's wandered Tokyo. Who knows where she's been staying? I have no idea what to do.

"As you know, Mochizuki Wani is a brutish, rude, and gross man. On the other hand, Tango Yumihiko is polite and smug like an English gentleman but is also an arrogant, vain, treacherous man, and a pervert. Utsumi Akira is the sole refreshing presence but typical of hunchbacks, his physique is hideous. All in all, he has nothing to offer. When together, all those three do is fight. Tamao finds this amusing and made it her business to invite them. I can't tolerate this.

"They quarrel and stare down each other. Sometimes the hunchback rages and sends the dishes on the table smashing to the floor. When one appears, another leaves in a huff. I've become both angry and sad. My mind is so jittery I can't leisurely read a book. When word got around, faces from the old days, the evacuees during the war, gathered under my roof to spend the summer. They said the place was perfect because Tokyo's bars and restaurants were shut down.

"That's their wish, but reality will save me. They aim to ease their boredom, but their presence suffocates me. Mokubei and Koroku's stay will bring me relief. They'll be a distraction. I need you to come, too. Mokubei and Koroku will be staying at the house. We're leaving Tokyo together the day after tomorrow."

"What about Utsugi-san?"

"Of course, she'll be with us. Kocho-san is coming, too. The theaters are closed for the summer."

Miyake Mokubei, a student of French literature, was the lover of the woman writer Utsugi Akiko, Kazuma's ex-wife. Being literary people, they discussed their situation and divorced. She's a beautiful woman, but Kazuma did not cause problems later. Mochizuki Wani did. During the evacuation, Akiko, Kazuma's then-wife, talked more and more with Mokubei. They decided to move to Tokyo after the war. Kazuma consented to a divorce. From the beginning, Kazuma's relationship with Akiko was troubling. For the most part, he is free of regrets.

Akiko was an extraordinarily sensual woman. During the evacuation, her relationship with Wani was more intimate than with Mokubei. However, Wani had no notion of absolute faithfulness and carried on with Tamao. Gossips spoke of his affairs with maids and women from the village. He thought of Akiko as a fruit or a snack after a meal. Fed up, she went with Mokubei, but her heart stayed with Wani. He was a popular author throughout Japan. His insolence, crudeness, and wildness probably charmed the passionate Akiko.

She was, instinctively, a doll-like woman and went to the mountain retreat because she could not suppress her jealousy or cut all ties with Wani. Mokubei was an intellectual, a scholar, and an oddball who fell in love with trifling women and let them lead him around by the nose. Consequently, he was a jealous man with a broken heart and more than a fool to accept Kazuma's invitation.

I accepted Kazuma's reason for these invitations but

also believed Kazuma hid a deeper reason for his enthusiasm over this plan. He had his eyes on Kocho. I think he wanted to seduce her.

Akashi Kocho was an actress and the wife of Hitomi Koroku, who hailed from a theatrical family. She embodied sex appeal and radiated sexual passion but preferred intellectuals over rough and wild men like Wani, who she hated. Hitomi Koroku was a stubborn pest and an indecisive, timid coward. He was a kind and friendly man but had difficulty making friends. Kocho loved Kazuma and would discard Koroku if Kazuma actively pursued her. She had a mind to pursue him.

In those days, Kazuma was a coward. Utsugi Akiko ran off with Miyake Mokubei. In the past, the women who left him suffered no regrets over abandoning him. Thus, darkness lurked in his heart. The evacuation guests ran off when the war ended. Of course, Koroku left with his wife, Kocho. Kazuma was a solitary man but summoned Spartan courage to see everyone off like a lover you desire more than anything. He seemed to be shut off in loneliness.

Once every month or two, Kazuma took the long journey to Tokyo. The changes in social conditions left a deep impression. In the spring of last year, he met his current wife, Ayaka.

During her college years, she wrote poems. Utagawa Kazuma, the genius of the intellectuals, was a foremost poet with the perfect amount of charm for literary women. Three or four times in those days, she brought her friends when she visited him. However, Ayaka had shallow interest and was indifferent to poetry. After graduating from the women's college, she never visited Kazuma again.

When he encountered her last year, Ayaka was living with a painter named Doi Pikaichi. Some said his paintings were unique. Others called him a genius, but I wouldn't go that far. He smeared lasciviousness all over a canvas that burst from surrealistic compositions. In a glance, the paintings were filled with charm that had both sensual and melancholy poetic sentiments. In reality, however, none of the severity of loneliness or nothingness was present.

He was a skilled businessman and a master who slathered colors in sync with the tastes of the age to fabricate similar works. The creation of the paintings was also commercial, and he was a master salesman. The post-war period was an age of hardship for artists. He contacted magazine companies and writers, made easy money by drawing illustrations, and had the unique style of a genius.

Kazuma seemed like a different man. He suppressed too much. The changes in the times marked the beginnings of his anger. His wife's infidelity spawned a rage that led to his single-minded, stubborn pursuit of a married woman.

Ayaka's beauty was exceptional. Her name was fitting. She was mysterious, loved amusements, and carefree. But she hated stubbornness and saw Kazuma's obsession and unbecoming aggression on his scowling face. She could be called a whore sent from heaven and hated poverty the most. The artist Doi Pikaichi drew illustrations and made good money, but high prices deflated his income. He couldn't afford a silk sock for one foot.

Kazuma was the scion of a prosperous family of sake brewers and owners of several hundreds of thousand hectares of mountains and forests. Although nothing to admire, huge sums of dark money fell into his hands. On each trip to Tokyo, he carried a small wad of bills from the cashbox. Even if the handful was smaller, the reduction wasn't apparent. In an environment where the people in the lower classes could not imagine the fistful of bills resembling tissue paper totaled 70 or 80,000 yen. Ayaka who loved amusements, delicious food, elegant clothes, and luxury fell in love with money. She simply gave Doi Pikaichi his walking papers and married Kazuma last autumn.

Doi Pikaichi's business acumen was indisputable. In a face-to-face business negotiation, Pikaichi told Kazuma the price was 200,000 yen to buy her outright, as one would buy freedom for a prostitute, and negotiating from 30,000 or 50,000 yen would take too much time. He began haggling at 100,000 yen and settled on 150,000 yen.

"What? That woman must be mine. If my flesh does not ... The pleasure in my body for her, like a European whore, makes me giddy. Am I a no-name hack poet? Soon she'll weep for me, apologize, and come home."

When Doi Pikaichi told me this, I thought this confident, made-in-Japan Don Juan was no good. Ayaka didn't see any difference between any man and a fart. She was an optimist who viewed the men of the world as objects to be chosen freely.

Doi Pikaichi's demand for 200,000 yen to purchase her was a blow to her pride. The wound was deep in this optimistic, beautiful woman's small pride because she thought of men as little more than flatulence. She filled with great anger. She did not fly into a rage or retaliate in revenge, but her fury showed on her face. She split up with him after a quarrel.

When I told Doi Pikaichi this, he roared with laughter. To him, the fight was stupid. Don't men give each other a chance to make up? Aren't fights between a man and a woman who are companions natural? A break-up after a bad argument is the key to getting closer. You see? He was the incarnation of confidence and conceit.

From the beginning, Doi Pikaichi's expectations were unrealistic. Ayaka thought nothing of him, but her marriage to Kazuma was unhappy. It was nothing like having an affair. Ayaka was a version of Princess Sotoori whose body glowed light beneath her clothes. A person able to see the allure in her beauty and youth radiating from her entire body saw her apathy, coldness, indifference, and almost no passion. Only shopping trips to Tokyo for extravagant articles gave her joy. She could buy the clothes and shoes that appealed to her. At the height of her happiness on the first night, she fell asleep in those clothes and shoes. She never did anything by the book.

Everything about her was adorable despite her considerable haughtiness of a queen like Cleopatra, selfishness, and inability to make allowances for the human heart. She never thought about a wife's duties or about her service to her husband. Thus, he was tormented by her indifference to anything he did. He failed in his futile efforts because she never saw him as special. He was ill at ease, regretful, and frustrated by any attempt to explain his resentment. He was ashen and overwhelmed. His expression betrayed one man's clumsiness, weakness, traces of agony, and distress.

Kazuma fell too much in love with his wife, Ayaka, and seemed to want to have an affair. He plotted to invite the evacuation gang for the summer and set his sights on Koroku's wife, Kocho. A rich boy like him was content to be loved and enjoyed pretending not to know. In particular, he was certain another man's wife secretly thought about him more than her husband. He enjoyed pretending not to know and toying with that love. This was his hobby and not an affair. He had little interest in jumping in and persuading her. He was not that smitten.

I thoroughly understood Kazuma's state of mind caused by his apparent sensual regret and shame for unexpectedly falling in love with his wife. Therefore, the unhappy part of him tempted the married Kocho and secretly depended on that love. He cruelly played with her pure love. He truly loved Ayaka but couldn't undo the harm he carelessly caused.

I called him a rich boy, but Kazuma was a forty-year-old, elite literary man and poet. Even if charmed by the devil, he was a man who had to bear the cross alone, and I didn't worry about him.

I had personal reasons for not wanting to accept this invitation. Of course, the outlaw Mochizuki Wani jumped on board. The plain pervert Tango Yumihiko and the cheerful hunchback Utsumi Akira marched in, became entangled, and exchanged glares and sneers. It was reasonable to want to call them a regiment of ghosts. Men and women in sticky entanglements resembling an old decayed spider's nest gathered under one roof. Aren't the wretched connections and entanglements unpleasant, vulgar, and hateful? I had a more forbidding reason not to join.

My wife, Kyoko, had been a mistress of Utagawa Tamon, Kazuma's father. Of his several mistresses, she received special favors. During the war, she had no reason to enter his home (his wife, Kajiko, was alive). He rented a house in the village and evacuated her there. She and I fell in love. When the war ended, I stole her, and we ran back to Tokyo.

Tamon's anger was violent. According to rumors, he could not suppress pent-up anger. Unfortunately, he was a powerful politician on the level of a minister and was banished to the place holding the greatest hope in my world. I became the hated villain for him to direct his fury. Last summer, his wife Kajiko died. He soon zeroed in on Shizue, a daughter in a respectable family in the village, and forced her to become his servant, a maid, and a mistress. His mood improved. After his banishment, his rested body favored and leered at the nineteen-year-old woman.

"I'm not like Mokubei and Koroku. Why should I go to your home? Even if your father's mood has changed somewhat, I don't want to see how uncomfortable it will be. Of course, I would tremble, but so would Kyoko. That's why I can't go."

"Please, don't be too quick and hear me out. I want to tell you, and only you, the whole story. This is my spiritual fairy tale and a bit of a popular true crime story."

He took a sealed letter from his pocket.

"Look at this. Someone's up to mischief."

This was written on ordinary letter paper.

Who killed Kajiko-sama?
It will all end on the first anniversary of her
death.
There will be hatred, curses, sadness, and anger.

The handwriting was poor. The characters were probably written to conceal the writer's hand. The ink was cheap, and stains dotted the paper. The stamp revealed the letter was mailed from a nearby town, easily reached by train from Tokyo. His home was seventeen miles away by bus when traveling the mountain roads. However, this country town is closest to his village and a convenient place for the villagers to shop.

"The text isn't clever … but it is literary."

"This letter is addressed to me, but I haven't written letters to criminals. If someone sees it's addressed to me, I may be targeted as a criminal. As you know, my mother was my stepmother. My father married her after my mother died. There is a three-year difference between us. She was 42 years old when she died last year on August 9.

What reason did I have to kill this mother? She had cardiac asthma.

"That's a scary diagnosis. The son of distant down-and-out relatives is a doctor called Ebitsuka; he walks with a limp. We paid his school tuition to study internal medicine. About five years ago, we gave him a house in the village, and he opened a practice.

"As the lone doctor in a mountain village, his practice covered more than internal medicine. He also needed to be a doctor of external medicine, ear, nose, throat, eyes, and even try his hand at dentistry. He objected to being summoned so soon, but my father refused to give him the time to learn every specialty because he was not in school to benefit the village but for my father's benefit. He forced the doctor to come after about one year in a research lab after graduation.

"The doctor is an academic and was dissatisfied. After he came, he was superficially obedient but disagreeable. He's forgotten his duty and lacks compassion. My mother got angry at the doctor, but dismissing him was a problem. She had to endure her dissatisfaction. A person with asthma suffers a terrible affliction. Mother lay on her belly, tearing at the tatami mat, and died in agony. She found no relief in countless injections.

"This is not exceptional but normal for cardiac asthma. A person can only endure so much agony. Death by another method may be indistinguishable from death by poisoning. Also, the bleeding and death spots that appeared on the corpse were different but nothing special. There was just agony. Death brought serenity to her face. She was buried without one person suspecting death by poison. This rumor reached our ears this year.

"The gossip began with the servants and merchants who came and went. They met around her deathbed and witnessed her agony. The never-ending talk was probably the embellishments told by the villagers who retreated to the mountains for leisure. If they asked Dr. Ebitsuka, his large eyes glared. He was the sort of man known not to respond to the obvious.

"His crankiness is aggravated by his limp and results in an inferiority complex. He's also an unlikeable man who hates to converse. At a recent gathering of the family for a meal, Tamao blurted out the villagers had been accusing me of killing our mother. Of course, she was joking. She's the type to play nasty pranks and is an odious woman.

"She came and may have mourned Mother's passing as Kajiko-san's only biological child but did not shed a tear. The person who kept her in line was gone. Now, she openly plays as much as she likes. But even she doesn't tell that stupid joke because it was murder. In fact, at that time, a plausible rumor named a certain person as the murderer. It was Nurse Moroi. You know her. She's a strangely sexy woman and must have been involved with my father.

"After you ran off with Kyoko-san, the fact is their friendship was understandable. A mother was killed, and the heir, targeted. Doesn't this new-style tragic human rela-tionship fit into village rumors? All gossip in a rural village is trite. This gossip inspired my sister to say that horrible joke. Of course, no one shivered because it wasn't grue-some. Everyone roared with laughter. Now, I can barely sleep."

Nurse Moroi Kotoji was about thirty years old. Women, particularly young women, are heroes and enthu-siasts. The average young woman dreams of becoming a nurse and going to the front if war comes. As a nurse, she's determined to volunteer for the battlefield, but Moroi was different, a cold woman with few dreams. She paid no attention to men's jokes. At nearly five and a half feet, she was unusually tall for a woman and had a well-proportioned, beautiful physique. Her face wasn't bad either.

The womanizer Mochizuki Wani, who she dubbed The Moody Perv, worked hard at imagining the night her innocence would suddenly turn to passion. He knew deep down she was a slut despite her distant, smug look. However, she never responded to his advances.

When war came, nurses became precious objects and were urged to go to the front. This nurse from an ordinary medical practice in Tokyo grumbled about being commandeered to the battlefield. Her superb ploy was to become a nurse in a village with no doctor and obtained permission to go there. She didn't go to Ebitsuka's hospital but was given a room in a private home and went to the hospital at noon. She made her schedule and became known around town. She had two other patients in the same home.

One was an elderly man called Nagumo Ichimatsu, an evacuee to this area. After his arrival, he suffered a stroke and was paralyzed. He was confined to bed. Ichimatsu's wife, Auntie Yura, was Utagawa Tamon's younger sister. She was semi-invalid and suffered hysteria caused by her innate weak nature. She locked horns with Kajiko.

Tamon had no enthusiasm for his immediate family and was not troubled by mundane matters. He wasn't bothered by his younger sister's family evacuating here, being a nuisance, falling ill, and having to provide them with medical care. His prominent family had money and material wealth. He forgot those people sponged off of him. However, women were different. His second wife, Kajiko, who was young enough to be his child, could not live graciously with them because of past animosity.

Auntie Yura had one son and four daughters. The son went overseas to work as an engineer and died on a submarine during the war. Two daughters are dead. One is riding the Manchuria Railway on her way to get married. The youngest daughter, Chigusa, was not married and evacuated with her parents. She and Tamao, Kajiko and Tamon's daughter, were worse than bitter enemies. Tamao was a beauty, but Chigusa was absurdly plain. Squinty eyes peered from her heavily freckled face, and she was piggy fat. Although plump, she had a sensitive nature and was warped by spite. Her powerful envy extended her malicious grudge to the meaninglessness of the wild Tamao. It was not Tamao's nature to hide her agenda, and she boisterously attacked Chigusa. This was the seed of her conflict with her mother. Kajiko submitted poems for publication in tanka magazines and was a gentle wife. However, she was pathologically fastidious, and her hate multiplied one hundred-fold.

Nurse Moroi's other patient was Kayoko, a woman with serious problems. Her mother was dead. Her grandfather and grandmother were the head manservant and maid in service for life in the Utagawa household. Both Grandpa Kisaku and Grandma Oden were kind-hearted, always smiling, and delightful servants. Kayoko was the granddaughter of this elderly couple, the child of their daughter, also a maid, and fathered by Tamon. Although Kayoko lived in a servant's room, she wasn't a maid's helper. Her clothes were not glamorous, but she was allowed tidy items with a metropolitan flair. The beauty of this attractive young woman was smart, pure, and bright, nearly translucent.

From the age of seventeen, however, she suffered from lung disease. In her fourth year in college, she fell ill in the dormitory and was briefly hospitalized. Since leaving the hospital, she slept and spent her waking hours in the maid's room and mostly read.

The twenty-four-year-old Kayoko was two years older

than the twenty-two-year-old Tamao. At twenty-six, Chigusa was two years older than Kayoko.

Kajiko agonized over the existence of Tamon's illegitimate child. The incident, which occurred before her marriage, seemed consensual. I don't know much about it, but her mother, the maid, hung herself after Kajiko came. After that, Kajiko weakened the curse she put on Kayoko. Because diet was crucial to her illness, she focused on special meals for Kayoko, proper clothes for her to wear so she wouldn't be embarrassed in the company of others, and told Nurse Moroi to care for her.

If Kayoko had a slight fever, the nurse did not take her to the hospital. Nagumo Ichimatsu and Auntie Yura asked her, although she was busy, to take Kayoko to the hospital when warranted by changes in her condition. Nurse Moroi was a heartless woman and lacked common emotions. She hated the Nagumo family with their excessive complaining, sobbing, and hysteria, and didn't provide them with good care. Her curse focused on Kajiko.

When Kajiko lay on her deathbed, the agony that made her tear at the tatami lessened just before her death. She asked if everyone was there. It was impossible to hear her words clearly, but she seemed to want the Nagumo family to be present. However, no one could understand her. Tamao sat closest to her pillow but had no idea what Kajiko was saying.

"This threatening letter is ridiculous. I have no experience in this sort of thing, but I'm not worried about the accusations in the letter. The evacuees in the village have free time. This is probably a prank played by an unstable loon. What I'm asking is terribly selfish. The truth is more than you, I need Kyoko-san."

Kazuma's face paled as it does when his drunkenness from sake fades away.

"I realize this is coming out of nowhere, but I've been passionately in love with Kayoko for a long time. But we are the older brother and the younger sister. My compassionate heart that adores the Holy Mother spiritually transforms the sexual passion.

"The problem was Kayoko's love for me was greater than mine. This story makes no sense because you can read stories like this every day. I am the older brother loved as a lover. But why are we told it is forbidden for an older brother and a younger sister to be in love? People say that's how it is, but why must we be like that? That's too rash.

"I don't want to be seen by the damn world anymore. I was defeated because I only thought of her love as the undiluted passion of a virgin. I was fine with dying. It's all too subtle. You probably can't believe this. There is nothing more sublime. What can I say? Kayoko is turning away from the world. She understands sin and is wise.

"She knows everything like a god. She's astute and sees her destiny. I'm unreliable. That's how it is. If god gently hugs you and whispers bad things, what do you do? I give up when danger comes. I will not touch her body. Even if I die, I cannot commit a crime against god, despite not feeling it's a crime.

"Kayoko squeezed my hand, and we kissed. It was a cold, sad kiss. You could say two people became one like water. It was dignified and sorrowful. Kayoko said, 'Let's get married. God will approve. Then we will die,' but I can't die. I'm not that naive. I'm a villain."

Kazuma shouted his words convulsively. He yelled, "I'm a Western boy by nature and don't move in one direction," but slowly calmed down like a beast in the zoo.

"But I'm a lowlife," he said.

"I understand. Anyone your age is a lowlife. You are deeply in love with Ayaka-san. Sometimes, you may want to persuade Kocho-san. Because Kayoko-san sees no man but you, it's not noble and not unexpected incest. In the world envisioned by you, isn't the root merely a virgin's charm and magical powers? When the root is identified, the truth is surprisingly flimsy. Are you angry? No? Actually, Ayaka-san not being a virgin bothered you and you surrendered. Love between an older brother and a younger sister is okay. You wanted to rebel a little. It's okay to vent. I thought you had and cooled down a little while speaking."

"When you talk like that, I'm saved. I don't think your words hit the mark, but I'll stop arguing. I don't believe I'm alone in this quarrel. I'm satisfied if I've gained your sympathy. I have a request. Kayoko-san has no friends other than Kyoko-san and thinks about her every day and becomes nostalgic.

"Kayoko-san knew her illness was serious but often walked over two miles up the mountain road to visit Kyoko-san. She was scolded but went anyway. She came down with a fever and was confined to bed but tried to get up. She escaped and went out. At that time, I saw Kyoko-san as a witch who wanted to kill Kayoko-san, and I hated her. However, the presence of you and Kyoko-san may comfort Kayoko-san.

"If you'll play that role, it would be hard to call me a coward because there's no one other than Kyoko-san. Sadly, she's already given up on me. I'd like you to come to distract my spirit. Of course, I'll be tempted, but I'm asking for Kyoko-san's help because all my strength is not enough."

That role is a problem. From the beginning, I couldn't decide on my own and had no response.

If I went back and told Kyoko, I would keep saying, 'I'm sorry.' They say only love sickness cannot be cured by the hot springs in Kusatsu, so a prescription from anyone would be no good. It must be left to those involved and the course of events. If Kayoko commits suicide, my conscience would be tormented. Kyoko would never want to go to the mountain villa again.

Kazuma gave up, persuaded by Kyoko's rock-solid determination. Mokubei and his wife, Akiko, and Koroku and his wife, Kocho, accompanied Kazuma to the mountains three days later.

2

ONLY SURPRISING ENCOUNTERS

O n the morning of July 10, I received this letter from Kazuma.

I've arranged for the Tourist Bureau to deliver tickets to you on July 15. Please come on the last train that day. I'm begging you. One of the three tickets is for Dr. Kose. Persuade or force him to come with you. I'm on my knees begging you.

I sense a frightening crime is about to take place. The blood of many people will be spilled. I'm asking only you and Dr. Kose to come. And Kyoko-san. Kyoko-san! Please come. I'll be waiting. I can see a sea of dark blood.

On the afternoon of the fifteenth, a messenger from the Tourist Bureau delivered the three tickets. The last train to N-town would leave at 11:35 pm and arrive the next morning at seven in time to catch the first bus.

Kazuma worked part-time planning advertisements at the Tourist Bureau.

I'm convinced Kazuma was threatening at times. That made it hard for me to go along with him. However, I easily fell in line. Was I somehow bound to him and couldn't help myself? First, Kyoko was reluctant to go, but the letter was too threatening. She was a graceful, elegant poet and was touched by the stunning incest of close relatives. She said she decided to go and joined me when I visited Dr. Kose to show him the letter.

Dr. Kose was not an actual doctor. He was eleven years younger than Kazuma and I, a youngster at twenty-nine years old.

Despite being a middle school student at seventeen, he became a pupil of mine under the pretext of becoming a writer. I couldn't reject him as a student to an inexperienced novice like me. If asked to go to the home of a wealthy family, he would say something strange like, "Young people are kindred spirits to young people."

Before long, he became absorbed in detective work and studied fashionable subjects like aesthetics in college. This outcome was not caused by not studying but recognizing his fate of being unable to enroll in any other subject at the college.

His genius for detective work was a wonder. When we showed him horrifying true cases, the certainty of his observations and his ability to precisely detect nuances in human psychology was frightening at times. He assumed the human mindset for contemplating a criminal act. He accurately partitioned everything, made calculations, and found the answer. What formula provides the foundation? We can't comprehend this kaleidoscope and the formal methods he employed.

To literary men like us, human beings are indispensable, and the maze of human psychology ends in infinite complexity. That's what makes literature convincing. To him, the human mind can be precisely dissected.

"If you understand people so much, why are your novels such crap?" he coldly asked me.

"Ah, ha, ha. Because my novels are crap, I understand crimes."

I was not trying to be funny or modest. My words were an enlightened view that sees through to the truth. His observations of people stopped at the low bar called criminal psychology. He seemed to construct observations confined to this level and never wandered into the infinite maze. That was genius.

Therefore, he couldn't write literature. Because the boundary line fluctuated in human observations in literature, he was a genius detective with zero sense of literature.

We recognized his undeniable detective skills and honored this unstudied idler with the title of Doctor. He never avoided learning challenging subjects. He stayed up late into the night to devour everything, except the trivial, from high-end products, like textbooks and entire sets of storytelling books, to obscene books, movie magazines, and sumo rankings. Nothing was too trashy not to learn.

When I went out to show him the letter and ask for his assistance, he said, "Okay, summering there would be nice. Will there be food and drink? But I can't go tonight."

"Why not?"

"It's hard to refuse, but please listen. A secret rendezvous. Do you understand?"

"Doctor, is that a yes? Is she one of those *panpan* prostitutes for the GIs?"

"No. There's something I've got to do. Sensei, I must be going now. I'll come tomorrow evening. I'd like to bring her along."

"That won't be a problem. Bring her."

"Never. I have no reason to bring a sacred virgin inside a pack of tigers and wolves."

"Doctor, are you interested in virgins? Well, well. I am haunted by a fellow with a foolish hobby."

My wife and I departed as instructed in the letter.

On this occasion, the train was a luxury tour. The trip was so tranquil I couldn't sit, sleep, or go to the bathroom.

We got off at N-Town and unexpectedly met a certain couple who rode the same train. I heard someone call my name and was surprised to see Kamiyama Toyo and his wife, Kisona.

During the war, Kamiyama and his wife visited the mountain a few times. He was a lawyer and Utagawa Tamon's secretary until eight or nine years ago. Originally, Kisona was an unregistered Shinbashi geisha and Tamon's mistress but had a secret affair with Toyo. He quit as Tamon's secretary but still visited from time to time. He looked like he had the brains for business as a lawyer and like a gangster with his sturdy, large build and muscular arms. Everyone in the Utagawa family had an instinctive hatred of him. Wherever he turned, he saw sour looks even on the servants' faces, and no one responded when he addressed them.

"And Kyoko-san. You've married Yashiro-sensei. He doesn't look the part either. That's it. A writer is mature. Of course, his path will be tough. I'm sorry, but may I ask you a question?"

I didn't answer.

"Yashiro-sensei, you're off to see Utagawa-san? May we join you?"

"You're going to see Utagawa-san, too?"

"Yes. What's going on? I received an invitation. Something curious is happening."

I lost all hope when we boarded the bus. It was the

creep, the last man I expected to meet. Doi Pikaichi was on the bus. Of course, he jerked his head in greeting but showed his contempt for everyone by raising his back without lowering his front.

"And where are you going?"

"Where am I going? I come to this place not much better than the goblin-haunted Adachigahara, where else would I be going? I'm going to Utagawa Kazuma's home. I guess you are too?"

I wondered why.

"What is your business?"

"Don't mock me. What business does anyone have with that hopeless poet? Because he promptly paid the ransom, I'll down as much sake as I like but haven't come so far down in the world to beg. He said to visit and spend the summer with sake and food. It's a strange thing to say, so I thought he was nuts. But if there'll be sake, being sociable is acceptable, isn't it?"

He spotted Kyoko and laughed with a snort.

"Are you with Kyoko-san? Of course, she's pretty and alluring, teeming with womanly virtues and fickle in love. Very sexy. What a shame. Am I too late? If I had evacuated to this village during the war, I would have embraced Kyoko-san. But why didn't I have the heart to enter the majestic Utagawa home with the rest, like you, Yashiro-san? Your novels are so childish. I can't read them."

What the hell was Kazuma thinking? What was his plan? I sensed the nonsense in his letter. Now, I'm getting anxious. What was going to happen? It would be better to know, at least, what he was planning.

We got off the bus. A young manservant was waiting to take our bags. I couldn't rest yet with the short two and a half more miles of walking up and down hills from here.

When we were finally close to Utagawa's home and

approached the location of the guardian god, Chinju-sama, two women walked toward us from the shade of some trees. Ayaka, Kazuma's wife, and Utsugi Akiko, Miyake Mokubei's wife, came out to greet us.

However, as Ayaka got closer to us, she stiffened, erect like a pole. Doubting eyes peered from her baffled face. Seeing this, Doi Pikaichi called to her.

"Lady Moneybags. Thank you for taking the trouble to receive us. I haven't rewarded you with loving care in ages."

He boldly walked up to her and looked about to embrace and kiss her.

"What are you doing here?"

Ayaka slowly moved to hide behind Utsugi Akiko. Pikaichi didn't expect that and hugged both women.

"Oh, good day.… and you are? Oh? Utsugi Akiko-san. Ah, the famous woman writer. I didn't recognize you. My, my, you're young and beautiful. I will leisurely greet each of you. Alluring women from the past await."

Pikaichi grabbed Ayaka's arm. She shook him off and briskly walked a few steps away.

"You bastard! Bum! You weren't supposed to come. Go home. Will somebody …?"

She looked at us in confusion. Pikaichi never stopped talking as he recklessly reached out to grab her, but she paled and fled. Paying no attention to her retreating figure, Pikaichi took out a handkerchief and wiped the sweat from his face.

Kazuma and the hunchback Utsumi were waiting for us at the house. The other guests were at the lake, bathing in the basin of the waterfalls.

I had no strength to speak. After a bath and a lunch of a sandwich and beer, I could no longer keep my eyes open. Bedding had been laid out in a room for me, and I fell asleep. The cool mountain air refreshed my body that gasped for air in the summer heat of the city. When I awoke, it was already dusk. One of my hopes was not fulfilled, the cries of evening cicadas. They probably would begin chirping at the end of the month. After I washed my face, a maid came to welcome me, then Kyoko returned.

"You're finally awake. Everyone has been served sake."

"I slept like a log."

I released a long yawn and joined them downstairs.

3
____

THE UNINVITED GUEST

I despised Mochizuki Wani. Few in literary circles liked him. He bragged about his clever writing style and held others in disdain. Decorum and manners were unknown to him. Kissing a married woman in front of others brought no shame. He might have been capable of rape, too. Although single, he bragged as though the women of the world were his.

However, he was a popular journalist and generous with money. His writing style dazzled because journalism values clever writing over ideas. Journalism bases its decisions on the phenomena of reality, not history. The arrogance of this first-rate writer was tolerated. Self-confidence and little conviction cannot create art. However, many saw his arrogance as a virtue. As if his lusty habits were proof of his genius, he was celebrated for his peculiar kind of nerves.

I thought, This will be a sight to see. After Doi Pikaichi added a seat, the disgusting beasts in literary and artistic circles would lock horns in a bullfight. Of course, that was Kazuma's plan, his grand success. I'm absentminded, which served to enrage them. I didn't realize they were riveted by the side dishes for the sake.

However, they betrayed my expectations. These men were astute in the ways of the world. Although coarse, these hoodlums cultivated sensitivity to humanity and justice and did not lock horns.

"Pikaichi, you don't drink sake?" asked Wani.

Pikaichi smiled. He rarely drank. This man probably did not need sake because he never drank to calmly and nonchalantly embrace and seduce a woman with others present. Drunkenness might make him drowsy and blunt his skills.

Whether drunk or sober, Wani seduced women and sipped sake.

Pikaichi jumped to his feet, rushed over to Kocho, and grabbed her hand.

"Let's dance, Kocho-san. I've secretly longed to have the honor of seeing you on stage. They say your face and figure are exquisite. And you're blessed with charm, daintiness, and pride. These are vices I like. Now, shall we dance?"

Kocho gently pulled back her hand and, in an icy tone, said, "No."

Wani roared with laughter.

"Pikaichi, please stop! Ah, ha, ha. Wooing a third-rate whore to be first like King Louis reveals your shallow knowledge. You may have trained in France, but you didn't absorb the teachings of the West. It's wrong to solicit a whore in public. A whore wants to be seen as a gentlewoman. She has a warped conceit. The best way to solicit her in public is to treat her like a whore. Observe."

He stood and raised Tamao's hand, began dancing, pulled her into an embrace, flopped down to the sofa, and kissed her. The unruffled Tamao raised her face and kissed to her satisfaction.

"Well? Pikaichi-san. Tomorrow night I will give you this. Trembling will not be allowed. I hate quivering men. Tango-san, let's tango."

Utsumi Tango shook his head. Tamao took no notice and walked toward him. The shaking head of the smug Tango resembled a doll's head.

"Well, Utsumi-san, once in a while, the footlights shine on you. Don't be overwhelmed and shrink into a corner."

A big-hearted smile rose on Utsumi's face.

"The footlights shine on me only when I play the lead role in *The Hunchback of Notre Dame*. That occasion calls for a co-star."

"Oh, yes. That's marvelous. This summer, we will perform it here. Hitomi-san, please write the scenario."

"Very good. I'll provide the stage props. We'll perform for the villagers and swindle that new yen from the peasants."

"The audience of farmers will flee from Pikaichi's props. We shouldn't do a play. With only actresses, can we do anything other than an erotic dance? Something like this."

Wani snatched and embraced Tamao and made her take off her two-piece dress, nearly snatching it off. Tamao, wearing a chemise, tumbled from Wani's arms but was undaunted. Her teasing face gazed at him, and she removed the chemise. She was in her bloomers.

"Is that enough? One more?"

A furious Kazuma grabbed his sister's arm.

"You can go, now."

"No problem. I'll save you the trouble."

Wani embraced Tamao.

"Stop this. You're vile."

"Don't be mad, Big Brother. Even if I were a demon, would I make a cute girl strip naked in public? Since you saved me from trouble, I'll borrow her and be on my way. The play is over. From here on, the drama belongs in my personal love affair, and spectators are not welcome."

Wani scooped her up into his arms, excused himself, and left for his room.

The pair did not return after five or ten minutes. They probably headed to a cheap bar or cabaret in town. Antics like this were a rare sight. Even Pikaichi was appalled.

"Well, the Utagawa home is an excellent brothel, better than what I've heard. I did not wander to far-off France, but I cultivated an interest in mountain climbing since my youth. Who will be my companion tonight? The accomplished woman writer or the poet published in *Bluestocking* magazine? Well?"

Utsugi Akiko, the writer, forced a smile and said, "It was a pleasure to meet you, but tonight, I have a previous engagement," she said and took the arm of her husband, Miyake Mokubei.

"We'll be going."

"All right."

Pikaichi jumped to his feet, deliberately walked forward, and opened the door between the living room and the hall. Like a hotel bellboy or a samurai guard in a palace, he politely lowered his head and saw them off.

That prompted the others to go to bed.

After retiring to our bedroom, Kazuma was soon at our door. He was seething.

"The truth is your behavior is disgraceful. If you came to help me, calm me down. I want to strangle someone."

I had no words to console him.

"Where's the time for a leisurely chat with you? What's

going on? I don't get it. You received the tickets from the Tourist Bureau?"

"Yes."

"Did you get my letter?"

"Of course, I saw it. I wouldn't be here if I hadn't. I didn't come with Dr. Kose; he's leaving tonight and will be here tomorrow."

"Dr. Kose?"

"What?"

"What about Dr. Kose? Why did you bring him up?"

"Don't you remember? In your letter, you said to bring Dr. Kose."

"My letter?" He looked astonished and stared at me.

"I didn't write that. I invited you and your wife, no one else. Oh, I get it. It's a trick. Someone else sent you a letter. Listen to me. What's going on? Who's behind this? I'm furious. Who's playing this trick? I sent invitations to you, Kamiyama Toyo and his wife, and Doi Pikaichi. All of you received your invitations. A messenger from the Tourist Bureau also delivered the tickets. I sent a letter to the Tourist Bureau to have the tickets delivered but for you two and the Kamiyamas. I didn't ask for Dr. Kose."

Now, it was my turn to be amazed. I never doubted this was his letter. The handwriting matched his exactly.

Fortunately, the letter remained in my pocket from my visit to Dr. Kose to invite him. I took it out to show Kazuma. He studied it.

"Someone broke the seal to my letter, rewrote it, and sent a forgery. These are my sentences. This part sounds right."

I've arranged for the Tourist Bureau to deliver tickets to you on July 15. Please come on the last train that day. I'm begging you. *One of the three tickets is for Dr. Kose*

Persuade or force (*Kyoko-san*) to come with you. I'm on my knees begging you.

I sense a frightening crime is about to take place. The blood of many people will be spilled. I'm asking only you *and Dr. Kose* to come. And Kyoko-san. Kyoko-san! Please come. I'll be waiting. I can see a sea of dark blood.

"Someone else wrote these [italicized] parts. I did not write this part [in parentheses]. This is a frightening crime. Where has that happened? I certainly wrote the ending, *a sea of dark blood*. At the time, I was troubled by dark visions of blood of the crime of an older brother and a younger sister. However, the rewritten part is an exaggeration. The thought you and Kyoko-san staying away upset me. I had to appeal to Kyoko-san's pure heart. I threw out the literary pride of a writer. Kyoko-san. Kyoko-san! I wrote the shameful text *I can see a sea of dark blood*. Kyoko-san, forgive me. What is the forger's plan? This may be the actual crime. Dammit. Now, I want to kill someone. Whoever it is. Bastard! I want to strangle him. During your stay, are there two or three people I can avoid killing?!"

Nevertheless, the handwriting was his. Upon closer examination, we found evidence of careful copying of his writing.

"What about the paper?"

"This is my writing paper."

"Where do you keep it?"

"In the desk in a corner of the parlor. I always keep paper, ink, and my pens there, and, of course, envelopes."

"Who mailed the letter?"

"During your evacuation here, the post office had no staff. The situation being what it was, I walked almost two and a half miles to post a letter. Now, they come here to collect the mail like they used to. It makes sense for the post office to take our mail when they deliver mail. When there's no mail to deliver, they'll come to pick up mail. We toss our outgoing mail in the wooden box at the entryway. Anyone could have switched the letter."

"Okay. Fortunately, Dr. Kose is coming tomorrow. It's perfect, right? The letter villain named him. Why did he summon Dr. Kose? If the rogue is trying to make a fool of Dr. Kose, that will end in a colossal failure. He's a genius in that realm. The rogue didn't think it through. No one surpasses him in finding criminals. He's becoming an unbeatable system and is an exceptional genius."

"Well, I'll see you tomorrow."

"Before then, we'll follow this crime, wander a maze, and haphazardly concoct a criminal. This task is impossible for a novelist who is not a criminal."

Kazuma went back to his room.

No sounds came from any of the rooms.

Kyoko said, "Something's not right. I'm frightened. A terrible incident may be about to happen."

"Why are you scared?"

"Why? I don't know. But I dread what may come."

"You may be right. A crime at a brothel? That damn Pikaichi. Calling this home a brothel was terrible."

"I spoke with Kayoko-san today, but it was an exchange of pleasantries. Perhaps it exceeded my expectations. She's worried about Kazuma. She told me people plan crimes. They selfishly fabricate them, and no one anywhere should think of crimes as normal."

"Crimes probably occur because of shame."

"Your splitting hairs looks like you want to see the dirt behind Kayoko-san's distress."

"I know. I know. The complaints of young women are unfathomable. I'm going to bed, but will I sleep?"

My afternoon nap was too long, but I was drowsy.

Somewhere down the hall, a woman was singing what sounded like a chanson in French. Tamao-san passed by and sang louder as she dashed down the stairs.

"Oh, is the great actress Tamao going to her room?"

Before I turned off the lights, I checked my watch. It was 11:15.

~

Author's Note: I am offering a prize for this detective novel. I will pay a manuscript fee to the most exceptional solution that deduces the murderer in this novel. This magazine will publish the details. I expect there will be nine or ten installments. The aim is to challenge everyone's wisdom. If no winner emerges, the manuscript fee will not be paid. The contest will end with no payment.

Sakaguchi Ango

4

———

THE FIRST MURDER

At 6:30 the next morning, July 17, we walked to the small Miwa Shrine, erected in the middle of nowhere on Mount Miwa. The origin of the guardian deity, the god of sake brewers, can be traced to the Nara era. The remains lay in a dense forest of towering trees. The shrine was a tiny doll-like house. A dense beech tree forest surrounded a lake that covered over seven acres on Mount Miwa. The deep green color of the water was an extraordinary ghostly shade. The legend of the guardian deity of Miwa mostly spoke of a courageous life and, like water, never dried up.

The scenery in this area burst with color and intense loneliness and buried in a silence that pierced the heart. To me, that was the great charm of this village. We strolled around and returned in time for breakfast at 7:30. We passed through the back gate and followed the sake storehouse to the front gate. One more monkey, Dr. Ebitsuka, was washing his body in the clean water flowing in the back garden and exercising.

I asked, "Ah, did you stay here last night?"

Ebitsuka glanced up but said nothing. He was an odd ball, a warped man. A bout of childhood paralysis left him with a limp. When naked, the difference in the thinness of his legs was obvious. He displayed hostility to all of us. We tried to converse, but he never gave proper answers. For that reason, he frowned in a corner during the drinking party held every night since the literary circle arrived at the mountain villa to play. He might have enjoyed his livid countenance.

We joined the others gathered in the living room and went to the dining hall where breakfast awaited. Utsugi Akiko looked out of sorts.

"I don't know why my head aches. I don't want to eat. Strangely, when everyone gets together, I can't sleep."

Kocho asked, "Were you up late last night?"

"No, I sleep too much but am still drowsy. Maybe being in the mountains makes me sleepy. My life is irregular, but I've strangely come to enjoy looking healthy the times it becomes regular."

In a loud voice, Pikaichi said, "A gentlewoman filled with vice loves virtue. That's what you are."

"Just water, please."

Ayaka asked, "Are you ill?"

"I have no virtues other than a healthy appetite. If my appetite vanishes, I may be sick."

Pikaichi said, "Perhaps it's morning sickness."

"Maybe Dr. Ebitsuka should examine you?"

Kazuma was worried about his former wife. Her husband, Mokubei, had been sullen and in a sour mood lately, so everyone steered clear of him.

"It would be horrible if you fell ill."

"Utsugi-san, you're a wise woman. Haven't you been at your peak lately? Your growth is vigorous," said the hunchback poet Utsumi in jest. Akiko had become the most popular and sought-after woman writer after the war. Oblivious to etiquette, she could dash off a creation in no time.

"Life is wonderful, so is death. Prosperous times like Utsugi-san's are curbed by divine punishment and a loss of appetite. Even gods aren't that powerful. Utsugi-san, have you become a genius?" asked Tango Yumihiko with biting sarcasm.

"Ah, ha, ha. Don't worry about the loss of appetite of a sinful lady. The slump probably comes from a body working too hard."

Pikaichi always sounded obscene.

The meal ended then Tamao appeared.

"Is there coffee? I sleep too much. I'm too drowsy."

"Of course, you are. You got little sleep," Pikaichi interrupted again. "Don't you want to eat? Wani-san is still asleep."

Only Wani had not appeared. Pikaichi cracked a smile.

"The man must be tired. Even with his physique, Wani is more drained than Tamao-san. It's an Utsugi-san novel. The subject of a picture doesn't become that indecent but is noble. Literature is obscene."

"I'll wake him," said Tamao coolly and bounced up the stairs while singing a chanson. Soon she went quiet and returned. Her face was pale, and the fire was gone from her eyes. For a short time, she couldn't speak.

"Wani-san is dead."

Kazuma's head jerked up. "What?"

"He's been murdered."

She staggered and dropped into the empty chair, dazed as a fossil. Kazuma slowly stood as his eyes darted around the group.

"Sunpei. Just you," he called to me. "The rest of you,

wait here. We'll go see. Just Sunpei will come with me ... and Ebitsuka-san."

The room was silent. Dr. Ebitsuka and I stood. The three of us left the hushed room.

Without a doubt, Wani was murdered. He was naked and stabbed in the heart. A dagger stuck out, as though his body stopped in an instant. Strangely, I saw little blood. In this plot twist, this fellow did not kill but was killed. It was hard to believe an actual murder ensnared me. I felt a strong sense of delight. But something gnawed at me like I was being tricked. His death was nothing. To the contrary, I wondered, Isn't he alive?

Dr. Ebitsuka checked for a pulse and turned over Wani's eyelids.

"He's been dead for some time."

"It was inevitable."

These words rushed from my mouth. Kazuma said nothing and stared. Finally, he seemed to come back.

"Well, we must leave this room. Don't touch anything. We have no choice. We can't cover this up and keep it from the police."

We went out to the hallway. I remembered to check my wristwatch. It was 8:22. We phoned the village policeman and returned to the dining hall. I urged my silent companions to speak, but Kazuma and Ebitsuka said nothing, so I spoke.

"Wani is dead and he was killed."

"It's murder? You're sure?" asked Pikaichi.

"We're certain he was murdered. Wani may be a faker like you but probably can't pull off the performance of tossing a dagger into his own chest."

I couldn't miss the transformation in Akiko's expression. Was she surprised? What was it? One person noticed my gaze and shot a stern look at me. It was Tamao-san.

She pointed at Akiko and screamed hysterically, "I know who killed him. It was the writer. Utsugi Akiko-sensei. She is exceptional. I'm sure she could kill."

Tamao stood and displayed the small object she gripped with her fingertips to each person as if revealing an article in a magic trick.

"This lighter is probably the Dunhill favored by Utsugi-sensei because no handsome boy is here to use a Dunhill, only Utsugi-sensei. It was on the desk beside Wani-san's bed. And there was no cigarette butt with a lipstick print in the ashtray on the desk when I left the room last night. That's the end of the story," said Tamao-san, tossed the lighter onto the dining table and yawned as she sunk into a chair.

Akiko looked like a criminal just found guilty. Her head hung down like she was sapped of strength. In time, she raised her trembling face.

"I killed him? That's a lie. A dagger? I know nothing about this."

I said, "Stop it. Who's the murderer? Someone killed him, but who wanted to kill him? All of us have a reason. It's wrong to name an all-star player for Japan, who deserves respect, as the killer. More than an internal struggle to find the murderer, our genuine hearts should be discussing a written appeal for the innocent."

Ebitsuka stood and grumbled, "This is a scandal. Obviously."

I was beside him and heard every word. He started to leave.

"Ebitsuka-san, we can't leave until the investigation ends."

"I don't have time for this. Patients are flocking to me. From dawn, they're being carried piggyback over seven miles up mountain roads. A murder? This is nothing more than the outcome of a game. The lives of farmers are little better than those of insects, but they're more precious. They're murdered along with the insects. Good-bye, all."

"A snob, a dandy, and a good doctor," said Pikaichi's rough voice to his back.

"You work hard to kill patients. We come across eyes colored like yours in mental hospitals. They let a madman take their pulse. The mountain folks are carefree."

The local police officer rushed to the house. Officer Minamigawa Yuichiro loved to read detective novels and, for the first time, chanced on an actual case. Every fiber in his body tensed. He stuck a paper stamped with a seal to the door of the crime scene. He faced the group, solemnly ordered them to not disturb the area, and then contacted headquarters.

"A serious incident has occurred. Hello, can you hear me? A popular writer from Tokyo, Mochizuki Wani-san. A popular writer. A famous writer. Don't you know him? He's the opposite of a literary hack. Uh, if it's not too much trouble, is there an officer who appreciates literature at headquarters?"

5

THE CAT BELL

The prefectural police headquarters was a little over five hours away. The annoying Officer Minamigawa Yuichiro did not go outside for a walk when we gathered in the dining hall to eat canned food.

"No, I can't. Evidence may disappear. I can't loiter in the hallway either. This is a crime. A strand of hair, a speck of dust from a shoe, something like that may be the key. It's all so subtle. If you are patient and cooperate for a few hours, you will be presented with the results of the powerful functions of forensic science."

His sole decision was to establish a path to the bathroom. Around 11:30, Dr. Kose came. I was eager to announce his arrival. This short man, just five feet tall, a 23- or 24-year-old man with a big round face and charming personality, looked like a monk who was quick to quarrel and agile but showed no signs of being a first-class detective. He appreciated and listened closely to Kazuma's and my explanations like he would be questioned.

"This is the fake letter. If you look closely, the truth is easily discerned."

"This is shocking. I can't tell them apart. Is this one Utagawa-sensei's handwriting? Wow, it looks the same. This is excellent. I can't tell the difference from the real one. Incredible."

Dr. Kose's horrible judgment was offset by his charm and big, round cuteness. He was courteous to the women, not weird or creepy, and popular with them.

"Kose-san, is there a nice lady in your life?"

"Huh? You're embarrassing me."

"You should have brought her along. Why not send her a telegram?"

"She's just a girl of seventeen and shy around strangers."

"So you two still have not kissed?"

"We did once. She turned bright red but wasn't mad."

"Well then, a honeymoon will be fine. I'll call her right now."

"She'd be uncomfortable in this house. She's probably unfamiliar with Western food and never gripped a knife or fork but is practicing right now."

While eating canned food, Officer Yuichiro vented his pent-up resentment by toying with Dr. Kose.

At 2:30, the car carrying the inquest judge, coroner, and more police officers arrived. At the request of Kazuma, Dr. Kose was given the same permission as a police officer to access the crime scene.

The forensic doctor concluded his examination. He retrieved many fingerprints from the crime scene. Detective Hirano Katsutaka, Head of the Investigative Division, had powerful insight in his mind's eye. At first sight, he suspected this crime was carried out with intelligence. Discernment came forth on the second, third, and fourth close examinations. Every colleague in the nation knew of this top-notch investigator, too good for the countryside, and called him Detective Suspicious. He examined the crime scene three or four times and ordered thorough searches of one thing or another.

"There's no blood for a particular reason. He might have already been dead?"

"We won't know for sure without an autopsy. In rare instances, when a sharp weapon is pushed into the heart, more specifically the heart pad, the result may be internal bleeding. But without an autopsy, we can't draw any conclusions."

The body was loaded into a truck and sent to the prefectural hospital for the autopsy.

"Wait a minute. What's this?" asked a detective from under the bed and picked up a small brass bell. This officer was Sergeant Arashi Hirosuke, the best investigator in the prefecture. His sharp six senses could sniff out a criminal by whatever means. In deference to his ability, his fellow detectives called him Eight-Foot Nose.

"What is that?"

"A bell."

It looked cheap, like a bell that hangs from a cat's collar.

"Is there anything else under the bed? Hey, Bookworm, you're a shrimp, dive under," said Eight-Foot Nose like an older brother. Detective Bookworm's real name was Naga-hata Chifuyu. He possessed eclectic knowledge picked up somewhere for some reason. He dabbled in German and understood a little about medicine but was never accused of having talent for detective work. He earned his nick-name because he'd overthink a simple crime; turn it into a complex, grotesque case; and devise an extraordinarily intricate explanation.

Detective Suspicious thought this case looked like a complicated murder carried out by Tokyo intellectuals. He thought Bookworm might be perfect for this case and brought him along to work alongside Eight-Foot Nose. His talent was to sniff out something eight feet ahead, but he was a nervous fellow. Despite his accurate intuition for crimes committed in the countryside, Detective Suspicious worried he lacked the ability to interpret a murder planned by an intellectual.

Bookworm disappeared under the bed and crawled around.

"Hey, hey, this is strange. There's a Western-style coat under here."

He pulled out the coat and examined it. Dust clung to a portion of the coat, indicating its use as a rag to wipe up something.

"What was wiped off? The top of this table? The desk?"

"Where is this dusty place? Do you know? Where was the coat?"

"Under the bed?"

"Look around there."

"Of course. There are traces of wiping around here. Something was wiped up under the bed. There are no residual blood drops or spilled water."

The coat was the victim's.

The in-depth investigation of the crime scene ended. But no fingerprints were found on the weapon this evening. Several fingerprints were taken from a flask and cup on the bedside table. When the fingerprints were matched, in addition to the victim's fingerprints, Tamao's fingerprints and Akiko's fingerprints were exact matches. Akiko's fingerprints showed she gripped the flask and drank from the cup. A tiny amount of brown liquid remained in the flask.

"Was the window open when you came?"

Demonstrating the value of this able man as the watchman, Officer Yuichiro said, "The window at the foot of the bed had been left open. The murderer probably entered there. There's no evidence of the use of a ladder or someone clambering up."

"Are there mosquitoes around here?"

"Are there? This area is famous for yellow fever mosquitoes. That looks like a pottery burner for mosquito repellent on the other shelf."

"I know. I asked because there are no incense ashes inside."

About fifty handwritten pages of a manuscript and about five hundred sheets of manuscript paper were neatly stacked on the desk and looked undisturbed, as did the rest of the room.

As they waited for the autopsy results, the police began the formal questioning. A group of investigators left for the day, leaving behind several men to spend the night in the police substation. Detective Suspicious went out to see off the group. He turned to one and said, "Tomorrow, please bring Eureka. From our perspective, the drawback is this woman with her lofty intellect gets embroiled in confusing messes. Remember, only bring Eureka."

I overheard this and was surprised.

"What? Who is Eureka?"

"Ha, ha, so you heard? She's the famous woman detective at headquarters. She works as a rural police officer but deserves better. Her name is Iitsuka Fumiko. She's a pretty, sexy lady who's a little brash and likes to tease. Her bad side is her carefree teasing and sweet-talking. In the end, she has the advantage and acts on her ulterior motive to henpeck and dominate men. Despite her success in convicting ten murderers in this prefecture, Eight-Foot Nose cringes and shows his disgust with her.

"At odds with that, she possesses the mind's eye of a genius. Somehow the inspiration pops into her mind. Whatever she's seen or heard pops into her head. She sits quietly and Bang! It's in her mind. Eighty percent of the time, she's wrong, but from time to time, she hits the mark. She's often right by skipping the reasoning and leaping to the conclusion. Things pop into her head; her mind works overtime. She may have the gift of inspiration that has the quality of a swift surge."

Detective Suspicious's team was seated at the dinner table. Eight-Foot Nose and Bookworm were given cups, too. Detective Suspicious had a sweet tooth.

"We'd be honored if you'd be forthright. It's painful as police to be greeted with sudden hostility. Police aren't a criminal manufacturing venture. However, a conversation on this topic during meals lacks delicacy. So rather than avoiding the topic of this case, let's not hesitate to take up the subject. Everyone, speak openly, sort out your feelings, and you'll feel better. What do you think? Can we talk freely in a calm discussion?

"This detached Western-style building is out of place in these mountains. Is it constructed from reinforced concrete?"

"Yes, the design is in the style of Frank Lloyd Wright. I think it was built about fifteen years ago. The main house is about 150 years old."

"In that case, the entrance key is a precision key."

"No one deep in the mountain locks his door. There's no fear of robbers, but intruders prowl at night. It's called night crawling."

A little annoyed, I said, "Officer, let's skip the useless chitchat. The murderer did not come from the outside. That's obvious. Your concerns are annoying."

"Please say whatever's on your mind. Literary work is

like that. We're accustomed to speaking our minds. We find beating around the bush strange and lose interest in providing answers."

"Well, Yashiro-san, you seem to know something about this case. We are blank slates who need to know. We don't know what you know. So you must tell us everything. We're listening. You said the murderer did not come in from outside. Why?"

"Because nothing was stolen. Who from outside would come here to kill him?"

"Why is it impossible someone other than the people staying at this house killed Mochizuki-san?"

"That, I don't know. But if you're looking for a murderer living here, most of us wanted to kill Mochizuki. Thus, the murderer did not have to come from outside."

"Naturally, but your explanation does not provide a reason why the murderer did not come from outside. He enters and leaves through the hallway and climbs the stairs to Mochizuki's room. He enters his room first. Mochizuki wakes up and is killed."

"The weapon, a dagger, was on display on a shelf in the sitting room. That means the murderer was familiar with the house's interior. He came with the intent to kill and took the dagger from there."

"Of course. However, I'm not inclined to conclude that's what happened. Was the dagger on display that day?"

No one answered, but Kazuma said it should have been there.

"Last night, everyone sat around this dinner table. After that ..."

"After that? After dinner, we always went our separate ways. However, Yashiro's guest arrived last night. They drank, talked, and danced until late into the night in the adjoining living room."

Tamao said, "Kazuma, stop. Officer, what do you wish to know? When he was killed? That's all. I will tell you. Wani-san and I withdrew a little earlier to his bedroom. I don't remember the time, but when I left his room, he was asleep. At that time, this lighter on the desk and the cigarette butt with the lipstick print were not there. And I don't smoke. I turned off the light and left the room. Earlier, Utsugi Akiko-sensei told us she owned this lighter. It's her turn to speak. Utsugi-sensei, please continue."

Akiko seemed ready and said, "I went to Wani-san's room around one. He was sleeping and snoring, loudly. I couldn't shake him awake, so I sat on a chair and smoked a cigarette."

"Did you have a drink from the flask at that time?"

"Yes, I did. I drank the rest."

"What did you drink?"

"Geranium. Wani-san seemed healthy but had a bad stomach. Instead of tea, his ritual was to guzzle geranium every day."

"Excuse me, but did you bring the lighter from another room?"

"Not always. But Wani-san did not smoke. Last night, I left without taking the lighter and locked the door on my way out. I returned one more time, but thinking about it, something was strange. I remembered I happened to have Wani-san's key. I searched and found it. I had a lighter and cigarettes and decided to go again."

"You're lying! I didn't lock the door," shouted Tamao-san.

"Well, the door was locked."

"Ha, ha. That's odd. What did you do with the key?"

"I returned it and locked the room. I deliberately left the lighter. Wani-san was awake and knew I was there. He seemed to know someone else locked the door. I came, too, but someone other than me came to lock it. Only Wani-san knew who that was. His protests made me leave my Dunhill lighter."

"That's a lie. A whopper. When I discovered Wani-san's body this morning, the door was unlocked. Didn't I enter his room without a key and discover his body?"

"Let's see. This is getting complicated. Does this house use the same key for each room?"

"No, they're different, but the same key works from the inside and the outside."

"Utsugi-san had Mochizuki-san's key. So who could have locked the door using the key from that room and removed it? Who has the same key?"

"Well, I had three copies made of each key. Each person was given a key. Another should have been collected and thrown in the desk drawer in the living room next door. And the last should be in the cash box."

"Eight-Foot Nose, check the drawer."

Kazuma and Eight-Foot Nose left to investigate. The ring of keys was missing from the drawer. Writing paper bearing the Utagawa family letterhead and envelopes were in a drawer of the desk in the living room. The guests were welcome to them.

"Does anyone recall seeing the keys in the drawer?"

"I saw them," said the hunchback Utsumi Akira like he was bored.

"When?"

"Let me see. I didn't bring manuscript paper and was rummaging around in there because I heard there was paper. I found writing pads and envelopes but no manuscript paper. This happened right after I arrived, more than a month ago. I couldn't tell you what month or day."

"There's a door between Mochizuki-san's room and the adjacent room. Is there a key to that door?"

"The door between those rooms is kept locked. The guests weren't given those keys. Of course, they're on the stolen key ring."

"Who was in the adjacent room? "

Detective Suspicious opened a map showing the location of each person's room.

a Kazuma's bedroom
b Wani
c Tango
d Kamiyama Toyo and Kisona
e Miyake Mokubei
f Utsugi Akiko
g Ayaka
h Dr. Kose
i Hitomi Koroku and Akashi Kocho
j Empty room
k Yashiro Sunpei and Kyoko
l Observatory
m Bathroom
u Kazuma's study
v Utagawa Kazuma and Ayaka
w Ayaka's living room
x Nagumo family's Japanese-style sitting room
y Yura and Chigusa
z Nagumo Ichimatsu

1 Utsumi Akira's bedroom
2 Japanese-style room
3 Japanese-style room
4 Pikaichi's Japanese-style bedroom
5 Dining hall
6 Billiards room
7 Lounge
8 Living room
9 Kitchen
10 Tsubota Heikichi and Teruyo
11 Back Japanese-style sitting room
12 Back Japanese-style sitting room
13 Tamao's bedroom
14 Japanese-style sitting room
15 Japanese-style sitting room

16 Buddhist altar room
17 Reception room
18 Tea room
19 Tamon's living room
20 Tamon's study
21 Tamon's bedroom
22 Dirt-floor room, inner entrance
23 Sunken hearth
24 Kotoji
25 Shizue
26 Yae
27 Empty room
28 Kisaku and Oden
29 Kayoko
30 Manservant's waiting room (dirt floor)
31 Kitchen (dirt floor)
32 Bathing room
33 Sake tasting room
34 Entryway
35 Fishing hut
36 Pavilion
37 Dream House

Figure 1.

"All right. Tango Yumihiko-san. I've read your work in magazines. Did you hear any unusual noises last night in the adjoining rooms?"

"I hear strange noises every night, so nothing caught my attention. Wani is dead, and from tonight on, I can sleep peacefully. How can I tell the difference between the sounds of love and the sounds of murder?"

In the wave that flowed into the adjoining living room after dinner, Eight-Foot Nose suddenly spoke to Ayaka.

"Excuse me, Ma'am. I'm sorry, but your slippers ..."

"Yes, they're Pantoufles house shoes."

"Pantou ... of course, they're not slippers but shoes. Do you always wear those shoes?"

"Some say they're hideous. Everyone teases me about them. But I love these flowery ones that look like toys. I have seven pairs of these awkward-looking, tasteless shoes. I'll wear this or that pair depending on how I feel that day."

"Do they all have bells attached?"

"Only this pair."

"Did you wear them yesterday?"

"Yesterday. Let me see. Yesterday, I wore them and another pair. Why?"

"A bell is missing. Do you remember when it disappeared?"

"I noticed the missing bell this morning when I put on my shoes. I was jumping, running, and stumbling a lot. I especially like these Pantoufles. They're cute. Aren't they? Don't you agree?"

"Yes, uh, of course. They ... well ... they're not seen much in our town."

After the police left, we had drinks. Mokubei, who doesn't like sake, drank heavily and kept silent. Utsugi Akiko, who didn't drink, sampled beer.

"Before we came here, we weren't married," said Mokubei in a low voice. Not used to heavy drinking, he was pale, and his eyes looked crazed.

However, this timid man couldn't look at Akiko and stared in the opposite direction.

"But isn't fooling around with another man under the same roof a problem of character? In addition to Utagawa, she was with me. Although she didn't see me as inferior to him, it's embarrassing now. We became her dogs. I feel a dog's shame. But it's a joke because that is her design for people."

Akiko was silent, but Pikaichi spoke up.

"Why don't we stop going round and round with this dialogue from *Hamlet*? If we can leave here, there will be instant karma and a rational outcome. Aren't those words praiseworthy?"

"Shut up. You brute. Speak to your friends, but you have none here."

"Who's a brute? The gentleman is appalled by an insult to his former wife. I used to hate male friendships. Utsugi-san is predictable. There is no Hamlet who insults a woman. If you're going to insult a woman, it's best to have the mental fortitude of a lion. A good idea would be to introduce foreign literature to this fellow who falls far short of the mark in ideas and living. He'll stay forever in Japan's countryside. Am I right, Utsugi-san? Let's be friends. First of all, you've lived with this fellow, but no matter how much time passes, he cannot portray a real man. Should we make this day our anniversary?"

"Which anniversary would this be for you?"

"Please, look at the Catholic calendar. No day goes by without commemorating something or other. We will also become Roman Catholics and must make all 365 days our anniversary days."

Unable to restrain himself, Pikaichi stood and took Akiko-san's hand. She pulled back.

"You're also a horrible person. You make fun of the suspect in a murder case."

"You sound so old-fashioned. Offering our kisses at

Wani's wake is sacred and true desire. Because constant flux is the true state of human life, life changes the day a lover is killed. This must be so."

"Tonight, I have a headache."

Akiko turned and left. Pikaichi followed, and several golf balls flew after him. One hit his head and another, his shoulder. Earlier, Ayaka had been playing with golf balls. Pikaichi swung around to see Ayaka leaning against a chair and looking the other way, feigning innocence.

"Damn you."

Pikaichi tried to leap at Ayaka to strangle her and knocked over every chair along the way, but I stood up. At the same time, Hitomi Koroku grabbed an empty beer bottle and stood. I pushed down Pikaichi. Koroku looked menacing. He was rumored to have been a famous left-wing fighter. Dr. Kose had a more peaceful state of mind than I. From his student days, he was the most influential man in the back streets. He could single-handedly fight about ten toughs and bring on a shower of blood. The doctor, our fighter, paid no attention, smirked, and enjoyed his sake. I was bold because I thought he would lend his power.

"Dammit. I'll be a knight and challenge them to a duel like they do in Europe. Each one will become my rival. If I steel myself, there's probably nothing they can do. Idiots," said Pikaichi. He raised his hands gripping a beer bottle from the table. He opened the bottles, drank from them, and went out to the garden.

Kamiyama Toyo said, "He must be knocked flat one time. How about surrounding him and punishing him with iron fists?"

Usually, he and his wife disappeared into the servants' waiting room to chat and rarely joined our conversations.

"You look muscular. Doesn't your business involve

gangs?" asked the hunchback poet with a smile and no compunction. No one got mad because he was not being malicious.

"I'm sorry. I look like that sort. But the truth is, I'm timid, and my build is deceiving."

"A man like me doesn't have the actual power to wave an iron fist for the sake of my wife. I may lack the capacity to love. The age is increasingly for beautiful people, and a ready iron fist seems necessary. What do you think, Mokubei, are there hunchback fencers in France?"

Chigusa said, "Utsumi-san, please write a collection of poems for me. The topic is for heartsick ugly women. All right? It will glorify me. If you do, there will be no need for an iron fist. No mocking. In return, I will praise and worship the good-natured hunchback."

I didn't like this homely young woman. Her mind was warped. Everything she said was the opposite of speaking the truth candidly and honestly. She called herself ugly but was vain inside. Calling herself ugly was perversely servile.

"There's only unnecessary heartache. I can only sing for the homely woman."

"Oh, that's out of character. Because we're alone, we say such things."

"It's awful the ugly woman must persuade the ugly man. The ugly woman burns with love for the handsome man. The ugly man values an agonizing death for a beautiful woman. Cyrano was not as ugly as I and more skilled at poetry. That has no value to me."

Utsumi held his head with both hands. His fingers were long, thin, and gnarled. His entire small face fit into his hands.

"When I retire tonight, I will write poems … for ugly women."

"Please wait. Let's take a walk. No? You wouldn't like that."

"I absolutely do not wish to."

"Not in this garden because Pikaichi-san is probably somewhere drinking beer. We should go this way to the beech forest," said Chigusa and picked up a pocket-sized electric lantern from a drawer of the wardrobe. She summoned the hunchback poet and disappeared outside through the dining hall door.

"That's horrible," said Tamao with a huff.

"Isn't that pitiful?" asked Kamiyama Toyo. If not him, there was no one to insert words at times like this when unpleasantness appears in the eyes.

"Is that pitiful? What do you mean by pitiful? Chigusa-san manipulates men like a beautiful woman. As for the hunchback poet, he's probably easy to manipulate. That is the queen's intention. It's disgusting. A crow plastered with peacock feathers is better than nothing."

The female race is genius at wicked observations. More than the beauty, the loathsome one stands out. For some time that day, Tamao had been drinking a lot of sake and was in a bad mood. She drank and drank in silence, and her expression changed.

"Today, I'm drinking plenty."

"Please stop, Tamao-san. Later, you'll vomit and feel awful," said Ayaka. Kocho lent her support.

"She's right, Tamao-san. Drinking that much is akin to poisoning yourself. Please stop."

"Yes, but ... just a little more. I ... I'm quietly drinking to see ghosts, the ghost of the murdered Wani-san. It's clear. I vividly see his expression when a woman lowered the dagger. It's a demon's face. A jealous demon's face."

"Stop talking like that. You've had enough for today."

"You're right. I'm sorry."

Tamao took Ayaka's hand and sobbed. Tamao's and her sister-in-law's feelings were in tune. When Akiko was the sister-in-law, however, she clashed with Tamao over everything, and they stayed on bad terms.

Ayaka seemed to hug the weeping Tamao while leading her away. When Ayaka returned ten minutes later, a maid ran in after her.

"Ma'am, the young miss is throwing up and in an awful state. Could you ask Ebitsuka-sama?"

Ebitsuka's face jerked up.

"Don't be stupid. Call a doctor to treat a hangover. She's not a queen. Go away."

His eyes looked threatening.

"Ask Kotoji-san."

"Yessir."

Kotoji was a nurse. The maid returned about thirty minutes later to report Tamao was peacefully sleeping. It was 10:05. Pikaichi's return was the cue for everyone to stand and go to bed.

"What's going on? I've come back, but you don't have to escape. Well, go, go. I will quietly lie down alone. It's best, I guess."

We ignored him and went to our rooms. The quiet was shattered by the smashing of porcelain or a sake bottle. Doors opened to see Ayaka running toward them with an altered look.

"Did something happen?"

"Yes, he … after I cleaned up, he suddenly …"

Ayaka stopped, tottered, and regained her composure, and dashed down the hall to her room. The bells on her house shoes jingled. I remembered the words of Detective Eight-Foot Nose and felt uneasy.

I knocked on Dr. Kose's door.

"How's it going? Have you found a target?"

"Please, don't overestimate me. I'm not Holmes-sensei. I'm completely lost. Firstly, more than crime, I'm overstimulated by the eroticism in this house. I must use all my powers to fight this stimulation and stop recalling the face of that girl in Tokyo.

"But didn't one of the bells on Ayaka's Pantoufles fall off where Wani was killed?"

"Yes, one was found under the bed."

"So what is it? Is Ayaka-san the prime suspect?"

"Oh no. The cat dangles a bell and can't catch a mouse. This map shows the layout of everyone's rooms. Who wished for this? Is Utsumi-san alone downstairs?"

"Uh, I don't know. Should we ask Kazuma?"

We headed to his room. Ayaka made us wait outside while she finished changing.

"Please, come in. Ayaka began staying in my room last night. Doi Pikaichi showed up, and she's scared."

"This is not normal. Someone's planning something, but I'm not sure what. If today's incident is a part of a plan, what will happen on the anniversary of your mother's death? Who has the key? Darling, fasten the door with rope. No, use wire."

"I'm not that nervous. With Kose's arrival, the criminal's lifespan is much shorter."

"Dr. Kose wants to know who assigned the rooms to the guests. Why is Utsumi downstairs by himself?"

"That was Utsumi's wish because going up and down the stairs is tiring, and the toilet is nearby. I guessed the others wouldn't mind. Ayaka said she didn't want to stay on the same floor, the second floor, with Doi Pikaichi. Despite there being empty rooms on the second floor, she was given the Japanese-style room on the lower floor."

"We don't use this Western-style building unless we

have guests. The three rooms on the second floor are next to the room used as a bedroom by Tamao-san."

"Does Kamiyama Toyo have some interest in your family?"

Kazuma paused then said, "Kamiyama was my father's secretary. He later quit but continued to come and go. He understands my father's weaknesses and may be blackmailing him. I've asked my father, but I don't know because he won't tell me the deeper reasons. My mother, who died last year, hated Kamiyama as much as she hated hairy caterpillars. Her dislike wasn't ordinary. I thought there might be a secret about Mother, but it's all my imagination. Anyway, my father mostly led a strategic political life. The seeds for blackmail abound. As his son, naturally, I didn't ask because I wasn't sure."

"He comes once in a while?"

"He probably comes four or five times a year. His current wife was the favorite concubine of my father long ago when she was a geisha in Shinbashi. He always came with her. She was dignified and stayed for several days like family. Last year, they came a few days before my mother died and happened to be here when she died. However, the day before she died, they avoided my mother on her sickbed and quarreled. I imagine this situation was the seed of blackmail not aimed at my father alone but also at my father through my mother. These are my simple musings."

I was astonished by Ayaka's splendid pajamas. Her elaborate clothing looked like Chinese clothes given a Western flair. Subtle craftsmanship created a colorful combination.

"Ayaka, is this nightgown your best outfit?" I teased. Kazuma forced a smile.

"She has fourteen or fifteen nightgowns that look like her best clothes. Around this time next year, there may be dozens more. She said it's a shame to wear the same night-gown two nights in a row. While cursing Doi Pikaichi, she changed. My clothes aren't in this room. Every day, she changes in the morning, at noon, and in the evening. She changes her hairstyle and puts on a necklace. Her perseverance is amazing but surprising."

Ayaka smiled lightly but said nothing. Although the subject was determined by her expression, she was confident in being greatly loved. How charming was the love of this woman? That may be because she was a woman born entirely for the night. Ayaka feared the murderer. However, that should have been nothing special. She was simply charming and beautiful and seemed to lack the innate instinct to think from different perspectives.

I returned to my room to an upset Kyoko.

"A little while ago, the master's chambermaid came to extend an invitation to visit him after breakfast tomorrow. I want to go, but my body says no."

This was not delightful news. Utagawa Tamon had a cold, drank too much beer, and destroyed his stomach. He'd been sleeping all morning when we arrived. He withdrew from the political world. Every day, out of boredom, he invited Go players from the village to play games. Sometimes he came to dinner in the Western building, but we hadn't seen him and secretly hoped his illness would last the course of our stay.

She said, "The maid Shizue-san is a cute girl. I heard she's eighteen and gets along well with Kotoji-san."

"Please stop. We've talked too much about human relationships."

I drank a little too much sake. Exhausted, I soon fell asleep.

6

THE SECOND MURDER

Before six the next morning, the police arrived and jumped into action.

The post-mortem lasted through the evening until the middle of the night. The findings revealed new facts. The forensics team traveled at top speed down the road and arrived before daybreak.

We awaited the arrival on the usual night train of Wani's students and the president and employees of his publishing company, who were scheduled to receive his remains around noon. After the post-mortem, Wani's body would be returned close to noon and immediately cremated, and the remains readied for the wake that night.

As we finished breakfast, the waiting police appeared in the dining hall. Detective Suspicious politely bowed and said, "I'm reluctant to tell you this so early in the morning, but a surprising fact emerged from the post-mortem. I'll be candid and ask for your advice. Before Mochizuki-san was stabbed by the dagger, he consumed a large amount of sleeping medicine. We searched but did not find any sleeping medication among his belongings. The result of the investigation clearly suggests someone convinced or tricked him into drinking the medication."

"Aah." Akiko released a soft cry.

"The sleeping medicine may have been in the geranium ..."

"Yes. Are there any clues?"

"Yesterday morning, my sleep was strange, and my head felt heavy. I thought that was odd and ..."

"And what?" asked Akiko, glancing around the group. "Tamao-san also said she was sleepy, and her head felt heavy. Perhaps, she also drank the medicine. Even now, traces of its effects flare up in my head."

Tamao-san was the one person missing from the dining hall. Her heavy drinking led her to vomit. No one was surprised by her absence from breakfast.

"Who usually made the geranium herbal tea?"

"Tamao-san invited Wani-san here as her guest, so either she made it or had a maid make it. However, from the end of last month, Tsubota Heikichi-san came to do all the cooking for his special customer. Occasionally, his wife, Teruyo, made the herbal tea. Herbal teas were made twice a day, once in the morning and once at night. Wani-san was given neither tea nor water. The only liquid he drank other than alcohol was geranium."

Chigusa diverged from Ayaka's explanation.

"It wasn't last night. Maybe, it was the evening before that Tamao-san made the geranium tea. I also helped with the cooking. Because there weren't enough portable stoves, Tsubota-san's wife asked to prepare the geranium tea in Tamao's place. Tamao-san got cranky when others took it upon themselves to do her work, so they had to get her permission each time. Tamao-san came with Teruyo-san, took the pot off the fire, let it cool, and poured it into the flask. Ayaka-sama was there, too."

"Yes, I cooked a meat pie because that's the one dish I can brag about."

"The second is grilled rabbit."

"Oh no, common folk like us hear you, and our mouths start watering," said Detective Suspicious and, out of character for him, crudely chuckled.

"Other than the two ladies, Tamao-san and Teruyo-san, who made the herbal tea, did any of the other five people see what was happening in the kitchen?"

"I don't remember each one, but the men came and went. Didn't Utsumi-san ask for ice shavings? Every day, he cools his feet with ice shavings. He's a strange one. Tango-san wanted cold water, and the kitchen had running cold, pure water. Hitomi-san and Wani-san came for beer. Kazuma-sama came from time to time for this and that. Utsugi-san was there, too."

"Yes, she was there the whole time. That day, they were making soba noodles. She watched and helped a little. When Tamao-san took the geranium off the portable stove, I was there, too."

"So the geranium was in the kitchen the whole time."

"Tamao-san cooled the spout with clean water, poured it into the flask, and took it to Wani-san's room. No one other than Tamao-san should have touched it," declared Chigusa-san, glancing around looking for support.

"Tamao-san poured the geranium from the pouch into the kettle that she placed on the portable stove, removed the boiling kettle from the stove, and filled the flask. Yes, that's what happened," said Chigusa with confidence.

I asked, "So was Wani-san killed by the sleeping medication?"

"No, the medication put him to sleep, then he was stabbed by the dagger. He probably drank geranium spiked with a lethal dose of sleeping medication. Utsugi-san and

Tamao-san may have drunk some, too, but the amount Mochizuki-san drank was about two-thirds of the geranium. The other two drank doses too small to kill."

"If the sleeping medicine could kill him, why do twice the work? What's the reason? Although the officer said he was put to sleep by the sleeping medicine and stabbed, he didn't say whether the person who drugged him and the person who stabbed him were the same person or different people. Is there proof this was the work of one person?"

"That's very doubtful. Why didn't one murderer kill him with the sleeping medication? That's the biggest unknown to us. We know two facts: someone made Mochizuki-san drink geranium containing sleeping medication, and he was stabbed while asleep. If one person carried out those two acts, the murderer didn't know the lethal dose for the sleeping medication. If the person knew, the aim was not to kill using the medication but to put Mochizuki-san to sleep. The dose was too small to kill."

"It might have been a prank. Who wouldn't hesitate playing that sort of prank on him? Someone may have been amused by playing a little prank to knock out Mochizuki to stop his philandering," said the smirking hunchback poet.

The officer thought a bit, then said, "Perhaps. Or it may have been a prank with little meaning. But if the sleeping medication was not placed in the flask, it was boiled in the kettle. We proved this by inspecting the remains of the boiled leaves in the garbage this morning."

"The kitchen that day was busy because they were making soba noodles," said Akiko.

Chigusa said, "Yes, it was very busy, but the electric stove for the geranium was in a corner near the door. We were busy a distance away by the window. With nothing to do in that corner, nobody worked there. Only Ayaka-sama was over there making the meat pie and whining because she hated the smell of geranium."

"Yes, I hate old-fashioned things like ointments and boiled medicines. They smell horrible, absolutely awful."

"Didn't Pikaichi-san catch a large snake outside the window that day?"

"A large snake?"

"It was a harmless three-foot-long rat snake. It ate a chicken. Open its belly and the evening snack comes out, so I brought a kitchen knife. Utsugi-san likes snakes and came to see it. I hate them and can't stand the sight of them."

"I'm afraid of snakes but like to look at scary things."

"Tsubota-san and his wife rushed over. He jumped out the window."

"Tamao-san casually grabbed the snake and held it up dangling," said the hunchback poet. Chigusa looked displeased and said, "Yes, she likes them that much. Hunchback-san doesn't have the strength to hang onto a suitcase. We hate the sight of snakes. Ayaka-sama, we didn't turn to look at Pikaichi-san. He was so awful like the storm god, Susanoo no Mikoto."

"Susanoo no Mikoto? Of course. Ayaka-san may be the sun goddess Amaterasu, but who is Chigusa-san?"

"She's Okame Hyottoko, the one with the funny face."

Chigusa was irate but submitted to the second-generation Cyrano.

"Pikaichi-san, usually, you randomly butt in and want to talk, but you're quiet today. Is it because Susanoo no Mikoto doesn't want to talk with the people of this world?"

"I am a well-behaved gentleman who follows the commandment: Only talk to beautiful people."

The door opened.

A young woman staggered in. She was the maid Yae. She grabbed the door, looked at everyone, and collapsed into a chair. While I wondered why she sat, she stood and soon told us why.

"The young Miss …" Her voice trailed off.

"What … happened?"

"She's been killed …"

Detective Suspicious turned to us.

"Everyone, stay here a little longer."

He left to search for the local policeman on duty, Officer Yuichiro, and went to the scene. He allowed Dr. Kose and Kazuma to accompany him.

About forty-five minutes later, Dr. Kose came back alone.

"What? Tamao-san's dead? How?"

"Yes. She was murdered."

"Poisoned?"

"Well, did she drink the sleeping medicine? We don't know. She was strangled. An electrical cord was wrapped around her neck."

Several women gasped; perhaps, they were Kocho, Ayaka, and Akiko.

"Not suicide, Kose-san, premeditated suicide," said Chigusa.

"Yes, it's a suicide made to look like strangulation. Tamao-san's case is clearly murder. Drunk and asleep, she would have been easy to kill."

I rushed to ask, "Did the murderer leave any clues?"

"Not one and nothing was stolen."

The room fell into a heavy silence.

"This is very strange. What's going on?" asked a suspicious Chigusa, lost in thought.

~

AUTHOR'S NOTE: It's unreasonable to settle on the murderer now. The murders occurred one after another. However, the readers know everything. I claim to have provided complex concrete evidence in the facts read by the readers to deduce the murderer. Dr. Kose will not deduce the murderer from anything but the facts known by the reader.

With an eye on the reward for finding the murderer, Eight-Foot Nose and Detective Suspicious will make a million impolite comments to remake the murderer because of the nature of their business, their deep suspicions, and reading our answers. They never tried to catch the murderer based, as usual, on deep suspicions. Out of fairness, for this reward, I will approach the solution as a reader, including in my dealings with the editor of this magazine. In other words, I will seal the solution manuscript and hand it to the editor before the deadline for the solicited solutions. The manuscript will be opened after the deadline and published. I will leave no room for doubt.

I intended to pester my friend Nagahata Issei, a doctor of forensic medicine; he has been my most inept rival for many years in pinpointing the culprit in detective novels. Therefore, the resentment runs deep. My problem is he'd certainly gather hints about the ulterior motive from my questions to see through to the secret. Through the good offices of Kooriyama Chifuyu, Dr. Asada Ichi of the Tokyo Medical University welcomed and instructed me on various matters. I greatly appreciated his help. I thought deeply and planned carefully by getting the name of an authority on forensic medicine to fool the reader. I set out to write a detective novel and carried out various plans. However, with you as my rivals, all of that was unnecessary.

Finally, here is the challenge. I challenge these people to find the solution: Edogawa Ranpo-sensei, Kigi Takatarou-sensei, Detective Suspicious-sensei, Eight-Foot Nose-sensei, Bookworm-sensei, and Eureka-sensei.

Sakaguchi Ango
August 7

7

THE AGING POLITICIAN CRAZY FOR DETECTIVE NOVELS

The cord of an iron was wrapped twice around Tamao's neck. The iron was kept on a shelf in her bedroom.

Most murders take place between midnight and two in the morning. A dead drunk or sleeping victim would offer no resistance. There were no traces of a struggle. The tidy futon covered her from the chest down. The mosquito netting hung undisturbed. According to the maid's testimony, she would have been sleeping with the vermilion paper lamp beside her bed turned on, but this electric light was gone and not found after searching the room.

One peculiarity stood out. Tamao's drunkenness made her vomit frequently. At her bedside were a washbasin covered with newspaper and a tray holding a kettle and a cup. Morphine powder had been tossed into the water in the kettle and the cup.

A small amount of the white powder spilled onto the tray. Eight-Foot Nose picked up and inspected the cup to discover a small amount of a white precipitate. He called the maid who nursed Tamao last night. She was Tomioka Yae, a cute, slightly plump country girl of 26 years.

"Was there saltwater in this cup?"

"Oh, no, it was pure water."

She said Tamao felt nauseous, and she hurried to fetch a washbasin. Next, she made saltwater in the kettle. Tamao gargled once with saltwater but hated the taste and switched to pure water.

The maid took the kettle and cup and returned with them filled with clean water. She also brought a bucket and rags to clean up the mess.

When she went to the living room to fetch Dr. Ebitsuka, he yelled at her. She left with no choice but to get Nurse Moroi. She believed Tamao vomited many times.

"The washbasin is full of filth. Please change it," said Nurse Moroi. The maid returned with newspapers in a new washbasin and took the dirty one to wash it.

Later as the vomiting ended, she heaved small amounts of gastric juices into the washbasin.

"The young miss gargled with water."

"Well?"

The maid stood looking vacant and about to cry.

"This white powder may have been here when you brought the tray."

On the verge of tears, the maid was probably a bit dim-witted and was flustered and blushing. Was it? Wasn't it? She said she didn't know. Her forlorn appearance made her look like her head wasn't good at thinking or recalling memories. Then her head popped up.

"When I left, the water filled eight-tenths of the cup."

In fact, the cup was eighty percent filled with water. The next day, the cup of water and the kettle were sent to headquarters. They reported morphine was detected.

Nurse Moroi said she merely rubbed the back of

Tamao, whose vomiting was caused by sake. She didn't give her any medicine or special treatment. The result of the post-mortem showed no morphine in her stomach, nor did her vomit contain morphine.

Like me, when Wani was killed, Nurse Moroi felt good and relieved by the sight of his corpse. She also wondered if he was truly dead and worried this might be a trick. This was just me talking, but her great hope was Wani would disappear.

Wani's and my writing styles were poles apart. Critics who hated me praised Wani. Critics who gave a low score to Wani gave me a high one. As colleagues, we were aware of our rivalry within our circle but felt little jealousy. Neither felt defeated because our writing styles were nothing alike.

Both Tango Yumihiko and Wani came here as powerful literary talents and held similar views on how to treat people and creativity. Thus, they found themselves at odds over who would win or lose in this situation. Without a doubt, sharp jealousy lived in Tango, who felt pressured by Wani's wild and uninhibited literary talent. He suffered because an author's jealousy surfaces in unexpected candidness about the other's popularity. Also, fame was entangled with an essentially troubled talent.

Tamao knew this. She liked Tango and Wani but was wicked. She was disgusted by Tango's torment rooted in his lack of literary talent. He was a smug pretender with an air of indifference. Tamao harbored awful thoughts about people like him and bullied him to hurt him viscerally.

I wanted to toast Wani's demise. I had been oblivious to and never given a moment's thought to crimes and criminals. However, Tamao's murder made me think about crime for the first time. I was forced to think about Kazuma's letter and the uninvited guest.

Naturally, storm doors are closed in midsummer because of the particularly cold evenings in the mountains. The doors were bolted, but locking doors was always lax, a habit in the countryside.

Tamao's bedroom was unknown and easily hidden from those of us staying in the Western building and those in the main house. Two high waterfalls were in the garden. One was about nine feet tall. The other was divided into three stages for a total height of sixty feet. A pistol shot would not be heard late at night over the sounds of the waterfalls. The area near the main house was directly below the waterfalls and filled with their sounds. Even in our Western building, not so much for the south-facing rooms, but minor noise complaints often came from our rooms on the north side.

We, literary people, are a breed of analyzers of the mind. If we brood over something, by nature, we cannot see the criminals without distinguishing between this and that. Even when we contemplate crimes, our limitations persist.

The elderly Utagawa Tamon, who invited us to join him after breakfast, wondered about the commotion. Fortunately, he did not come, but Shizue came and asked me to visit him if possible.

"Shizue-san. This has been an awful experience."

"Yes."

Shizue raised her innocent, beautiful, and well-proportioned face to look at me. Her eyes reflected wisdom, clarity, serenity, and always looked knowingly at beautiful things.

Is this cute, innocent young woman truly old man Tamon's mistress? I couldn't believe it. Her body was a young woman's.

"Was Utagawa-san unusually upset?"

"No. He's calm. His usual self."

We went to see him. Tamon looked as he always did.

He didn't look angry. Thinking about it, I was worried for no reason. This man exemplified a big shot and was probably a prominent figure in Japan. He was carefree and lived a life of contentment.

"It's wonderful you came. We were thinking about making the rounds to see everyone. However, a cold, a stomachache, or some other ailment keeps me in bed. I'm resting my fragile body to fight this illness. I was mad at you at one time but no longer. This feels like old times."

Tamon was in a pleasant mood, like a loving father. His unbelievable calm upset me, as if one of his two children, his daughter, had not been murdered. I never thought he was bluffing. He must have known about the people who kept a distance from his family's circumstances. He was agitated and confused by those people rather than the shocking personal affair. I heard he was furious at Kyoko and me. Anger and sadness may be distinct emotions, but I felt the need to rebel a bit and raised my head to say, "Today was a horrible day. I understand your dismay about this unforeseen event."

"No, no."

The old man interrupted. In addition to interrupting, he had one expression. His one look was hard-to-please.

"This may be my fault as well. Because I'm like this, my children were also born peculiar. It was inevitable. But I cannot understand one thing."

Tamon shut his mouth, then his face brightened.

"No, I may be worrying unnecessarily. Because I'm giving my body a break, I'm pondering various trivial matters."

"Can you share them with us? Often, some unexpected dim intuition hits a vulnerable spot."

"Well, let's bring this talk to an end. I can't offer much hospitality, but I'd like to commemorate this occasion. This is a small souvenir of the Ming Dynasty painter Zhu Da I acquired on a visit to Beijing. Its deep spirit, vast and infinitesimal quiet, and solitude pierce the soul.

"For Kyoko, I have this necktie pin from a stay in Paris. This inexperienced country samurai thought this surprising ornament dangling before him would have gone unnoticed. It's an 18-carat diamond. I can walk around with this around my neck. No one thinks it's a diamond. They think it's a glass ball. I go out drinking with it secretly hanging down and am safe even in Japan. My late wife thought it was a joke and took no notice. It recently reappeared after I tossed it somewhere and forgot about it."

Although Tamon was lighthearted and philosophic in thought, an 18-carat diamond might be a valuable item. Eerily, the small Zhu Da object was a rare object in this world. He treated a beloved woman from his past affectionately, like a daughter. This made us boil over with natural feelings of comfort and warm hearts.

To my surprise, I noticed various books on the bookshelves in the room were mostly history books. However, half of the few novels were translations of detective novels, including works by Kuroiwa Ruiko and S.S. Van Dine. The novels were mainly translated works like *The Count of Monte Cristo*, *Les Miserables*, and *Gone with the Wind*.

I asked, "Do you like detective novels?" Tamon nodded.

"I loved reading Ruiko since I was a boy. During my travels overseas, I remembered my hobby of detective novels to kill time. Okakura Kakuzo, a lover of detective novels, could not have evening dinner and drinks with me because his family thought his health was too fragile. We chatted about half of Conan Doyle's detective novels.

When we got to the climax, he stopped talking. I asked why, and he said that was enough for the day. He teased me and said to come later with another book if I wanted to hear more. Doyle fit well into this strategy of dinner with drinks. Recent mystery novels have a subtle flavor and are muted and intricate. Thus, they are interesting to read but not suited to the dinner with drinks strategy.

"I love detective novels, too. Which do you prefer?"

"I like the novels by the English woman writer, Agatha Christie. Van Dine and Ellery Queen are filled with futile pedantry, too much suspense, and self-importance. I don't enjoy reading them. Long ago, I simply walked to Maruzen to buy this detective novel."

He picked a Western book from a stack in a corner of the bookshelf. They were all detective novels. If Crofts's work was there, so was Freeman's, the *Redheaded Redman* or *Zigomar*.

"In that case, you must have ideas about this case."

He said nothing for a few moments.

"Did the same person kill Mochizuki-san and Tamao? If so …"

He shut his mouth, then said, "Who could it be? Yashiro-san, what do you think? Do people kill willy nilly? Any person may commit any crime. It could be anyone."

Tamon's eyes sparkled and stared at us without hiding that light. His mouth trembled. He seemed to have more to say but changed his mind.

8

ONLY ONE HAS AN ALIBI

I left Tamon's room and returned to the Western building. As I walked past the room where Tamao was killed, a voice called to me. A woman in her thirties comfortable in Western dress was inside.

"Hello. Excuse me. Who are you?" she asked.

"Who's asking?"

"I'm with the police and want to know who everyone is. Your name, please."

"Oh, of course."

I released a burst of air.

"Ah, you're Eureka-sensei!"

"How rude!"

Eureka raised her lovely eyebrows and said, "What is it? You visitors, both the men and the women, are of no account. The mad love affairs of writers and actresses are horrible. You trouble your wives year in and year out and end up in this kind of mess."

"You're absolutely right. How did you know? Did it pop right into your head? Who's the murderer?"

"Be quiet."

"I'm sorry. Excuse me."

I was about to walk past when she grabbed my wrist and pulled me back.

"What is your name? You are impertinent."

"You're Eureka. What does your intuition say it is? Threatening someone to get their name is a violation of the Constitution. Ah, ha, ha."

I angered Eureka and escaped.

I calmed down in Kazuma's room with Dr. Kose, Kazuma, and his wife, Ayaka. We leisurely chatted until three in the afternoon.

The president, the publishing manager, and a young employee of the publisher of all of Wani's books, and a student of Wani arrived a little before noon to claim his remains. However, his autopsied body had not been returned from police headquarters for cremation. This village has a crematorium worker but no crematorium. Firewood is stacked in the open air and burned. The process lasts one night.

Like setting a small fire, the businessmen added to our gathering of people unfamiliar with real work launched plans from a different world. Where did they come from, and why? They prepared the room to receive Wani's body, negotiated with the priest, and communicated with the crematorium. They also came with a black curtain and, in no time, transformed the front parlor into a funeral hall.

I wanted to speak in confidence with Dr. Kose. Finally, I had the chance.

"The truth is I have information I want to tell you alone. Last night, I returned to my room but couldn't sleep and went for a walk. I'm not sure about the time, but I believe it was around eleven. I think Kyoko was already asleep and didn't notice."

"Yes, I vaguely remember seeing you on your way back."

"I intended to go out the dining room door to the beechwood forest. I changed my mind at the back door and went around to the garden. A walk around the lake took me to the Dream House on the hill. From there, I thought about going to the small pavilion and the top overlooking the waterfall basin. The fishing hut below and the burning lamps were visible from there.

"I glimpsed a woman's figure disappear into the darkness but could not see where she came out. I'm sure she came from the fishing hut. She seemed to walk around the outside of Tamon's bedroom and returned to the kitchen door. I knew it was a woman but couldn't tell who.

"A short time passed, then a man exited the fishing hut. First, he washed his hands in the lake water. It was Dr. Ebitsuka. He was wearing a short-sleeved shirt and pants. While wiping his hands with a handkerchief, he climbed the hill in the garden, turned, and went after the woman who disappeared. That's all I saw. I stayed ten more minutes and then came back."

The Dream House was a miniature version of Prince Shotoku's Hall of Dreams. The fishing hut was a teahouse modeled on some hall in Yamato. One room was a tatami room; the other was furnished with a Chinese-style desk and chair.

"Well then, Ebitsuka-san spent yesterday in the fishing hut. Recently, hasn't he been staying there every night? Because I took no notice, I didn't know whether someone from the village was staying somewhere in the house. The formality of receiving permission from each owner wasn't the custom in this house. The two lives of the owners and the servants were independent. Ebitsuka-san was like one of the family in this house, so he usually spent the night when he visited at night to socialize. This wasn't unreasonable because the mountain road from the hospital was nearly two and a half miles, and he walks with a limp.

"We had a car before the war. Since the war, there's not even one rickshaw in the village, let alone a car. Ebitsuka-san is a strange fellow. I don't know when this started, but he doesn't want to sleep in the main house and stays in the fishing hut. If there's an emergency, he phones from the hospital. Something like that might have happened last evening."

"I'll ask Yae."

Ayaka used the telephone in the room to call the maid Yae, but she'd gone to the village on an errand. Nurse Moroi came.

"Moroi-san, did you go to the hospital?"

"Today, I met with the police and was there until close to noon. Also, I tended to Nagumo-san who complained of a stomachache this morning."

"Yura-sama?"

"No, her husband."

"Was there an emergency at the hospital last night?"

"No, there wasn't."

Nurse Moroi stared coldly at Kazuma when she answered.

"Well, were you at the hospital? Last night, you had no reason to see Ebitsuka-san."

"I had no reason to be there."

"Did Ebitsuka-san stay at the fishing hut last night?"

"This morning, he was in this house. I know nothing about last night."

Moroi stiffly turned to the side and presumed to ask, "Are you satisfied?"

"Yes, thank you. My questions were strange. Please, don't be offended."

"If there's a problem between Dr. Ebitsuka and a woman, perhaps you can ask Chigusa-sama? On nights the doctor stays in the fishing hut, he usually leaves the hut one time during the night. Everyone probably knows, but all of the servants know. Chigusa-sama has no reason to sneak off, instead, this has something to do with honor."

She stared at us and bowed her head exactly forty-five degrees, turned, and left.

"A smug, warped woman. Is her body temperature ice cold?"

"Is her skin surprisingly soft and velvety? Maybe she's chubby and warm," said Dr. Kose. The women were startled. His words did not fit his interest in virgins."

"Well, Doctor, is there a plausible suspect?"

"No, not one."

"What evidence have the police seized?" asked Kazuma.

The doctor linked his hands behind his head, rubbed his hair, and gave an unfortunate smile.

"No, not one. The police are dogged in their examinations, but it's all so elusive. First of all, they've found no grudges, infatuations, or any other motive."

"But it's unlike an opportunistic crime, like robbery by a vagabond, and closely resembles premeditated murder. Have any discrepancies appeared in the details?"

"Have they?"

"The great doctor asking me is malicious. Are you asking without laughing at the opinion of an amateur detective? Tamao-san left Wani's room at 11:15 pm. I was still awake. I heard Tamao-san singing a chanson as she bounded downstairs. That prompted me to look at my watch and turn off the lights.

"Tamao-san left Wani's room without locking the door. A little after two, when Utsugi Akiko went to Wani's room, the door was locked. When she came back with a key and entered the room, Wani was still alive. He was asleep and snoring. He didn't wake up even when shaken. Akiko-san deliberately set down the lighter, locked the door, and left.

"When Tamao-san discovered Wani's body the next morning, the door was not locked. What on earth does this mean? Well, Doctor?"

"Uh, I was awake and heard Tamao-san singing the chanson when she left. What could that mean?"

"What do I know? I know the murderer had a key. The door was locked one time while Wani was alive. After he was killed, the murderer left without locking the door. When you and Utsugi-san unlocked the door and entered the room, the murderer may have been there."

"Yes, perhaps he was," said the doctor.

The faces of Kazuma, Ayaka, and Kyoko changed momentarily. Unknowingly, I was on edge, too.

"Oh? Really? My evidence isn't substantial. Where was the murderer?"

"Yes, well, if Utsugi-san is telling the truth, perhaps there's no other possibility than his being there. Under Wani-san's bed. There's no other hiding place. Detective Suspicious, Eight-Foot Nose, Detective Bookworm shared that expectation. That's still the expectation."

The women sighed to relieve their stress.

"How could he be in there?" cried Ayaka.

"I'll explain how and may be made a fool of by the murderer. I still can't hypothesize anything. Surprisingly, the murderer may not have been in the room at that time."

Kazuma asked, "Is there proof of the assumption that the murderer was not there?"

"Yes. He, the murderer, is a technician and prepared various schemes. Of course, we may want to believe that, but he may have been incredibly unprepared. I don't know what to believe other than, from the beginning, the fellow failed and was harmless but found himself in a fix. The unique problem was the murders of Wani-san and Tamao-san."

Kazuma jerked up his tormented face.

"On the night of the day before yesterday when Wani was killed, I was awake and working until three in the morning. Ayaka fled to my room and fell asleep on my bed, so I got up and wrote. Since last year, I've been writing an essay on French symbolist poets but have made little progress.

"I think it was around one when I heard a key being inserted into the door of the adjacent room. I said I fell fast asleep late at night, but I easily distinguished this sound from the waterfalls. I couldn't hear footsteps or tell whether the person was entering or leaving."

The doctor nodded and said, "Of course. If I were the murderer, I'd probably muffle the harsh sound of keys. Was it Utsugi-san? Ayaka-san was sleeping here the entire time."

The question caught Kazuma off guard.

"Yes. The night before and last night."

"Utagawa-sensei, you worked until three in the morning."

"Yes. But this is the night before last. I went to bed much earlier last night."

"Ayaka-san rested the entire time until three in the morning."

"She slept through it all."

"Well then, we've finally established an alibi for one person. We can't prove anyone else was not the murderer. Tamao-san slept in a special place that facilitated her murder. The place and the situation said kill me. When is the anniversary of the death of your mother, Utagawa-sensei?"

Kazuma's expression changed with the word *anniversary*. For a little while, he was bewildered and at a loss for words.

"The ninth of next month. What day is that?"

"I don't know. Is there a link to that threat and this murder case? I've found nothing. I don't know whether the murderer killed Wani-san and Tamao-san. As for the threat, there may be a need for caution."

Word came that Wani's body had arrived.

9

―――

**THE ROAD BACK FROM THE
CREMATION**

When the sutra recitation and incense burning ended in the funeral hall, the coffin was loaded onto a large handcart and immediately taken to the cremation site. The male guests: Kazuma, Mokubei, Hitomi Koroku, Tango Yumihiko, Dr. Kose, Pikaichi, and even Kamiyama Toyo, slowly followed the coffin.

The hunchback poet gripping what looked like the cane of a forest witch emerged from the entryway. Ayaka-san stepped out of the party of women who lined up to see the men off.

"Utsumi-san, this may be too much of a strain. They're probably half way there by now, if you don't mind my saying."

"Yes. If you go, you'll be leaving the women alone. We'll be lonely," said Akiko.

"You're popular, Quasimodo-san," shouted a smirking Chigusa.

"I'll be on my way. Don't get carried away. I'm not so dim to think you want me to be a pretty lady's toy."

He was an indelicate man. By nature, a homely person

82

is warped and vulgar. The hunchback is an odd fellow whose words are out-of-bounds and crude. He sticks out and has a curious attraction to the foolish, uneducated, and crass Chigusa-san. With good humor, he carelessly laughed.

"Well, I must be going. If I don't give the requiem, Wani will not happily become bones."

The man far behind the others walked away at a steady pace. Ayaka accompanied him outside the gate to see him off.

The cremation site was in a dense forest on an impassable back mountain at the bottom of the mountain. The procession passed through the beech forest. A grassy plain covering three hundred square feet surrounded the conical mountain where turtledoves sang in the forest. Firewood for the cremation was piled high beside the cemetery guard's night shed.

They chanted sutras again and lit the fire. As the large limbs of the arrogant brute turned to smoke and disappeared, my emotions intensified.

We left when his bones finally appeared the next morning. As twilight faded, a thin haze swiftly floated up from the valley. The mountains darkened to purple, and the evening cicadas had not yet disappeared.

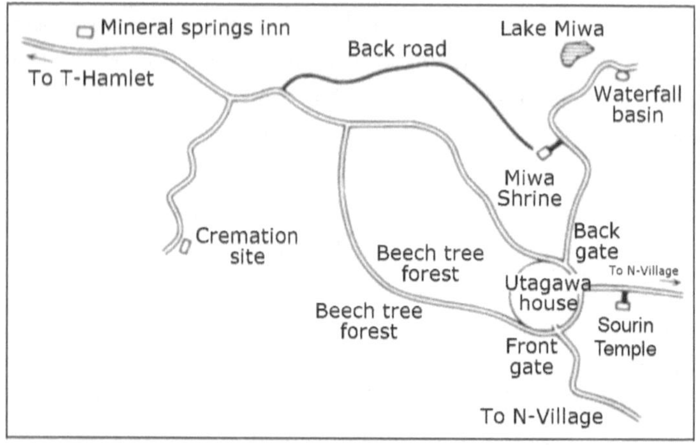

Figure 2.

Of course, Utsumi was exhausted, and pain paled his normal complexion.

Pikaichi said, "Hey, Hunchback-sensei, get in the cart, I'm pushing. You may be superstitious so I'll confess, it carried the coffin. You idle your life away and live a life of indolence, but you're a marvel of creation whose life will extend to old age. Get on and ride."

"The transformation into a monster is longevity. It's not a problem. Get on."

Utsumi didn't hesitate to climb on. Two peasants pulled the two-wheeled cart. Pikaichi pushed from behind for the vigorous climb up the valley road.

The group of priests and monks, Kazuma, and Kamiyama Toyo left first in a bunch. Tango Yumihiko, Koroku, Mokubei, Dr. Kose, and I leisurely followed.

Yumihiko's cynical face whipped around to look at us.

"I don't know about Tamao-san, but one of these four killed Wani, except for Kose-kun."

The cool Mokubei said nothing, feigned ignorance,

and kept walking. The honest Hitomi Koroku gasped a little.

"Why? Why us four? Well?"

"If the murderer is one of us, it's probably you. Why did you say that? Whenever you have the opportunity, you get too many ideas and speak to manipulate. Is the truth you killed both Wani and Tamao-san?"

"That's why I'm saying one of us four."

"Why don't you speak clearly about yourself? Aren't you a writer, too? All of us are writers; therefore, we must use words responsibly, right? We are not detectives."

Yumihiko was a little self-conscious but slowly broke into a sarcastic smile.

"For instance, a robber killed Wani. That is not interesting at all. Perhaps, Kazuma has a problem with his younger sister and Wani's rudeness pushed him over the edge, so he killed them both. It happens all the time. That's interesting, isn't it? I killed Wani and Tamao-san. This is also quite possible. And because it is highly possible, and if true, isn't it interesting?

"We are not detectives but writers. We must search for the truth and not discover murderers. Am I right? I seem to be fabricating a murderer. Don't Wani's and Tamao-san's killings make compelling subjects? By using them, wouldn't creating the possible murderer also be an interesting diversion for a writer? I think it's our duty to flush out a common criminal. What do you think?"

Koroku was angry and did not respond.

"What kind of literary talk is this? Can you stop talking about business? There's a good chance I could do it to Wani and you. However, my style is very practical. How can this murder case be considered practical? The possible murderer, in addition to being novel, is not commonplace.

Right? This crime is not cliched in terms of human nature."

Mokubei looked about to rain questions on him in a quiet voice when Koroku left in a huff.

"Tango has a secret design. Could he be the murderer? The truth is banal, but can the truth be he has no defense? A fellow like you shows contempt for others. Wani was an insolent man but was candid and had a lovable side. Compared to his openness and cheerfulness, Tango was clearly a few steps behind Wani as a writer. Secret designs, deep thinking, and negativity are not a writer's qualifications.

"Wani never minced words but thought one should think from another perspective and think deeply not superficially. All writers always have their own way of thinking. Am I right? Wani's work is concise and decisive compared to Tango's current work, but the roots of his thinking are deep. Therefore, his scale of his work was far-reaching.

"Tango stuck to miserly thoughts, which made his thinking shallow, his problems narrow, and the literary value of his works small and stingy. If you start talking about the murderer in a murder case, it's surely for your own defense. It's best to come to the point. Did you kill Wani? Did you kill Tamao-san? You're not the killer but are you afraid of looking like the murderer? It's because Kose-kun is here, too. Are you aware of that?"

Tango's smirk stayed.

They climbed from the valley and entered the village road.

"Excuse me, but I will take leave here for a relaxed stroll home," said Tango Yumihiko. He parted from the group and walked in the opposite direction towards the village where he'd come upon a hamlet with a mineral springs. The mineral springs inn, though called an inn, was not famous enough to attract guests from other regions. It was nothing more than the public bathhouse of the hamlet.

I had a sudden realization. The inn sold general goods and over-the-counter medicines. Goods bought before the war were still on sale, but the customers were gone. During the war, they stocked the sedative Calmotin. In those days, I became drowsy if I drank sake and didn't need sleeping medication. Recently, however, I've been suffering from insomnia. I planned to see if the mineral springs inn stocked Calmotin, which I wanted and planned to buy if I went to the village. Tango's departure reminded me of this, so I left and followed him. I walked about two-tenths of a mile when I met Tango coming back.

"What happened? I thought you were going to the mineral springs inn."

"Yes. I was, but there's something else I have to do. Excuse me."

It was another half mile to the inn. This hamlet had fifteen buildings.

The proprietor of the inn was a shrewd man around forty years old with a pale, intelligent face. He listened to my situation and said, "You see. Tokyoites are astute and from time to time found their way to this establishment to shop. Not selling would have been a good idea because I didn't know the current prices. I suffered a great loss in the past by unknowingly selling too cheap. Now, there's nothing left."

"Please, have a look. If there's any, of course, I'll pay the black-market price."

"I don't know the black-market prices. Anything costs 100 times more, 100 times, okay?"

"Medicine is nine times higher than in the past. Food

may be 100 times, so medicine should be 100 times higher, too. For that price, would you please search for the goods?"

Bundles of old medicines were in a cardboard box in the corner of a shelf. He examined each one, but there was no Calmotin. After the proprietor went to so much trouble, I couldn't leave without buying something. I bought a couple of gastrointestinal medications for deworming and went home. All the medications were ordinary.

"What's Calmotin for?"

"It's a sleeping medicine."

"In that case, about three months ago, Utagawa-san's guests, Nagumo-san, Utagawa-san's sister Auntie Yura-sama bought it. She bought it all. I had sleeping medicine then."

Night fell on my way home. The beech tree forest was dark and walking, perilous. In the remaining light, I slipped down the side road behind the mountain of the Utagawa house and came to the junction with the mountain path to Mount Miwa. From there, I intended to go around to the back gate but on my way down the hill, I ran into Kazuma in front of that gate. He was coming from the side road in front of the Zen temple.

"Oh, it's you. Are you in a hurry?" asked the surprised Kazuma.

"I went to the mineral springs inn to buy Calmotin. I was looking for unsold leftover stock from the war. Unfortunately, Auntie Yura-sama beat me to it."

"Really? The leftover stock at that inn was discovered lately. People have written asking me to buy things.

"I'm coming from Sourin Temple. I went to make arrangements for my sister's funeral. Despite waiting a long time, no one came. I sat in the main temple and got lost in thought for half an hour."

A pocket electric light moved slowly toward us from the

hill at the front gate. It was Dr. Ebitsuka. He was surprised to see us and stopped.

"Good evening," he said. "Has the great man Wani become a sliver of smoke?"

Wani finally became a sliver of smoke. Although a part of me was delighted, when the limping doctor said the same thing, my intestinal worms were no longer calm. He joked and was sarcastic about all of us and not just Wani. Whenever he spoke, I wanted to slug him. My mind conjuring terrible thoughts like this bewildered me.

Earlier, I told Kazuma this. And when I left the other three to climb up the valley to take the village road, I said I was going to buy Calmotin at the mineral springs inn. I had completely forgotten Wani ingested sleeping medicine in the geranium. Today, wasn't a different white powder spilled at the pillow of Tamao-san's corpse?

Like in a bad play, I deliberately showed I regularly used Calmotin or some sleeping medication. I was miserable, worrying whether everyone suspected me.

Dr. Ebitsuka left us at the entrance to the dirt-floor room. We walked around the garden to the Western building. Were those the four monks at the cremation spot this afternoon now in the front parlor of the main house and mixed in at the dining table chatting with Tamon and Yura?

Kazuma approached the edge of the parlor.

"What? The priest was here? I didn't know that and sat in the main temple waiting for him for thirty minutes."

"He's a poet and unfamiliar with the ways of the world," said Tamon, clicked his tongue, and glared at his son.

"After the service, I always invite over the priests and monks for the *odoki* meal, an ancient custom in Japan."

"How may I help you?" asked the elderly priest, smiling at Kazuma.

Before the war, this priest was famous throughout Japan and taught Indian philosophy at universities. He was from this village and withdrew to the village's Zen temple during the war. He looked like a simple priest and a poor old man, not a scholar.

"Not now, you're having your meal. I'll ask tomorrow morning."

Kazuma entered the living room. The meal was ready, and everyone was waiting for him.

When he sat at the table, Utsumi said, "Today, I rode back on the coffin cart. The peasant pulling the cart said something peculiar. I thought a murderer was among the notable guests, but that may not be so.

"One of the evacuees to the village is a young demobilized soldier. He's a literary or political buff and seems a bit nuts. An erotic writer like Wani is a terrorist, a cancer in Japan, who must be killed. He showed a knife hidden in his breast pocket to a villager and said he killed Wani with it. This man said he truly hated Tamao-san because she was the sort of woman who would ruin Japan. The police are keeping an eye on him."

Kazuma looked troubled and said, "That evacuee is from this village. He's a discharged military man, a draftsman or something, called Okuda Tonekichiro. He was discharged; his home burned down; and he doesn't know where his wife and child are. He's a little off. His time on the battlefield warped him. He was in North China and is devoted to Confucius. Even now, he put a bulletin in a window of the evacuee room to announce Confucian studies or a study group on *The Analects of Confucius*.

"This is just hearsay. Perhaps under some false pretext, he ran into Wani on the streets. But Wani whacked him, and he was crushed. Wani would make quick work of this slender, lanky man. He probably ran off crying like a small dog with his tail between his legs. This former soldier said Wani was an erotic writer, but the soldier is peculiar. Also, Ayaka has received strange letters."

Ayaka also looked concerned.

"But they weren't love letters. I was sure they were connected to Wani-san. I was fooled by an erotic writer like Wani-san."

Ebitsuka spoke these unpleasant words.

"He may be insane. That makes sense. After killing Wani-san, he came to my hospital to have his wounds treated. The wounds were scratches. He spoke at that time. This muscular man is a gang member. All physical strength and vigor are not cultural. But what is it? Perhaps it's an illness. He said things like that. And he sent a letter to 'Utagawa Tamon's Monstrous Bitch.' She didn't respond. He didn't name her. Perhaps there may be many bitches. He said all of them made concessions for each other."

"Hey, bush doctor of the haughty gentleman, why don't I drag you out of here?" asked the enraged Pikaichi. "Are you some kind of miserable asshole? Pompous bastard. A lackey who fights the truth and claims the world is fine. What kind of man are you? Why don't you take a seat with the obnoxious crowd?"

Pikaichi walked over to him, with a grunt, lifted the chair where Ebitsuka sat, carried him out of the parlor, and set him down.

Pikaichi returned and sat. The doctor limped back inside holding the chair. He looked calm but sulky and returned to his original seat.

Without getting angry, Pikaichi asked, "Does the Notre Dame professor have an immature mind because of his injury? He can't run and play. I'm sure the murderer is a part of this group."

"Why? Is it impossible to sneak in from the outside?" asked Utsumi.

"Idiot. Where is the evidence showing someone other than us could have committed this murder? The murderer was able to lock and unlock Wani's room. That is crucial. Therefore, this feat had to be the work of the dignitaries."

Enraged, Kazuma screamed, "We're not detectives. Why don't we stop talking about murderers?"

"What?" spat out Pikaichi.

"Very well. I'd like that. Erotic stories. This is good. Only this. The dining table is always like this. As the men and women present drink, against all decorum, their point-less talk covers literature and the arts. Your works are immature no matter how much time passes. Wani-sensei wrote his novels for adults. Thus, we'll discuss eroticism and act erotically often. Tonight, I will not pick a fight with Utsugi-sensei. I prefer the frigid primness of Kocho-san. Maybe, it's the fault of being Japanese, but I'm interested in Buddha statues, specifically, those from the Asuka era. The erotic dancers of Java or Bali have the colorful eroti-cism of the Asuka era. I want to hug their waistlines."

Pikaichi stood and danced by shaking his hips like natives of the South Sea Islands. He also knew their songs. His hand gestures, hip movements, and singing voice were vivid. The women were astonished by his exact reproduc-tion of the harsh voices of those islands. The tint in their eyes changed from hatred to praise they wished to hide.

10

MADNESS

The time was 9:40.

Aunt Yura-sama came to the living room and scanned the group. She asked Dr. Ebitsuka, "Where's Chigusa?"

"Don't know."

His tone was unfriendly. Akiko sitting beside him said, "I haven't seen Chigusa-san at all. She wasn't at dinner. Right, Ebitsuka-san?"

"I don't know."

"Ayaka-sama, do you know what happened to Chigusa-san? Was she at dinner?"

"No, I didn't see her."

"What happened to her? I thought she was here, but where is she?"

The old woman left on her unsteady legs. Since her stroke, she struggled to walk and dragged her legs. Going up and down the stairs was a battle. None of the rooms was suitable, so she endured the inconvenience and nearly crawled up and down stairs. A bedpan was handy at night.

All of us were drunk. Pikaichi drank an amazing

amount. Even Utsumi had numerous cups of beer. In this night's gathering of murder cases, sensitive nerves and pain were inevitable. A murderer among them was the unpleasant thought foremost in their minds.

Ordinarily, Mokubei didn't drink sake. When he did, it was because he was easily duped, mostly by Tango, who ensnared him for a little while. Whatever the situation, the spearhead was quickly pointed at Ebitsuka.

"Famous finicky doctor, would you please sit here? What? No. Very well. You will listen in private to explain our madness. But from my perspective, I have no doubt you are the one who is insane."

"Now that's an insightful remark."

Pikaichi was very amused and took command of the group.

"Listen carefully," he said, "I hate to expose the scandals of men, but in your case alone, I've lost all desire to restrain myself.

"You disdain the private affairs of our literary crowd. Aren't you intimate with a particular young lady nightly in your quarters in the fishing hut? And Kayoko-san hates your examinations. If no one else is present, she refuses to be examined by you. Judging from the gossip at Gonsuke's Bar, didn't you grab Kayoko-san's hand and stare at her tits for a long time? Recently, you've become heartsick because you were obsessed with the darling maid named Shizue-san. You insinuate someone has an illness in her chest, or an abnormality in her organs, or the need for frequent medical examinations. These three incidents occurred here. What are you up to at the hospital? Even by judging from the three cases here, compared to the love and lust of literary people like us, your obvious slight peculiarity, negativity, and perversion are outrageous."

"Yes, that's it," said a delighted Pikaichi. The women

pretended not to hear and talked amongst themselves about what to do. This may have been the fault of their social compassion and politeness. However, Mokubei's words relieved pressure by instantly freezing the women's social tendencies.

"A famous doctor, a true gentleman. Ladies and gentlemen, please look at his eyes. Those eyes shimmer. They are the eyes of an insane man. Eyes that killed people. The eyes of a murdering demon starved for blood and not satiated even when looking at a sea of blood. He cannot hide his true character. Look. Look at him."

Mokubei paled from intoxication and oozed menace. His sunken eyes radiated evil but were no match for Ebistuka's eyes.

"From the beginning, I was aware of his progression. He shook with anger. From a frenzied rage, the dazzling light of a madman stayed in his eyes. The flash in his eyes was certainly able to pounce and kill a person. The light unmatched in fury could tear someone from limb to limb, randomly kill, or commit any act of a madman."

The women gulped air.

Mokubei glared at Ebitsuka.

"Without a doubt, he's deranged. His craziness may be schizophrenia, or he suffers from delusions. I think I'm pure and part of the justice faction. You invent an opportunity to play with Kayoko-san's tits, get closer to the women, and play with Shizue-san's tits. You aren't aware of what you're doing. Are you a pervert and crazy? Your fastidiousness that fantasizes about the impurity of others is a disease of a madman. Everyone, isn't that true?"

Ebitsuka's eyes gradually burned and opened as wide as possible. He was at a loss for what to do. He had no idea what to say or do. In an instant, everything was possible. An eruption of sorts seemed to occur.

The sounds of dragging feet preceded the entry of Aunt Yura-sama holding the hand of Nurse Moroi.

"Chigusa is nowhere to be found. Where could she be? Do any of you have any idea where she is?"

A different fear swept through the room.

"It can't be. Is it another murder?" shrieked Pikaichi. "Calm down, Yura-sama. That girl is in heat. Excuse me for saying, but didn't she come because her whole body surged with sexual desire?"

No one answered.

Nurse Moroi spoke quietly like a drowning person speaking underwater, "Yes. Chigusa-san went out for a secret rendezvous."

"What are you saying? You knew."

Yura-sama looked helpless and astonished at Nurse Moroi's cold face.

"Chigusa-san received an invitation for a date on a slip of paper. I saw her fluttering around. I didn't read the note. She went out around six."

"Where did she go?"

"I don't know."

"Who was he, her date?"

"I can't say," she said in her forbidding tone.

Again, the room went silent.

Ebitsuka swung his arms like a bear. His behavior was odd. Maybe he was overexcited. He turned with a start like he was about to jump up. He briefly touched the hip on his lame side and left the room, swinging his arms. At the entrance to the hallway, he turned and screamed with all his might, "You idiots!"

His small stature created a strange, hoarse voice that sounded like it would break. Next, he executed an energetic about-face and walked off.

"Wha, ha, ha, ha. Wha, ha, ha, ha."

Pikaichi released a maniacal laugh.

"This is a total farce. Isn't this a murder farce? From the beginning, this house has been a farce. Why do you all look so serious? I want to say brothel. Am I right or off the mark? Is this a lusty group or a nest of sex maniacs?"

"Shut up! You lowlife! Go back to Tokyo! Go now!"

Ayaka shook with rage. Her nerves twitched as if jolted by electricity.

"What the hell's wrong with you? Say that one more time!"

When she finished, Pikaichi's expression changed. He was a demon. The silence was like the scalpel of the murdering demon living in Ebitsuka. Pikaichi became vicious, a demon, a crazed savage animal without a human face.

He sprang and grabbed Ayaka. He swung her around then flung her away. Ayaka stumbled forward onto all fours. Her clothes ripped. She banged her knees and couldn't stand.

We moved to help her up, but she jumped to her feet. This woman didn't look brave, but she raised her head and said, "You thug! You criminal!"

"You bitch!"

We were still in shock when he slapped Ayaka and knocked her down. His arm strength worked quickly like an arrow, and we weren't ready for the next shock. He raised a large flower vase off to the side.

Fortunately, Hitomi Koroku carried himself like a warrior. Pikaichi threw down the vase. It hit no one but smashed to pieces on the floor.

Pikaichi tossed out Koroku with the supernatural strength of a raging bull. When Ayaka sensed his menace, she turned her body and fled. She flew into the dining hall and escaped into the garden.

Pikaichi was already after her.

When we caught up with them, Pikaichi had shoved Ayaka against a pine tree in the garden and was slapping and pushing her so hard she was gasping for air.

We piled on and dragged them apart. When they were about sixty feet apart, the women left with Ayaka. Pikaichi was panting, so we let our guard down. He darted off again.

Ayaka realized what happened and sped off. She moved her slight body with ease and amazing speed in a straight line like a fish. She reversed course and flew back inside through the dining hall. During our chase, she reached her room and locked herself in. Pikaichi stumbled running up the stairs and failed to catch her but was close behind.

Pikaichi was kicking her bedroom door like a raving maniac. We caught up and rushed him.

"You bastards."

We chased him off.

"You ugly bitch. Come out and I'll kill you. I'll strangle you. Throttle you!"

Pikaichi grabbed his shirt collar and closed it around his neck. He smashed his foot into the door but fell flat on his face with his arms and legs splayed.

The commotion probably lasted close to an hour. If we approached, he stood and leaped at us while howling like a wild beast.

We gave up and withdrew to our respective bedrooms.

I could hear Pikaichi getting up every ten or twenty minutes to kick the door to Ayaka's room, fall flat on the floor, and scream.

I gave up and fell asleep. I was later told Pikaichi screamed for the next three hours. When someone tried to wake him in the morning, he was exhausted, out like a light, stretched out, and face down before Ayaka's door.

Ayaka was unhurt. Pikaichi was quiet and calm the next day. However, a murder occurred in an unexpected place.

The hunchback poet had been murdered in his bedroom. We split up to search for Chigusa and found her body in the forest on Mount Miwa.

Author's Note: The title *The Nonserial Murders* has various problems. In a word, *nonserial* indicates a different murderer may have committed each murder. Often, a great detective appears. Detective Bookworm showed up first at the house. The title provides clues and good hunches but provides little to interpret.

Iizuka, aka Eureka, sent a letter from far-off Kyushu and wrote seven or eight will die. And the murder victims will be killed one after the other. This terrible trick of Eureka was impressive. It just popped into her head. No one could fathom how she achieved that simple trick.

The murderer is deduced from the title. That trick comes from *The Casebook of Inspector Hanshichi*. Detective Suspicious was skilled at guessing the murderer from the cover design of a detective novel but has not captured an actual murderer since the Meiji Restoration.

I have my doubts about the titles of detective novels. The great detectives appear to be close to the level of the sloppy casebook of Hanshichi. More than ridiculous, this is lamentable for law and order in Japan.

Now may be the time for Dr. Kose to briefly explain serial and nonserial. I ask you not to be too easily led around by the nose by the murderer. Writers are in a muddle without rivals.

Based on the addition of a challenge and the views of Edogawa Ranpo's detective stories, among detective novelists, Kikuo Tsunoda is the master of pinpointing the culprit and respectfully presents challenges in his great detective novels. Next, there is Professor Shikiba Ryuzaburo.

The reward presented by me, the author, will average around 10,000 yen. I'm sorry it's not much. I wanted to give an 18-carat diamond, unfortunately, I can't afford one.

Sakaguchi Ango

11

THE WAY HOME FROM THE
CREMATION

The next morning, I left my room to go for a walk and found Pikaichi splayed out face down in front of Ayaka's door.

I went out the back gate and headed to Mount Miwa. Waving my walking stick in that direction, I called out, "Halloo!" to Kamiyama Toyo and the manservant Grandpa Kisaku.

"You're up early, Kamiyama-san. You look stylish in your knickers for your morning walk."

"I'm an early riser. This is no joke. Sleeping all day is for literary folks and burglars. This is not a walk. This is a search. Chigusa-san went out yesterday evening and never returned. Yashiro-san, these words may invite bad luck, but should we be thinking, Has it happened again? Despite my appearance, I have a weak heart. Taking a walk revolts me. I can't walk the mountain roads in what looks like a jungle."

"Have you conducted a broad search?"

"I searched the roads frequently traveled. I'm going to walk from Miwa Shrine to Lake Miwa."

The three of us went around to the back of Miwa Shrine and looked up the mountain of dense forest. Low, striped bamboo grew rampant in the area and entangled with weeds and vines. Gloomy darkness and stillness weighed down on us.

"This is surely a jungle where you go to get murdered. Yashiro-san, I'm not walking into that. Never."

"What should we do?"

Kamiyama bent down and picked up something.

"This can't be. This is women's rouge. How did it get here? Oh, look over there. Have those weeds been stepped on? What if …"

He took five or six steps in and found a handbag that had been thrown out. Its contents were strewn around. After ten more steps, he found Chigusa-san lying like she was asleep in the shadow at the base of a large tree. She was blindfolded by a *furoshiki* wrapping cloth and had been strangled by a waist sash.

The area showed no signs of resistance or fighting.

"It looks like she didn't fight back. The trampled weeds we discovered first were not where she was killed. Her body was carried here and abandoned. She hadn't been raped. If this murderer respected the woman's chastity, was he being a gentleman?"

The pants suit she wore was not disheveled.

We notified the police. Kamiyama and I guided the party of detectives and Dr. Kose to the crime scene.

When we returned for breakfast, we walked into mayhem. Utsumi Akira had been stabbed to death in his bedroom.

He had not appeared at the table for breakfast. Ayaka went to see and found him still in his pajamas lying on a pool of blood in the middle of the floor. He had three stab wounds on one side, two on his chest, and two on his neck.

A knife had been washed and placed on the dresser. The murder washed his hands, too. This knife was on the display shelf with other knives in the sitting room.

One of Utsumi's slippers was about two feet away from his feet. The killer discarded the other beside the door in the room. Utsumi wore these slippers in the toilet next to his bedroom. The murderer left no other evidence and no fingerprints.

The crime scene investigation ended. The doctor from the prefectural hospital took Chigusa's corpse. The main hall of Sourin Temple was turned into the autopsy room for the autopsies of the two new bodies.

They estimated Chigusa was killed between six and seven on the evening of the 18th, and the hunchback poet, between eleven and midnight. Utsumi seemed to have been reading Laclos's *Les Liaisons dangereuses* in bed. It appeared he put the book face down, got out of bed, and was killed. He might have gone to the bathroom and was killed on his way back to bed. Or Utsumi let his killer into his room. Perhaps before he realized what was happening, an acquaintance with murderous intentions stabbed him from the back to his side. He staggered, tumbled forward, and was stabbed in a frenzy. The knife to the heart was the fatal blow. And when he was face down, the murderer stabbed him in the neck. In short, he was killed by someone he knew. Terrified he could survive, the murderer persisted in the crazed stabbing.

Around eight-thirty after dinner, Detective Suspicious gathered all of us in the living room of the Western building.

"Now, I have to toss out my respect for etiquette. No one can be crossed off the list of suspects. Therefore, I must be blunt and ask for your cooperation in this investigation. I'm requesting your alibis from the lighting of the fires after the chanting of sutras at Mochizuki-san's cremation until dinner. Let's begin with the general situation. Kose-san, what time did you leave?"

"Well, I have a careless nature and rarely check the time, but it was around the time of the secret rendezvous," said the doctor, forcing a smile.

Kamiyama Toyo said, "I looked at the time. The chanting was over and the fire lit. I was thinking about going home when Yashiro-san asked for the time. The young master, Kazuma, answered. When I looked at my watch, it was 6:06. Kazuma-san said it was 6:09. My watch is a cheap Movado but was a good buy that's never off by more than one-tenth of a second. How about that? But I'll sell it for 100,000 yen. Ah, ha, ha."

Eureka's loud, shrill voice said, "Yashiro-san, don't you wear a wristwatch? Why did you ask the time?"

"I left it on my desk yesterday. Eureka-san, is it your rule to wear everything you own all year long?"

"What? Aren't you being rude, addressing me as Eureka-san?"

"Be quiet."

Detective Suspicious stared with a hint of menace.

"Now, did everyone return together?"

No one answered, then Kamiyama Toyo said, "First of all, the painter Doi Pikaichi helped push the large handcart. Utsumi-san was riding on the cart. This group left first. Two young men pulled the cart. With Doi-sensei pushing, the cart powered by three dashed up the valley with amazing speed."

"Why was there a handcart?"

"To carry the body."

"Why didn't the cart return immediately after bringing the body?"

"This is not like the rickshaws and one-yen taxis hired

in the cities and towns. The young men in the countryside help at the master's house and don't rush back home. They help stack the firewood or do other chores because the cremation site has few workers."

The head detective turned to Detective Bookworm.

"Are those two young men coming?"

"Yes, everyone there yesterday was summoned. They're in the other room."

Two young men, Wasaburo and Kiyoshi, were called in.

"Where did Utsumi-san ride to?"

"To the mountain road behind the mansion."

"Was it the mountain road that goes to Mount Miwa?"

"Yes, we went up for the first 200 feet, then down the hill for the next 200 feet and parted."

"Why didn't he ride to the back gate?"

"From there, the hill went down. He said, 'That's enough. I'm getting off.' Riding downhill seemed to make him sick."

"Doi-san, is that what you remember?"

"I don't know. I quit pushing the cart. I pushed hard from the cremation site and up the valley for about a quarter of a mile. After that, I strolled around. It was an ordinary road with no incline. Pushing the cart pulled down the road by the two young men was nearly identical to pushing a Datsun motor car."

"You didn't stay with the cart?"

"The cart runs at a terrific speed. The bouncing up and down is horrible. They rattled around a curve and were gone. When I reached the road where they parted on Mount Miwa, I didn't see the hunchback."

"Did anyone notice Utsumi-san on the mountain?"

No one answered.

"Doi-san, was Utsumi-san here when you returned?"

"No, I got back first. Utsumi was second. After that, I have no idea. I had no reason to keep watch."

"Do you know what time that was?"

"I'm not sure, but when I returned, Utsugi-san was the first to greet me. She may have a sense of the time."

"It was around seven, maybe about ten minutes before seven? I have no sense of time, either."

"Was everyone else together?"

Kamiyama Toyo said, "I was with Kazuma-san and the priest. The others came much later."

I said, "That's true. Tango, Mokubei, Koroku, Dr. Kose, and I nearly crawled back as we engaged in a rambling war of words. When we climbed out of the valley, Tango left us and went to the mineral springs hamlet. This could be called a type of lyrical stroll caused by the awkwardness of verbal disputes. Next, I went to buy medicine at the hamlet. I crossed paths with Tango, who had walked about a tenth of a mile to the hamlet and turned around. I bought medicine at the mineral springs inn. It was getting dark when I started home. I bumped into Kazuma at the back gate. Dr. Ebitsuka was there, strolling with a philosophical gait. He carried a glowing electric lamp in his breast pocket."

"Kamiyama-san's party returned together."

"That's so. Nobody left along the way. At the back gate, the priest returned to the temple."

Kazuma said, "Yes. That's why I thought the priest was at the temple, so I went there to speak with him. I called out to him several times, but there was no response. Then I waited in front of the main hall for thirty minutes. When I gave up and went home, I met Yashiro at the back gate and found the priest sitting in the living room."

"Of course, I see. Utagawa-san, did you see anyone at Sourin Temple?"

"I returned by that road and did not see a soul, which means I have no alibi."

"Tango-san and Yashiro-san returned alone. The rest, Hitomi-san, Miyake-san, and Kose-san, were together."

Mokubei shook his frosty face.

"No, I was alone, too."

"Hitomi and Kose-san followed the periphery of the beech forest. I went by the back road, so I walked the road Utsumi's cart passed down."

"You met Utsumi-san there."

"Excuse me, but I saw absolutely no one. That road winds through a dense mountain forest. This road has no vegetable or rice fields, and the villagers never travel it."

Dr. Ebitsuka came late and entered alone.

"I'm sorry to keep you waiting. I was in the middle of something when the call came. Every evening without fail, I come to this house, but there was an emergency tonight."

"That's ridiculous. Why must you come every night?"

The doctor looked about to straighten up, his eyes flashed arrogance, and muttered, "Ridiculous."

"Ebitsuka-san, what time did you come here last evening?"

"Why would anyone need to remember that?"

"We'd like to know the time you left the hospital."

"I'm not a timekeeper. No one other than the keeper of a temple with a bell lives by watching the clock."

"When we visit someone's home, we know what time it is and the time we'll arrive. I think that's a natural thought. Don't you agree, Ebitsuka-san?"

With piercing coldness, Mokubei said, "If that's not so, he would be even stranger. Ebitsuka-sensei, do you understand? What the detective said is true. People who leave their house to visit another's must always be conscious of the time."

Perhaps Mokubei still remembered last evening. The academic Mokubei possessed a woman's vindictiveness and harped on one thing.

"Explain it to suit yourself. That is a detective's job. My job is to examine sick people, and that is my responsibility. I know nothing about anything else."

"Yashiro-san and Utagawa-san were with Ebitsuka-san at the back gate. Yashiro-san came by the usual back road, the road taken by the cart. Utagawa-san came from the Zen temple. Ebitsuka-san came from the village. What time was that?"

I said, "Let me see, it was around eight. By then, the day would be over. Was that so? In this area hidden by the mountains, sunset may come sooner."

The detective said, "I see. Doi-san returned first around seven or six-fifty. Next, Utsumi-san, Kamiyama-san, and Utagawa-san. Utagawa-san returned or went out immediately. Next?"

"Hitomi-san and I came back," said Dr. Kose.

"Then came Miyake-san. Tango-san. Yashiro-san. That's everyone. Which one of the women went out at that time?"

Utsugi Akiko answered, "All of us were in the living room. Others were in the kitchen, but they may have been together."

"You say together. Who was together?"

"Kocho-san and I were in here. Ayaka-sama went to the kitchen and came to speak to us. Kamiyama-san's wife did so, too. I think Chigusa-sama was not in this room."

"Who was the last to see Chigusa-san?"

"I was," said Nurse Moroi, who joined them. She seemed full of self-confidence to intimidate the others.

"I saw her exit the back gate around six. A minute earlier she had shown me a piece of paper."

"Did you read the paper?"

"Yes. The homely woman and the hunchback were to have a rendezvous that day from six-thirty to seven behind Miwa Shrine for a private conversation. Utsumi-san was enchanted by her and said she was special."

"Utsumi-san asked me to pass her the note." Ayaka-san looked troubled and ashamed and said with slight amusement, "Utsumi-san was confused. This *rendezvous* was not used in the ordinary sense. It's the opposite. I prefer to call it a secret meeting of the evil spirits of the rivers, forests, and mountains. The wish for a simple meeting says a secret meeting of the homely woman and the hunchback of evil spirits. He intended to write poems devoted to ugly women his whole life. Chigusa-san lived for those poems. The poems for Chigusa-san were not written."

"How do you know?" asked Pikaichi. His words were bathed in scorn.

Hitomi Koroku asked, "Did he write those poems? Detective, did you examine Utsumi's manuscripts?"

"I looked through them, but they're outside my field of expertise. Kose-san, are those the manuscripts?"

"They are, but just titles are written."

Detective Suspicious's demeanor changed, and he scanned their faces.

"Last night was a boisterous night," he said with a laugh and glanced at Pikaichi who said he knew nothing and looked away. The detective turned his attention to Ayaka. Her kneecap, both arms, elbows, and fingers were bandaged. She looked embarrassed but had the essence of a beautiful woman and gave the clear impression she felt a general sense of freedom. The detective's gaze moved to Dr. Ebitsuka.

"Ebitsuka-san, you were furious last night. So why didn't you go straight home?"

"I went straight home," said Ebitsuka. His entire face seemed to burn with anger. He may have been grinding his teeth. Detective Suspicious's eyes stopped on his bandaged hands.

"How did you hurt your hands?"

"I fell on the mountain road last night."

"Ebitsuka-san has a bad leg, and he takes four and a half hours to walk from this house to the hospital. He left here last night at 9:30."

This was the first time I heard that Ebitsuka, who stayed over every night, went home last night. I strained to hear, but Ebitsuka's large eyes lit his face, and the detective did not stare back.

"By an unfortunate coincidence, a medical emergency arose last night. It happened a half hour after midnight. A phone call arrived from the hospital. Nurse Moroi searched for Ebitsuka-san in the fishing hut. Ebitsuka-san returned home one and a half to two hours later. Doesn't Ebitsuka-san take four and a half hours to walk the road home?"

"I kept walking."

Ebitsuka tensed his shoulders and nearly spat out his words.

"Hmph. I keep walking. I don't go straight home. You idiots. To sweep away the air sullied by shameless people and restore myself, I must wander the back mountain roads as a stranger. That's how I injured my hand. Is this an inn for dogs? Hmph. A bunch of dummies. Hmph."

"Did you meet anyone? Visit or talk to anyone? Did anything like that happened?"

"Hmph. Who in this village would I want to visit? Ridiculous."

"Chigusa-san had been killed by 9:30 last night," teased Mokubei. Ebitsuka shook with anger and clenched his fists.

His radiant eyes filling his face stared at Mokubei, who gulped.

Detective Suspicious turned his gaze to Ayaka.

"Miss, last night was a disaster for you. Are you healing?"

She smiled.

"Thank you. My left knee is a little sore. The rest are scrapes."

"You escaped into your bedroom. Doi-san chased you, banged and kicked your door, and carried on until midnight."

Pikaichi looked unfazed. Unafraid and anticipating the detective, he said, "I don't remember it well. Detective, I don't remember becoming a tiger. Wouldn't anyone who's dead drunk be a bit out of it? The others surely know more than me about my behavior last night."

The detective nodded.

"People who got close were grabbed. Is that so, Kazuma-san?"

"I had no reason to approach him, but I had to when he entered my room. He grabbed my collar, pushed, and kicked me. Finally, I managed to escape back into my room. Kose-san grappled with him, too."

"I was also close to the bedroom. His face busy grinding his teeth peeked out the door. His hands swung up, then he shouted and rushed out. That was the first hour."

Kamiyama Toyo nodded.

"Yes, the uproar lasted until around eleven. He took a fighting stance in front of the door. His eyes glared; he was angry like the guardian god Nio at the temple gates. He had the prowess of a splendid warrior. From around eleven, he landed on his butt in the hall. The door supported his back. He sang and shouted. I may not look like a reader, but I laid down on the floor and read. At eighteen minutes after midnight, Doi-san's angry voice weakened then ceased. I quietly opened the door and peeked out. The drowsy painter Doi's back had slid off the door."

Detective Suspicious nodded.

"Kamiyama-san is a lawyer by profession and attentive to time, which is vital. Thankfully, you know a great deal. From your wife's bedroom door, he could see the length of the hall. That's why he leaned against that door. He could watch everyone come and go. Doi-san, could you tell us who came and went?"

Pikaichi looked a little tickled and embarrassed.

"Well, I may have screamed and chased after anyone who came in or went out last night, but my memory is fuzzy. After I leaned against the door and sat on my backside, everyone was asleep and no one came in or out. Let me see."

He thought hard but recalled nothing.

"Doi-san, you never left the front of the door. Not even once?"

Pikaichi scratched his head.

"Maybe to urinate. I really don't remember."

"No, he never moved from the front of the door," stressed Kamiyama Toyo. "The yelling voice at the same place didn't pause for five seconds. Would anyone have heard better than my wife? Probably not, but my wife can peacefully sleep through a tiger's roar."

His words put a serious look on Ayaka's face.

"I remember every moment. Until a little after midnight, the tiger roaring outside my door never stopped. Since the tiger appeared on this mountain, I usually slept in my husband's bedroom. Last night, however, I ran into my bedroom. I did that because my custom is to lock the door from the inside in my room, and I intended to do so immediately. Fortunately, I was far enough ahead of him and managed to lock the door. I thank his usual laziness."

Kamiyama Toyo asked, "Don't criminals enter through windows?"

"Why do you think that?"

"The painter Doi endured at his post. Doi-san says he doesn't remember, but he must have a reason for trying to kill someone. A murderer intentionally enters an intoxicated state in his mind and sets to work with deliberation.

"You may be right."

Detective Suspicious was an experienced man and never revealed the true aim of his investigation to us. But I heard from Dr. Kose that the murderer left no signs indicating an intruder from outside.

This murderer never devised a strategy to enter through a window or a door. He didn't carry out a queer little stunt. In other words, there were no clues. When a plan is executed, psychological footprints are left and are easily controlled, as in my novels. However, an amateur detective has nothing to cling to when that's not the case.

After the questioning ended, Detective Suspicious broached his target topic.

"As all of you know, four people have been murdered over three days in one house, an unprecedented event in Japan. Reasonable government administration in this situation demands all the residents living in the same mansion, despite leading innocent lives, do not escape from being considered suspects. I'd appreciate everyone's cooperation in showing me your rooms and belongings.

"Out of respect for you as cultured people of the highest caliber, I will be candid about the thrust of this investigation. I surmise from the gruesome loss of blood by Utsumi-san, the murderer's clothes are bloodstained. I

assume the murderer has either hidden, cleaned, or other-
wise disposed of those clothes.

"This is why we are asking to see your rooms and
possessions, but you are not required to show us. We are
simply appealing to all of your fair-mindedness and
common sense, seek your cooperation, and wish to be
shown everyones' powerful counter-evidence in our investigation."

The distinguished women, in particular, were upset
about showing their belongings. An unusual mood took
over. In the end, Dr. Ebitsuka did not cooperate.

As in all examples of nothing coming out of a great
fuss, the only piece of clothing stained with blood belonged
to Ayaka. Her clothes were dotted with drops of blood
from Pikaichi's attack. The blood was hers. Utsumi's blood
type was B and hers was O. There was no controversy.

We showed everything to the bottoms of our trunks,
but not one clue emerged.

12

WHY WAS THE HUNCHBACK POET KILLED?

We were influential men but trembled at the murders committed over three consecutive nights. A door locked by a key was not enough. We were on the verge of nervous breakdowns in the wretched misery of being wrapped with a cord and tied to the bed. With no lock in the Japanese-style room, a man like Pikaichi was no exception and could not get a good night's sleep but managed naps.

I found out Dr. Kose measured the time to travel the road from the cremation site to the back gate with painstaking accuracy. He carried a stopwatch back and forth over the same road for five days. One day, I joined him in his experiment.

"Normally, I take forty to forty-five minutes to walk this route."

Considered to be exactly midway between the cremation site to the back gate, the path along the mountain stream about a foot wide dropped down to the bottom of the valley. The narrowness of the path was a concern at a glance. To go down to the bottom of the valley, you had to navigate rocks and cross the valley. The trace of the path was faint and curved around into the dense forest.

Dr. Kose guided me through the weeds to this path. I gulped and stared. Below us, I saw Miwa Shrine. We were beside Miwa Shrine.

I shouted without thinking, "Of course, I understand now. The murderer came in from this path and killed Chigusa-san. During the murder, Utsumi came from another path, passing by on his way home. No, that's not it. The killer might have tricked Utsumi into coming in order to kill him and met him looking harmless."

"In that case, Utsumi-san was killed as a precaution?"

Dr. Kose grinned.

"I didn't understand why the murderer came down this path. If you see this path, excuse me for saying, but I must add Miyake-san, Tango-san, and you to the list of suspects. This story is complicated."

The walk from the cremation site to the back gate took forty to forty-five minutes. Coming without the handcart and sprinting may take thirty minutes. Because a round trip to Miwa Shrine may take twenty-five to thirty minutes on Utsumi's legs, Pikaichi arrived home between 6:50 and 7 pm, about five to ten minutes before Utsumi. This was not the time of the rendezvous. Chigusa-san had already been killed. Therefore, she didn't appear, and Utsumi didn't know Chigusa-san would never come. If he met Chigusa-san, he would have returned later or accompanied by Chigusa-san.

"Does the rendezvous note read by Nurse Moroi exist?"

"We're looking for it, but we haven't found it among Chigusa-san's belongings."

I was repelled by the woman called Moroi with her conceit and affected intellectual countenance. Until Ayaka received the request and passed it to Chigusa, I thought if I was not in Chigusa's play, this was Nurse Moroi's trick.

The hypothesis was someone killed Tamao by placing morphine into the cup and water pitcher at her bedside. Morphine was secretly stored at Ebitsuka's hospital. The elderly Tamon was addicted to morphine and hid it in this mansion.

One day, Tamon invited Dr. Kose and I to his study. When our conversation moved, as it often did, to talk of the murders, Nurse Moroi happened to be there to give Tamon a vitamin injection. I was nasty on purpose.

"Moroi-san was the last person to see Chigusa-san and Tamao-san alive. She may have put the morphine into the cup and pitcher at Tamao-san's bedside. This style appears in a modern detective novel. A nurse is likely to have morphine. That sort of stupid trick shouldn't work. However, if the clue is too suspicious, nothing is suspected. Was the strategy to anticipate that vulnerability and deliberately play a trick? Moroi-san is a woman whose intellect is unequaled. Excuse me for saying, she's also a deep thinker like you. As in a riddle, we three literary hacks variously become suspects."

Although my rudeness has been unbridled lately, instead of civility, the guests in this house were told outright, "You may be a murderer."

Nurse Moroi glared at me.

"Yashiro-san returned late from the cremation site and was alone."

"You're right. However, Moroi-san has a superb physique. Excuse me for saying, but she may have the upper body strength of a small man."

The grinning Dr. Kose said, "In Wani-san's case, it was the shoe bell. In Tamao-san's case, it was morphine. But in

Chigusa-san's and Utsumi-san's cases, no incriminating objects were left behind."

Tamon, who found fault in everything, said, "Of course, that is interesting. But there's one issue."

"There can't be," said Dr. Kose, self-consciously in denial.

"It's not easy to fake the truth for something like the mystery of one's focus. The person in question is arrogant and would be hard to save. Yashiro-sensei, isn't that like literature?"

"Politicians are like that, too. However, Kose-san, this crime was planned to the smallest detail. All my doubts surround Utsumi-san's case. While danger shined in Doi-san's eyes, he had to kill. This unavoidable riddle was undeniable on that day. The riddle's solution may be a lead in a corner of this case."

"How would you go about solving this riddle?"

Tamon did not answer. I said, "It may have happened because Utsumi saw the murderer. However, because he did not know Chigusa-san had been killed, how would he know to suspect that person as the murderer? Therefore, Utsumi had to take his last breath that night."

Dr. Kose made a strange comment. "It was a crisis. Well, a dangerous bridge was crossed."

"Perhaps the most dangerous bridge."

"Why?" asked Dr. Kose with a smirk. "Killing Utsumi-san would have been a slight challenge if Pikaichi-san were in his room, the lower Japanese-style sitting room."

Tamon's bright eyes looked at the doctor, but he said nothing.

13

THE BLESSED VIRGIN IS A
GIFTED LIAR

A week passed without incident. I woke from an afternoon nap on July 26 to a visit from Kayoko.

It was Kazuma's birthday. In celebration, a special meal of steamed rice and red beans was cooking in the kitchen of the main house. The kitchen in the Western building was also bustling. To my surprise, Kayoko had been invited to dine with us.

Kayoko was a fine-looking blessed virgin. Oddly enough, compared to her, Ayaka was more like a young woman, more colorful like flowers, and didn't look married. Her devilish mysteriousness easily kindled hostility from others of her sex. And her peculiar attractiveness to any man might have evoked jealousy. Kayoko had a special relationship with Kazuma. I was pained by her intense animosity and acute sensitivity whenever Ayaka's name came up.

Her excessively violent hatred or jealousy diminished her and elevated her rival. Even a pure virgin like Kayoko gave the impression of being difficult to listen to. One is struck by the feeling that a jealous, beautiful demon actually exists.

Kayoko was religious, probably the fault of her poor health, and looked like a prophet.

The discovery of the bell from Ayaka's house shoes under Wani's bed brought her under suspicion as the murderer. Some were stubbornly convinced Wani and Ayaka were in a relationship. Those of us who knew that wasn't true had difficulty handling their overexcited nerves.

"But Kayoko-san, that's wrong. In Wani's case, only Ayaka-san has an alibi. She was asleep in Kazuma's bed. Kazuma stayed awake writing until daybreak."

"My brother is trying to protect Ayaka-san, but she hasn't said a word."

When Ayaka became the topic of conversation, Kayoko showed her irritation. However, as we chatted, Kazuma and Ayaka dropped by to see me.

"Oh, Kayoko-san, what a surprise."

Ayaka's big charming eyes looked delighted like pollen ready to fly off.

"This evening's meal will be enjoyable. Kayoko-san sits quietly like an aromatic, tall mountain plant deep in the mountains. Everyone senses her presence like a flower."

I expected Kayoko to resist this flattery and be annoyed, but nothing like that happened. With a happy smile, she said, "It's you who smells as lovely as a flower bouquet."

From total silence, she spoke like she was infatuated and enchanted by Ayaka's gorgeous appearance.

I was astonished. Women begin as young women of pure daintiness. All of them are innate liars, diplomats, and politicians. Nevertheless, I felt Kayoko was an awful woman.

I believed she was a solitary person. Her one friend was

Kyoko. She was not open with others and always lived with reserve. By chance, her being with Kyoko allowed only me to know the sincere Kayoko and not just the reserved Kayoko. All women show their hearts, but men rarely get a chance to touch the depth of a woman's heart.

Kazuma was serene, not troubled in the least by unexpectedly being put in this predicament.

"Kayoko, how is your health? Weren't you suffering from a slight fever until a few days ago? As this incident unfolds, this visit is anything but relaxing. Lately, haven't you been reluctant to take Ebitsuka-san's medicine? You can't be overly sensitive and must take the doctor's medicine."

Kayoko raised her melancholy face.

"Yes, but I don't think my life will be long."

"Don't say that. Kyoko-san, don't you agree?"

"Yes, dying young is nonsense. When you have bright hopes, you'll quickly decide to recover from illness."

She spoke with authority and declared recovering from illness is simple, the sickly woman may not have agreed.

Kazuma turned to me.

"Dr. Ebitsuka has been a problem lately. A teacher called Okuda Tonekichiro of the Confucian Analects Research Association arrived a short time ago carrying a letter of invitation from Ebitsuka-san. He wanted to give a lecture on *The Analects of Confucius* to my guests. He came for a business meeting and asked when would be a convenient time. Sergeant Arashi Hirosuke, aka Eight-Foot Nose, stopped by, so after making his request, Okuda left. Ebitsuka-san's letter of introduction was idiotic. The lecture would benefit everyone. The text diverged from common sense, for instance, he claimed Okuda is a genius and a sage. What was he thinking?"

"Is the teacher of *The Analects* in his right mind?"

"Fanatical followers are probably lunatics who all demand fanaticism."

"Wouldn't it be interesting to hear a charming lecture? For now, he's like the people who appear and disappear in Tango's novels. In that case, the teacher may be interesting and amusing when flattered in various ways. Since the end of the war, Hitomi Koroku populated his recent works with weirdoes, oddballs, and lunatics. In these times, this type of lunatic at war's end may play the leading role."

"A navel-baring review and the analects teacher are as different as clover and the moon. That's the truth. Don't the novels of the sensei called Ango Sakaguchi seem ready to embrace the navel-baring review and the analects teacher? Actually, I'm here because Eight-Foot Nose wishes to ask us something?"

We exited the room, leaving Kayoko and Kyoko. Eight-Foot Nose was waiting for us in Kazuma's room. Ayaka left for the kitchen to help prepare dinner.

Eight-Foot Nose was accompanied by Eureka.

"Please, excuse this interruption."

Although Eight-Foot Nose was a lout, he could demonstrate proper manners at times and lowered his head.

"Today, I wish to hear about the circumstances of the literary circle. Mochizuki Wani-san appears to have made quite a few enemies."

"Which enemies?"

"His enemies in literature. When Mochizuki-san died, who was happy?"

"There was no one who was not happy. His author friends hated him. He was a crude and rude man. At first, I was overjoyed."

"All writers are jealous," said Eureka in a shrill scream as if on the attack. "You have no self-confidence because you lack talent ... and are jealous. Such a disgrace."

"Because nothing pops into my mind. I'm unhappy. We are certainly stupid."

"When Mochizuki-san died, the market for your manuscripts expanded."

"That is true."

"Yashiro-san, although jealousy of his talent existed in literary circles, is murder unthinkable?"

"It may be considered. As one of many possibilities, isn't murder highly unlikely? The murderer may not act at all times and in all places. Firstly, if a particular person is killed, the reason to improve your talent vanishes. Jealousy among writers is not a problem of fame but a problem of talent. It makes no sense because if you kill, what becomes of your talent? This sort of murder rarely happens."

"Of course, you may be right. Independent of the art, killing a person out of jealousy in the arts is possible but uncommon. As for killing, if talent does not change, then the only option is to kill. I have a terribly rude question. All of you are living in the whirlpool of these incidents. This is not one incident. Four of your acquaintances were killed one after another over three days. No one is brave enough to be a police informer. Every heart has its suspicions. I believe someone has an idea. That may be my suspicion?"

"Well, how much should we impersonate amateur detectives?"

"To a reasonable degree. Natural human feelings make sense. I have a bold request, but I want you to tell me your secret thoughts. Of course, this will be done in a manner to avoid offense. One method will be half in fun. I'd like you to vote for the murderer. I will preside over the vote because we have hit an impasse. In fact, Yashiro-san suggested this as a joke. What do you think? It's half in jest and will be entertaining."

"This isn't a worthless exercise. We amateur detectives

probably have a suspect. Perhaps the result will be none of us has pinpointed the murderer. I've held that position from the beginning. There's no logical basis to ask who is the murderer."

"That's fine as a start. 'I don't know?' is an acceptable response from anyone who does not know. Or, someone may not be certain but has a vague idea or suspicions about someone. I will be grateful to hear any secret suspicion arrived at by each of your idiosyncratic methods."

"Excuse me for declining to preside, but you yourselves should preside. Standing at an impasse has no value. So you don't have a method where you have no responsibility. Using ordinary people as pawns diminishes the merits. Wouldn't Eureka as the moderator be interesting?"

"You've said a lot. Merits? Merits or demerits? Which do you have? Didn't you take up with Utagawa-san's mistress? You have the nerve to brazenly come with your mistress to her former lover's home. That's not much better. The gall. You may think you have merit, but what the police do is not divine judgment. You have a fair understanding of yourself."

This proposal reeked with menace but was serious. Playfulness had to be erased from a vote for the murderer.

14

THE BLESSED VIRGIN AND THE LAST SUPPER

W e didn't sit around the dining room table but assembled in the living room. The hard drinkers were sipping whiskey when Dr. Ebitsuka entered with a tall, gangly man shaven bald and about thirty years old. His sharp cheekbones and pale complexion made him look malnourished. The cuckoo clock in the room struck seven.

Dr. Ebitsuka with an air of self-importance said, "People, I introduce to you, Okuda Tonekichiro-sensei. More than a researcher of *The Analects of Confucius*, he is the most sincere and faithful practitioner of *The Analects,* an aesthete, and a holy man."

The holy man's desperate face quivered as he gaped at them.

"They say man does not live by bread alone."

Pikaichi seethed. His veins stood out on his scowling face.

"Hey, hey, that's not from *The Analects*. His words are outrageous. Isn't that a compromise sermon between Japan and the West? An insane monkey. Thin or withered, the artist is an unadulterated version of the thing itself. Unlike

125

a lady's maid, the insane monkey withdraws and doesn't become a side dish for sake."

Hitomi Koroku took over.

"Isn't this unpleasant? Ebitsuka-kun, it's irresponsible for you to show up at our gathering. We never gave you permission to bring a stranger. What nerve. We are not guests in your home. *The Analects of Confucius* preach etiquette, but isn't the teacher of *The Analects* betraying them by his presence here?"

Also angry, Kazuma said, "Ebitsuka-san, I am the host of this gathering and will not allow this intrusion. Please take your companion and go. It would be best if you don't attend this gathering."

Caught off guard by Kazuma's words, Ebitsuka's lips trembled and, for a short time, he was silent. As expected, the sarcastic Tango slowly spoke in a quiet, serious tone.

"In Tokyo, I can't hear the preaching of a holy man of *The Analects*. I'm not a stickler about the common sense theory of courtesy. His insufficient knowledge of courtesy may make this holy man one of the greats. Won't recklessly chasing him off while he masters real worth go against the performer's readiness?"

"That's enough. You're the type who speaks formally. Not knowing what you like or dislike, you speak in what seems to be a novel way. Therefore, your writings will forever be fake. Wani and you are as different as the moon is from a soft-shelled turtle."

Pikaichi jumped up and placed both hands on the shoulders of the holy man and spun him around.

"Well, you walked here. You are violating the law by committing the crime of house intrusion. Since I will pardon you without appealing to the authorities, disappear. Please leave. Left. Right. Left. Right."

Long ago, this holy man offered no resistance and was

laid flat by Wani. He was treated at Ebitsuka's hospital. He paled more at the appearance of an extraordinary man not surpassed in dignity by Wani, lost his words, and stumbled as he was pushed out the dining hall door. Ebitsuka followed and disappeared through the door.

Dinner was ready and on the table.

Pikaichi said, "I have no idea what to do about that freakish doctor and have a low opinion of the artistic fraud named Tango. His conceit makes him unbearable. Kayoko-san. Yours is a lovely name. You certainly feel through your heart muscles. Compared to a fraudster like Tango, you probe the depths to the essence. Miss, please take this seat beside me. Like you, I have a profound spirit and do not tease or pester. Will you tell me a few stories on matters you have contemplated with your discerning and quiet spirit?"

He offered her a chair and sat beside her. Fortunately, Kyoko was a distance from Kayoko. For some reason, Kayoko liked Pikaichi. To our amazement, she regularly engaged him in conversation. However, when a virgin latches onto this sort of man, he may be easily tamed.

As always, Kamiyama Toyo's wife, Kisona, and the maid Yae served. The meal's courses were too much by half. Ebitsuka went around to the main house and entered the dining hall from the living room. However, no place was set for him. Kisona said, "The food is ready. And now a seat for the doctor."

She retrieved a chair from the corner. Out of character, Kazuma glanced up with an indignant look.

"Ebitsuka-san, the temperaments of the people in this gathering and you are at odds. Nonetheless, you see this gathering and look for a seat, but the others are offended by your presence. I'd like you to leave. Please have your meal in the main house."

"Ah, that is correct, but I also have a different temperament. I am a sacrifice who secretly harbors undesirable thoughts caused by the police confinement order," said Pikaichi, tapping his chest.

"Compared to the beauty, quiet, and insight of Kayoko-san, a woman like Ayaka somehow seems stuck with peacock feathers. Excuse me for saying, Utsugi Akiko-san is a popular woman writer, but the way of her soul, the correctness of her position, the dramatic depth of her soul, and silence, as expected, in some ways surpass the blessed virgin Kayoko-san. Forgive me for saying, but isn't my pure heart that praises Kayoko-san splendid?"

"Oh no, I recognize Pikaichi-san's pure heart more than anyone," said a blushing Utsugi-san with flirtatious eyes.

"For Kayoko-san, any amount of praise is fine. Women truly see me as trash."

"No, Akiko-san, excuse me, but I'm well acquainted with your indulgent character and your childish demands. Your generosity is exactly like that of a *Bluestocking* poet like Watatsumi."

"If Utsumi-san were alive, that truly detestable fellow would put Pikaichi-san in his place."

Taunting Akiko, Hitomi Koroku said, "In the end, Utsumi was hateful. What can you say about his humanity?"

"He was made of human flesh," said Mokubei and turned his disgusted face away from his wife.

Pikaichi ended by saying, "I despise the man who despises his wife with lusty scorn."

Ayaka stood and whispered something to Kyoko seated next to her. Both left the dining hall. Several minutes later they returned. Kyoko came over to me.

"I went with Ayaka-sama to the bathroom. She was

afraid to go alone. She said she saw a figure hiding in the garden. I'm terrified. Please, come have a look."

Ayaka seemed to have also spoken to Kazuma. He stood and joined us. I stood and called over Dr. Kose. Guided by Ayaka, we went to the bathroom in the hallway connecting the main house and the Western building. The hallway bathroom was next to the room where Utsumi was slaughtered. Naturally, the women avoided it. From the hallway, we could see a human figure outside in the front parlor of the main house. We went to challenge whoever it was and found Detective Bookworm.

"Oh, it's the detective."

"I'm a little relaxed, but I am on watch."

"Every day?" asked Kazuma.

"Yes. You are sleeping, and we are watching."

"A detective may be hidden in the bushes in the garden. Who's the guard on the top of the garden falls?"

"Let me see. I haven't met him. Is it Eight-Foot Nose? No, he should be on another assignment. I'm probably alone on patrol."

Ayaka-san was relieved. Kazuma and I stood and went to the bathroom. I returned first. Because everyone went out in groups, we did, too. We crossed paths with Mokubei and Kamiyama Toyo returning from a trip to the bathroom.

The coffee was brought in. When Yae set the coffee on the table before Pikaichi, he picked up the cup, stroked, and played with it.

"So uncivilized. You always play with your cup," said the staring Yae.

"Because you're so rough, the cups are chipped."

Yae didn't care for Pikaichi.

"Give that to Kayoko-sama. This one has more chips."

The other day during Pikaichi's rampage, he turned

over the table and chipped and broke many coffee cups. Since then, there have not been enough cups. She made a point of always giving a chipped cup to Pikaichi. Being the child of a maid, Kayoko was resigned to being treated worse than the guests. Yae always gave Pikaichi his special cup. Kayoko was given a cup with more chips than Pikaichi's.

"This cup will be yours, Kayoko-san. It has fewer chips," said Pikaichi and exchanged cups with her.

She stirred the coffee and took a few sips. A strange look then alarm washed over her face. With vacant, staring eyes, she tried to gently put down the cup but dropped it. She jumped to her feet. Her eyes opened wide. Clawing at her chest, she fell forward, crawled onto the table, and collapsed. A stunned Pikaichi tried to grab her, but she slipped through his arms and sunk to the floor.

Pikaichi wrapped his arms around Kayoko and raised his hysterical face.

"Call the doctor. Now! Hurry! Call the doctor. Don't you understand? Dammit. What are you waiting for? Hey, I said call the doctor. Fools."

Kyoko and Kazuma flew out the door. Dr. Ebitsuka appeared in no time, maybe in one or two minutes. He took her pulse and lifted her head. Pikaichi's voice boomed like a deranged cracked bell.

"Nobody move. Nobody go outside. Don't move anything on the table. Kayoko-san was poisoned and is dead. It should have been me. Dammit! Some bastard tried to poison me. Look! Kayoko-san is dead. Sit down. Go back to your original positions."

Pikaichi raged as his crazed eyes burned fire. His shoulders shook violently with each breath.

Shizue opened the door in confusion.

"Is Dr. Ebitsuka here?"

Wondering what happened, Ebitsuka stood and turned. Kamiyama Toyo shouted, "Yes, he is."

"Can you come immediately? The master has taken a turn for the worse."

As she spoke, she saw Kayoko but suppressed the urge to faint.

Kamiyama Toyo's booming voice roared like a funeral bell.

"It's eight-fourteen."

AUTHOR'S NOTE: A visitor, Ozaki Shiro-sensei, a writer who lives in Ito, was announced. He asked if Sakaguchi had a written detective novel and whether "I" was the murderer? Sakaguchi Ango's novels always turn "I" into the bad guy. Therefore, the criminal is "I." He already knew the answer was yes and demanded sake.

Dazai Osamu-sensei, a writer living in Mitaka, told a magazine writer the murderer had not yet emerged and would appear in the final installment. The author will feign innocence but he has decided. "Ma'am, beer, please. Well, I'm counting on you."

These two did not take up the author's challenge. I'll omit a detailed explanation because the reason is obvious.

The hero without rival was Four-Foot Nose-sensei of Kyushu. He appeared at my home after a trip to far-off Tokyo.

"Is it okay, Sakaguchi-san, if I guess who the murderer is now? I'll write the rest later. Are you listening? May I speak?"

Omens are overdone, but something is missing. One person creates an outline, and another secretly executes all of it. Isn't that the trick found in Ellery Queen's *The Tragedy of Y?* Of Eureka and Four-Foot Nose-sensei, the people of Kyushu favor Eureka more or less and are foolhardy.

Four-Foot Nose-sensei, who lives in Kuki, Saitama Prefecture (plus Four-Foot Nose-sensei of Kyushu total to Eight-Foot Nose) is the husband who obeys his wife and loves the tranquility of a pleasant household. He writes detective novels where the women are naked. These novels become detective novels of desperation. Sakaguchi-san, are you crazy? It's bad, even if Eight-Foot Nose becomes Twelve-foot Nose.

This month's challenge did not uncover a person of quality to present. This person does not live in this world. I overestimated the Japanese people. Merely by writing a detective novel, I was surprised and regretted discovering the desperate lack of insight in our native land.

Sakaguchi Ango

15

THE SUGAR POT AND PIKAICHI'S SLEIGHT OF HAND

Kayoko's body was carried out. We packed into the living room with Tsubota Heikichi, his wife, and the maid Yae. The police sealed off the dining hall and kitchen.

Detective Suspicious and his team finished the post-mortem and followed Shizue and Nurse Moroi to the living room. The time was just after nine-thirty. After examining the dining hall and the kitchen, the detective stood before us.

"Ladies. Gentlemen. I apologize for disturbing you tonight, but we must meet with you. We can't bear the shame of our incompetence. In our defense, our rival is an evil genius."

Losing his usual cool, Detective Suspicious was a little upset, full of fighting spirit, and showing excitement unbecoming his age.

"Tonight, two people were murdered in two different places."

"Two?" shrieked Utsugi Akiko reflexively. Detective Suspicious nodded.

"Yes, two. Utagawa Tamon-sama and Kayoko-san. However, the plots shared a common thread. Both were killed by poison mixed into food. Kayoko-san was killed by potassium cyanide and Utagawa Tamon-san by morphine."

This was a shock. The morphine that killed Tamon was not put in his coffee but his pudding.

The Tsubotas were questioned first. As usual, Tamon avoided meat and ate lightly seasoned fish, which was not on our menu. Today's menu was sweetfish grilled with salt, carp *sashimi*, soup, chilled tofu with toppings, and *oshitashi* spinach.

Tamon ate pudding after his dinner. He ate a jellied dessert with lunch. Since the spring, Ayaka had been making these desserts for him.

The morphine simmered with the pudding and was not sprinkled over the ingredients.

Ayaka said, "I can't imagine how it happened. While I prepared the pudding, nothing out of the ordinary occurred. I don't recall ever leaving the area. Nothing suspicious took place."

"What time did you make the pudding?"

"I believe around four. A detective stopped in looking for Yashiro-san then checked his room. He greeted Kayoko-san, who happened to be there, and later went to the kitchen. I placed the cooked pudding in the refrigerator."

"Ma'am, what about the sugar?" asked Tsubota's wife, Teruyo. Ayaka's eyes opened wide. When she looked at the wife's face, Ayaka flushed and her eyes shined.

Detective Suspicious asked, "Why do you care about the sugar?"

Tsubota's wife answered, "The master's body couldn't tolerate sugar, and he didn't eat ordinary sugar. He only ate foods using beet sugar. This sugar was kept in a special sugar pot."

Right away, the detective inspected the sugar and soy sauce in the dining hall. He thoroughly inspected Tamon's private sugar pot and discovered a large quantity of morphine inside.

The glass sugar pot was half full. Until that day, no problems arose when cooking with that sugar.

"Was the sugar used in any dish other than the pudding?"

"It was only used in the dishes for dinner," replied Tsubota Heikichi, nearly flinching. He paled.

"Before the pudding, when was the sugar last used?"

"In the tea served with the sandwiches at lunch. I put tea and sugar into two cups of milk and boiled it."

"So you put in a fairly large amount."

"Yes. I probably used nearly the amount used in the pudding."

"Did Utagawa-san drink all of it?"

Tsubota couldn't answer, but Shizue answered, "He drank it all."

"You served?"

"Yes."

"Nothing strange happened after that."

"No, nothing."

"When did you prepare the tea?"

"The master ate lunch at 12:30 and dinner at 8:00 in the evening. About ten minutes before, Shizue-san always began bringing in the trays to be on time. I probably made it exactly ten minutes before 12:30."

Detective Suspicious nodded.

"Did anyone touch the sugar pot between 12:20 and 4:00 that afternoon?"

Tsubota Heikichi looked ashamed.

"You took absolutely no precautions."

"I was not in the dining hall the entire time."

"Yes, you returned to your room during the afternoon break and rested until around three. I believe you stayed in the kitchen until about 1:30 to clean up?"

"Yes, I washed the dishes. Kamiyama-sama's wife helped and returned to her room around 1:30."

"During that time, did you see anyone in the kitchen?"

"After lunch, everyone napped. Until around three, people rarely appeared in the kitchen. After three, we returned to the kitchen. Beginning with the lady, Utsugi-sama, Yashiro-sama's wife, Tango-sama, Kamiyama-sama's wife, and others appeared, but not one of them touched the sugar pot."

"From 1:30 to 3:00, no one should have been in the kitchen."

"Yes, that's true. But around two, Moroi-san informed me the sweetfish had been delivered."

"You received it?"

"No, she told me it was in the refrigerator. She spoke from outside the door then went home. The custom here is for the staff to nap after lunch. Everyone knows that and is careful not to disturb anyone's rest."

Detective Suspicious looked excited and stared at Nurse Moroi.

"Recently, you closed the hospital."

"From 8:00 to 11:30 in the morning. The master ordered it after Chigusa-sama's murder and Yura-sama's worsening illness."

Nurse Moroi was calm as usual. Even an important man like the detective changes his demeanor depending on his companion, but Nurse Moroi's lack of expression was like water. Whether speaking to a grand duke or the dauntless Detective Suspicious, she looked up with defiance.

"Was bringing the sweetfish your job?"

"At that time, I was the only person on staff awake in this house."

"No one was in the kitchen."

"No, there was one person."

The room tensed. Detective Suspicious prepared his body by concentrating the power below his navel.

"Who was it?"

"Kayoko-sama."

Everyone's confusion was palpable. Determination filled the detective's body.

"Moroi-san, you reckon the dead tell no tales."

Nurse Moroi gave a detached nod.

"Yes, perhaps but it is foolish not to believe my words."

"What was Kayoko-san doing?"

"She said she came for a drink of water. She left as I put the sweetfish in the refrigerator. When I left the kitchen, Kayoko-sama was sitting in a chair in the living room reading. Yashiro-san's wife came in but said she was on her way to take a nap."

"I also saw Kayoko-sama in this living room. It was about 2:40. Yes, she was reading," interjected Kocho-san.

It was getting closer to eleven. Detective Suspicious was irritated.

"Now Kamiyama-san, your occupation requires an eye for keen observations. Please tell me about dinner."

"All right, allow me to speak for everyone."

He was accustomed to this role. He wasn't like this a short time ago, but after being named the group's spokesman, his bearing changed. Even Detective Suspicious seemed inferior and settled his breath when Kamiyama entered the hall and took a seat to be questioned.

"Exactly when the cuckoo clock struck seven just before

dinner, we gathered in the living room for drinks, beer for some and sake for others, and waited for the table to be ready. I must add that this cuckoo clock is about four minutes late.

"When the clock struck seven, Dr. Ebitsuka entered with a pale, lanky man dressed in a military uniform named Okuda so-and-so. He holds study groups on *The Analects of Confucius*. Ebitsuka-san introduced his companion. This holy man began to preach. He told us 'man does not live by bread alone.'

"The painter Doi glared at this holy man. He deemed him an idiot and asked if that phrase originated with Confucius. This man hated the lecture mixing Japanese and Western ideas addressed to authors who see things as they are.

"Hitomi Koroku-san forgot his manners and fumed. Only Tango-san tried to be an ally of the holy man. In the end, however, the host, Kazuma-san, did not allow this home intrusion. The painter Doi turned him around and marched him outside through the dining hall door. 'Left. Right. Left. Right.' Ebitsuka-san left with him. I was worried at that time. Ebitsuka-san, you had taken off your shoes and came from the main house. Were you walking around barefoot?"

Dr. Ebitsuka rolled his bright eyes and did not respond.

"After this prelude, the main event finally begins," interrupted Pikaichi.

"Allow me to say what happened next. Close to the end of the meal, the lady of the house whispered to Kyoko-san, and they both left the dining hall. They soon returned. After they spoke to Yashiro-kun, Kazuma-kun, and Kose-kun, all five left the dining hall. Then confusion reigned. Two or three came and went, but I don't recall who.

"Then coffee was brought in. Detective, please listen.

Only my coffee cup was chipped. The rim was chipped. Although I did smash a coffee cup, isn't it strange this household could not find a replacement? For almost a week, I've been told, 'You broke this, so it's yours,' and was always given a chipped cup.

"That maid there said this. Please ask her. She's behind this and has a plan. Who instigated this? There's no need to go into detail; everyone knows. According to some plot, potassium cyanide was put into my cup. Unfortunately, Kayoko-san's cup was also chipped.

"Her cup had more cracks than mine, so I exchanged cups. That caused the tragedy. Why not ask Eureka about the spiked coffee for us? She'll hone in on it immediately. Immortality. Detective, if you question the people who came and went in the dining hall after the meal, the murderer will emerge."

"Why did you exchange the coffee cups?" asked Detective Suspicious, somewhat amazed.

"It's obvious. My life's objective is to work like a dog or a horse on behalf of the ladies."

"That's a lie. You put the potassium cyanide in your cup and gave it to Kayoko-san."

Ayaka shook in anger and stared daggers at Pikaichi. He looked dismissive and ignored her. Her rage exploded.

"He is known for his magic tricks and knows enough to trick children and drop poison into a coffee cup. Be it *Hanafuda* playing cards, dice, or gambling, he's a skilled cheater. His fingertips are a magician's."

A Go board was beside Pikaichi's sofa chair. Pikaichi picked up a Go stone. Teasing Ayaka, he held the stone between his fingertips and stretched out his arm. The stone in his fingertips appeared and disappeared freely like a living being to tease her. As Pikaichi played his magic trick, he calmly said, "May I have your attention? This feat will demonstrate the love story of black and white fantasies. Behold!"

He grasped another stone, a white one, to add to the black stone and held both stones. His skill in making the stones appear and disappear with ease was bizarre. Pikaichi deliberately stared down Ayaka.

"This is not the madness of a murderer. Why would I kill Kayoko-san? One has a motive to kill. This motive must be sought first. Now! May I have your attention?"

Detective Suspicious seemed to be pushing his excitement down to the depths of his heart but calmly smoked a cigarette and scanned the group. He slowly turned to Ayaka and said, "Why did you leave the dining hall with Yashiro-san's wife?"

Ayaka blushed, and Kyoko didn't speak up. With no way out, Ayaka said, "We went to the bathroom. I was too scared to go alone and asked Kyoko-sama to come with me.

"I looked out the bathroom window toward the mountains behind the larger waterfalls, I could see someone, a human figure, hiding. Light from the pavilion and lanterns at two locations lit that area. I could barely make out a figure blending in with the dark places. The form I saw stayed near that border and disappeared into the darkness. I was scared and asked my husband, Yashiro-san, and Kose-san to investigate. Detective Nagahata was also there and joined our investigation."

Detective Suspicious nodded.

"So Bookworm investigated immediately."

"Yes, I ran off right away but found no one. I didn't race straight there but went once around the Western building and through the maze of garden paths."

"But he was alone, and that was too much for one man," said Detective Suspicious, addressing his underlings.

"Did everyone return to the dining hall?"

I said, "I returned after going to the toilet, and so did Kazuma and Dr. Kose."

Kazuma and Dr. Kose nodded.

"Did you three return to the dining hall together?"

"There was no particular reason for us to return together and we didn't."

"Yashiro-san, did you and your wife return together first?"

"We peeked into the kitchen and spoke to the maid. But I don't remember staying together. Kyoko-sama might have returned before me."

"But we were mostly together. I spoke to Tsubota Teruyo and glanced around the kitchen for a short time with no particular purpose in mind."

"Was coffee being prepared in the kitchen at that time?"

"It was ready."

Ayaka deliberately stared at the detective, but her voice was naturally soft despite her determination.

"We returned to cups of coffee ready for us on the table in the living room."

"Was coffee in the cups?"

"Yes. We added sugar and milk in the kitchen then carried in and set up the coffee."

Detective Suspicious left the dining hall, went over to Pikaichi's and Kayoko's cups and scrutinized them. The rim of Pikaichi's cup had one large chip and one small one. Kayoko's had two large chips and two small ones.

Detective Suspicious raised his head and looked at the maid Yae.

"Which cup was for Doi-san's exclusive use?"

"That one, Sir," she said with confidence and pointed to the cup with fewer chips.

"Are there any cups without chips?"

"No, there are not. They were all damaged somehow during the war. No new ones have been purchased."

The detective nodded.

"Only cheap goods are available now because prices are outrageous."

Then he turned to Kazuma and me.

"Did you see the coffee cups on that table?"

We both nodded.

"A few others left. Who were they?"

"I left," said Kamiyama Toyo. And Mokubei said, "Me too."

"Did you see the coffee cups on the table?"

"When I returned from the bathroom, the coffee was being carried into the dining hall. Several may have still been on the table. I wasn't paying much attention and don't know."

"When I returned, all the cups of coffee were gone. While Dr. Ebitsuka gripped a coffee cup and was drinking, I looked at what had been brought from the kitchen."

The detective looked surprised.

"Ebitsuka-san wasn't in the dining hall?"

"I ate in the kitchen."

His answer was frosty and blunt. Kamiyama Toyo spoke up.

"This explains one scene. Doi-san jumped into the middle, suddenly moved from the prelude to the finale. Ebitsuka-san left during the meal, probably persuaded of the inevitable by the holy man, but later returned to the dining hall. When he did, Kazuma-san said he wanted Ebitsuka-san and his guest to leave because of their unusual personalities. At that point, they left the dining hall."

The fact that Ebitsuka was in the kitchen eating for a

long time after that shook the few doubts we had. Meanwhile, Pikaichi looked upset. He looked like nothing made sense and kept his mouth shut out of irritation.

"Where did you eat in the kitchen?"

Ebitsuka stared back in protest and didn't reply. Teruyo answered for him.

"Depending on the nature of the food, the busy places in the kitchen change, he moves around here and there. Sometimes he eats sitting in a chair and other times, he stands."

The questioning ended and the police left. A troubled-looking Pikaichi said, "Detective, I am fed up. I can't go back to Tokyo, can I?"

"That's right. I can't force you to stay, but if no emergency has arisen, it's best if you stay a while longer."

"Is that so? Well, there's no emergency. I'm working on drawings for a fall exhibition and not worried. However, I'm not feeling good. Since yesterday, I've been preparing my meals."

"You can't. You are awful. You're a villain who will poison us all," shrieked Ayaka.

Detective Suspicious interrupted.

"I see. What should we do? I'll send Eureka every day to prepare your meals."

"I understand. That's fine as long as I'm alive."

A knowing look flashed in a heartbeat.

"Although a murderer may be among this group, if I stare, be afraid."

Next, the wakes were held for Tamon and Kayoko. I fell asleep a little after two.

16

___

THE SECRETS OF THE UTAGAWA FAMILY

The police requested an examination of Tamon's will. They easily opened the safe. However, the will was not a formal document, only signed by Tamon, and dated July 24, 1937, two days before he died.

The will shocked Kazuma.

Tamon confessed Kayoko was his only living daughter after Tamao's death and wrote his entire estate should be equally divided between Kazuma and Kayoko. And before the division, he wrote Yura-sama and Katakura Seijiro each be given 200,000 yen.

"Who is Katakura Seijiro?"

"A secretary who served this family his whole life. He fell ill this spring and retired. He's seventy-six."

Detective Suspicious took a copy of the will, asked for Katakura's address, and left. The discovery of the will probably deepened his concern over finding a strong motive for Kayoko's murder.

However, the detectives unknowingly crossed paths with the elderly Katakura when he was driven here by a family member to pay his condolences. He was ill and had difficulty walking. He prostrated himself before his boss's corpse and did not raise his head for ten minutes.

The detectives found out about his destination and returned. In the room holding Tamon's body, they listened to Katakura's story. Kazuma and I took seats and listened.

"How many years did you serve this family?"

"Well, I began at the age of sixteen and turned seventy-six this year. That would make it sixty years. Back then, the value of this family's fortune was a small 100, 120, or 130,000 yen. They were once a prominent wealthy family. I'm surprised by the changes over time and the huge change today, but that probably should be expected given the defeat."

Katakura's health was in decline, but his mind was sharp. He had no qualifications but keen insight. The police altered their attitudes.

"Is it true Kayoko-san's mother committed suicide?"

"Yes."

Katakura shut his eyes and spoke like he was mumbling a Buddhist prayer. Detective Suspicious filled with sudden compassion as he observed this old man.

He looked at the elderly man and said, "Katakura-san, of course, we have examined the old records of the police and the town administration. We gained a superficial understanding. However, the family you love and gave a lifetime of good faith has secrets. Forcing a cruel confession from an elderly man is heartless work. Katakura-san, you may think of us as demons. However, when you consider the bizarre sequence of crimes that struck this house, if our cruelty does not pinpoint the truth, we may never find the murderer. As public officials, we've heard nothing about old wounds to this family, please, tell us the truth."

Serene understanding quietly filled the old man's eyes. They reflected acceptance of the detective's heart.

"A portion of the old timers said Kayoko-san's mother did not commit suicide but was murdered. Is this a fact?"

The old man closed his eyes. He paused a few moments then answered.

"Detective, I know nothing about that. Thinking about it now, my rashness might have caused problems for this family. Later, the storeroom where she hung herself was demolished. The knot was tied behind her head. She hung from a ceiling beam in the storeroom, crashed to the ground when her sash ripped, and died.

"The sash was Kajiko-sama's. The footwear she wore was left at the scene. Kajiko-sama's belongings were separated from this other person's. I had a revelation as I examined them. Kajiko-sama's *geta* sandals had been hidden. The neck cord was also loosened, hidden, and replaced by a rope.

"Those living deep in the mountains back then say the rope was untied and artificial respiration performed. Getting away with calling it suicide was easy. This secret was leaked. The rumors persist to this day. At first, I was reckless and believed with near certainty, most probably, it was suicide.

"Kajiko-sama had a strong disposition and suffered from hysteria but was thin, weak, and didn't have the strength to strangle anyone. Dispassionate, objective eyes would come to that conclusion. For a moment, I was convinced and confused. At that time, unfortunately, the master's secretary was in this house, and took me to the scene. That horrible man was Kamiyama Toyo."

We were struck by a thunderbolt. More than the detective and I, Kazuma was in shock. He paled. His body stiffened like a stone.

The detective expressed his sympathy with a nod.

"I understand. The rumors claiming Kamiyama Toyo blackmailed the Utagawa family were not lies."

Katakura said nothing and rested for a minute.

"In addition to Kamiyama's blackmail, this family has another secret. The young master may not know about this either. If this incident never happened, I intended to seal all of this with me in my coffin. This trouble worries me. Today, I came to be questioned and to tell the young master these things."

The old man rested again.

"When the master was twenty and a student in Tokyo, he fathered a child with a maid at an inn. This child was adopted into the Ebitsuka family, distant relatives. He broke off connections with the woman. As the child grew, his nature was warped. He swindled, blackmailed, robbed for a living, and died in prison. He married by the time he was twenty and died leaving two children.

"The younger brother of the two orphans is the man known as Ebitsuka Koji, the doctor in this village. He is the grandson of the late master. His older brother Gentaro died three years ago, leaving three children. The oldest grandchild is around eleven and being raised by his widowed mother, who lives in Village M, about two and a half miles from this village. These days, they no longer have any connections to this family and receive no allowance."

Detective Suspicious couldn't string two sentences together. Kazuma lost all color.

"When the master's out-of-wedlock child was adopted into the Ebitsuka family, Ebitsuka-san was a gentle man and kept his promise, never revealing the child to be Utagawa Tamon-sama's seed. Thus, the child is registered as his son. Till the day he died, this twisted man who swindled, blackmailed, and robbed for a living never knew he was the oldest son of Utagawa Tamon-sama. Of his surviving sons Gentaro and Koji, Koji is a genius but has no idea he's Tamon's grandson. The only man who knew this secret was the awful man, Kamiyama Toyo."

"He told Dr. Ebitsuka."

Katakura did not answer and stopped talking.

"That bastard Kamiyama used this to blackmail Kajiko-sama. Initially, she was unaware of this secret and in shock, so she came to me for the truth. Kamiyama told Ebitsuka everything and started a lawsuit over the distribution of the fortune. But that wasn't enough for him, and he embarked on blackmail. I might have thought about killing Kamiyama more than once. It would have been wonderful if someone had. A waste of a life. This is so regrettable. Unfortunately, he won't die."

The old man's tears poured down.

Eight-Foot Nose inadvertently moved forward on his knees, breaking the silence.

"The rumor of the poisoning of Kajiko-sama had some substance. Hmm, one more time from the beginning, a new root must be dug up."

Detective Suspicious said coldly, "Can the white bones from a year ago be dug up and a poison emerge?"

He turned. "Katakura-san, there's just one more thing. Kazuma-san, with the deaths of Tamao-san and Kayoko-san, are there any other living children of Tamon-san?"

"There's no one else. He only had a few children."

17

THE CASE OF THE NONSERIAL
MURDERS

Despite the authorities' efforts, they did not discover one piece of incontrovertible proof.

Most of the suspicions that turned Kamiyama and Ebitsuka into suspects were explained. Even when Utsumi was killed, Kamiyama on the second floor did not fool Pikaichi's eyes. As for Ebitsuka, he should have been able to kill Utsumi Akira downstairs with ease. However, when Chigusa was murdered, both of their alibis held up.

Kamiyama Toyo returned from the cremation site with the priest and Kazuma and chatted for a long time with the women in the living room. His proof agreed with the women's story.

Around eight, Ebitsuka arrived from the village and bumped into Kazuma and me at the back gate. Detective Suspicious questioned him closely about when he left the hospital, but he was silenced by Mokubei and never answered. As a result of the investigation, his patients confirmed he examined three successive patients from 6:00 to 7:20. He didn't have the time to commit this crime. From 7:20 to 8:00, he was walking from his last patient's home. Because he walked with a limp, it was no mystery, he took more time than a fit man.

Many witnesses testified Kamiyama's wife, Kisona, was busy helping to prepare the *odoki* and never left the kitchen. The researcher of *The Analects of Confucius* went to a village nearly twenty miles away that day. A witness in the village to this fact provided his alibi.

In addition to the authorities' work, I was aware of Dr. Kose's meticulous investigation of Ebitsuka and Kamiyama. He failed to break their alibis.

"Doctor, these murders may have been committed by different murderers. Maybe, the cases related to the murders of the Utagawa family, Chigusa-san, Wani, and Utsumi were carried out by different people. Although the murders were committed serially over time, the motives, the murderers, and the distinct cases may be mixed together. Does that make this a case of nonserial murders?"

"You may be right. The character of this case probably should be called a case of nonserial murders. When I record this for posterity, I may call it *The Case of the Nonserial Murders* because that is the murderer's objective. In other words, which case was premeditated by the murderer? I am placing great importance on tricking the murderer because this criminal fears the discovery of the true motive. If we find the motive, we find the murderer."

"Well, are all the cases the work of one murderer?"

Dr. Kose nodded while grinning.

"That is certain. This gathering of shady characters under one roof is not by chance but by the will of the murderer. I, too, was politely summoned, isn't that a bit aggravating?"

The doctor smiled awkwardly. I realized he already knew something.

"So what is the murderer's true motive?"

Dr. Kose laughed out loud and said, "If I knew that, I could name the murderer. However, these are frighteningly well-planned crimes. Every aspect was meticulously calculated. This crime may be the most intelligent and grandest ever in Japan. This murderer is a genius. Ignore the intelligent stinginess and cheap tricks, and you have a superb crime.

"The cheap tricks already left footprints in the design of a machine to tie a door to a thread and naturally close the door or to fake a locked-room murder. Has the murderer's mental state been explained yet? The scariest part is always describing the murderer's mental state.

"The heavy silence for terrifying everyone is proof of the murderer's a demonic murdering genius. What is the murderer's true motive? Which murder was the murderer's true objective? As the murderer warned, the murders will probably end on August 9. However, the murder connected to the true motive may not necessarily end on August 9. The intended murder may have already been committed."

"If that's so, will these extra murders have to be committed under strict security?"

"That means the true motive must be hidden. What will happen on August 9? It may be the climax, but I have doubts. This murderer gave advance notice of August 9. The firm date of August 9 is not the stupid obligation it appears to be because this murderer killed two people in one day. He always strikes in unguarded moments. If he kills someone with poison, the survivors become vigilant. Therefore, he poisoned two people in quick succession. I think the poisonings announced the end. Perhaps he does not anticipate another murder. This is the murderer's character. Therefore, I think August 9 should be faced head-on."

However, Dr. Kose was not confident.

I knew the doctor visited Katakura and the home where Ebitsuka was raised despite his suspicions centering on Kazuma. I knew this was true because the doctor said to Kazuma, "Utagawa-sensei, I can't imagine you, Ebitsuka-san's uncle, did not know. Kajiko-sama didn't know and thought your father confessed all to you, the heir in this family, but that's beyond reason."

Kazuma was overwhelmed. I spoke in his place.

"Doctor, you don't know because you weren't here. I was a witness when Katakura-san came to reveal these secrets. At the time, Kazuma paled and looked stunned. Despite being a great actor, his expression wasn't fake. The truth in his heart was exposed. His face didn't lie. That expression of truth was more certain than a lie detector."

"That may be so. Your literary method involves several egotistical and arbitrary steps and may be certain, like a lie detector. Utagawa-sensei did not truly know this until now. How odd the family heir didn't know at least what Kamiyama Toyo knew. If Kamiyama Toyo didn't know, I could agree with you but ..."

Kazuma felt awful and was livid.

"I did not know a thing. I am the heir and alone would inherit because there are no other heirs. My father was a nihilist. He used to say, 'Your generation is fine doing as you please. If anyone dies, any grave is acceptable.' He possessed a trait unbecoming a member of an old family: he understood little of the idea of family. Like all things are essentially nothing, he gazed at the faces of cold human loneliness. He may not have realized it, but his understanding of literature may have been more profound than mine. Problems such as small secrets like old wounds didn't exist. These incidents occurred and became serious. If these incidents had not happened, wouldn't this be irrelevant?"

Dr. Kose was slightly embarrassed.

"That's true. However, if this incident took place in the household of a man like me with no wealth, it may be as you say. But it's reasonable for the incident to become the seed for Kamiyama Toyo's blackmail. When I imagine the distribution of this family's fortune, the amount of money to be distributed may not be insignificant."

"If Kamiyama Toyo files a civil suit, and the suit is legitimate. I will not respond to the blackmail but distribute the inheritance to the Ebitsuka family. More than a tangible result, I'll have a taste of justice."

Kazuma was panting as he spoke, but Dr. Kose even suspected me.

"Sensei."

He appeared at our room and grinned at Kyoko and I.

"Although Utagawa-sensei said that, but he's different. Did you know Ebitsuka-san is a grandson in this family? Someone close to Kajiko-sama, a maid, or Kayoko-san would know enough to attempt blackmail. Did Kayoko-san know? I have doubts about her."

Through his smirk, he said, "Ma'am, you were Kayoko-san's friend. Did you happen to hear this story from her?"

His straightforward actions as a detective unsettled Kyoko because a dagger from an inside pocket was suddenly waved around and flung at her.

"Oh, Kose-san, you're horrible."

"No, Kyoko-san, please don't be offended. I must rely on your forgiveness of my rudeness and ask these questions. The fact is, you were Tamon-san's lover and probably heard a bit of this story from him—"

"No, that never happened," she said, infuriated.

"I'm terribly sorry," said the doctor still grinning.

"Sensei, is Tango-sensei single?"

"I believe so."

"Does he have a lover?"

"I'm not sure. I haven't heard anything like that."

"I wonder what designs Tango-sensei had on Tamao-san."

"How often has he been in love? How much does he think about such things? I have no interest in thinking about that pervert."

"When he became a great author, he became fussy and had difficulty socializing."

Everyone was a suspect. I was also a little disgusted. I thought too highly of Dr. Kose. Compared to him, Detective Suspicious was not impetuous but was cautious, honed in on a target we did not understand, and enjoyed diving single-mindedly into the investigation.

One morning, when I went out for a walk to Mount Miwa, an elderly couple in distress was squatting in the road. On a closer look, they were Yura-sama and a man I'd never seen before. He must have been her husband, Nagumo."

I approached and ask what happened. Yura's troubled expression changed to relief.

"We seem to be having difficulty walking. We're old and could do this ten days ago, but today, we can't."

"I heard you've been ill."

"Yes, but this morning he felt a little better. His aching legs and hips were fine. I thought he was overdoing it. He wanted to see where Chigusa's body was found. Although he was an old man complaining, I agreed and we set out on our mission. Also, I thought it was an old man's pain. As I said, we could do it today but wouldn't be able to tomorrow or the day after tomorrow. We keenly feel the uncertainty.

"If we didn't do it now, we may never be able to go. What has happened can't be undone. We're fine with dying. More than a four- or five-year-old who can't wait for tomorrow, we have no more patience. In the end, we are tired. Just this spring, we walked to the mineral springs without tiring."

"Yes, yes. You came up in the conversation other day at the mineral springs inn. I was there to buy Calmotin."

"Calmotin? No, that medicine——," said Yura-sama and blanched.

"Who is this man?" asked her husband, still crouching.

"He's a guest in the Western building. His name is Yashiro. He's Kyoko-san's husband."

"Oh, yes, him?"

I offered my hand. He took it and stood. I thought about carrying him on my back, but he was a big man, thin but almost six feet tall.

"Should I send a cart to fetch you?"

"No, no. I can walk."

He walked holding onto my shoulder.

"Moroi-san has a hard heart. If a patient goes out for a walk, she's concerned enough to go but will say, 'Go if you wish to die.' That's outrageous? If tipping is encouraged, I'll do it no matter what. Please slip her some huge amount of money. That woman is a helper who administers drugs and a demon who would not hesitate to poison without a second thought."

The old man clamped onto my shoulder while gasping and struggled to say, "Yes, she is."

Moroi Kotoji seemed to live a regrettable existence.

He asked, "How is her pregnancy coming along?"

Yura said, "Pregnant? Is she pregnant? By whom? My

brother had been ill since her arrival. Aside from that, Ebitsuka-san would marry her if she were pregnant.

You can't count her companions: a postmaster, a schoolteacher, or a farmer who recently came into money. The rumor is she sleeps with the one-hundred-yen bills she earns. Because she has no affection in her heart, her dearest friend is money. She's a ghastly person."

If we hadn't met Kamiyama Toyo along the way, I would have been late.

Kamiyama is a big man, about five-nine, and carried Nagumo on his back with no trouble and walked shoulder to shoulder with Yura.

I thought Moroi Kotoji, a mysterious woman, played a mysterious role in a corner of this case and must be fiercely condemned.

Who is this woman with a greedy and amoral heart?

I promptly investigated her alibi on the day Chigusa was killed during the evening of July 18. I failed.

On that day, Moroi was the last person to see Chigusa leave through the back gate. From six to seven at night, Nurse Moroi massaged Tamon and stayed in when done.

18
———

THE SEVENTH VICTIM

The day was August 3.

Lately, I've gone to my job at the mineral springs inn around noon. Of course, it was quiet there, too, but somehow the Western building of the Utagawa home was quieter. The sturdy reinforced concrete blocked most outside sounds.

More than the quiet, I was tired of the monotony. With each successive incident, I hid my feelings to prevent the others from knowing my mood and wore a matching expression. I felt confined and went to the inn.

These feelings weren't unique to me. Recently, everyone often disappeared during the day. Some took the bus to town. Tango visited the village to challenge the Go players to games. Kazuma fell into an agitated melancholy and went for walks to who knows where. Pikaichi and Kamiyama Toyo never went out but engrossed themselves every day in betting on their billiards games. Both were around 300-point players. Sometimes Dr. Kose joined them. He equaled them in ability, was a skilled player, and had the personality of a born gambler. The previous night, those three decided to play all day today, from morning to night. Although they could lose entire fortunes, their enthusiasm was over the top. Kamiyama Toyo woke up early each morning to have his bath.

I heard Kyoko left early to go shopping in N-Town and visit old friends.

Around nine o'clock, when I was about to leave for the inn, Ayaka saw me.

"Yashiro-san, do you have a moment?"

Her eyes twinkled.

"You're going to the springs today. May I go with you?"

"Today is Monday. It may be crowded."

"What? On Monday, there are no crowds. The inn is deep in the mountains."

She may be right. A few days ago, she said she wanted to try the springs and would come with me. Only on that day, the inn was packed. I could barely do my job with all the noise. People were always crowded in the tub. Ayaka couldn't bathe in the baths for both men and women. Unlike the hot springs in the cities and towns, the guests at a hot springs health resort in the mountains simply enjoy the baths. They go in and out the bath for most of the day like harm would come to them if not in the bath.

A joyous Ayaka carrying a towel, soap, and a bath kit followed me.

At the beech forest, we caught up to Tango Yumihiko dressed in a summer *yukata* kimono. Apparently, in no hurry, he swung his stake while strolling. He gazed with great amusement and cynicism at the two of us and Ayaka's kit of bathing utensils.

"This is amazing. Madam, you're going to the baths?"

"Are you going to the mineral springs, too? Shall we go together?"

"Today, I am promised a game of Go at the postmaster's club."

"But isn't his home that way?"

"Yes. I enjoy Go, but when we meet, I'm in a bad mood. In any kind of meeting, I'm out of sorts. When I walk toward the meeting place, naturally, my legs aim in the opposite direction."

"You're a born contrarian. You should go to the mineral springs inn since your legs are pointed that way."

"It's as you say, but my legs turn on their own."

While talking, they turned from the center of the beech forest into the deep forest with no road.

"I'm an eccentric."

"With your warped personality, it's best not to be seriously involved with anyone. If I say white, you're the type determined to say black."

That day, the hot springs inn was deserted. Most of the bathing guests who came to the countryside in groups of two or three were nearly gone. Entire families came on outings to the mountains. Many guests had disappeared. The special quality of groups is their vitality.

With few other guests, Ayaka saw no need to request a chaperone and relaxed in the tub for over thirty minutes.

She peeked into my workspace.

"This is quite a stylish room for the countryside."

"It is. Only this cottage is special."

The room looked over a mountain stream. Outside my window, the mountain fishermen politely greet me as they pass by.

"This isn't the yard, is it the road?"

"In the mountains, yards and roads are the same. This road probably runs from there down to the valley. That's where the sediment settles. It's a popular fishing spot in this area. Look here. Even I bought a fishing pole. Sometimes, I take a break from work and fish out that window."

"You fish?"

"I have yet to catch one because it's a bad time. My fishing gear is the cheap junk sold in this inn. It's hard to catch sweetfish, salmon, or char."

"I'd like to watch you fish someday. Well, I'll be on my way. Goodbye," she said and went home.

The rare guest, Ayaka, came and was now gone. I was a little excited and couldn't work. Simply showing her how I dropped the line would have been no good. I ate lunch, took a nap, then returned to finish a little work.

Between 8:00 and 8:30, four or five people returned home. According to the bus schedule, both the last group coming from N-Town and the group heading to N-Town arrived around seven. The times for buses in the countryside are not fixed and must be given a window around thirty minutes long.

Recently, many people often went out. Most returned during dinner. They arrived in this village around seven. The problem was the last bus to leave N-Town was around five and arrived in the village around seven. Even men on faster legs took an hour to reach the Utagawa house.

On this day, Mokubei, Kyoko, and Kisona returned on the last bus from N-Town. Kazuma and Tango returned on the last bus from F-Town. The F-Town bus traveled between N-Town and F-Town. The buses going in either direction from N-Village, midway between the towns, took less than two hours.

The last bus from F-Town was late. Kazuma and Tango returned to the house around eight-thirty, but Utsugi Akiko never appeared.

"Was Akiko-san on our bus?" I asked Kazuma. He said, "No."

She wasn't on the last bus to leave N-Town.

Kyoko said to me, "Ebitsuka-san was on the last bus from N-Town. Today is Sunday, so his hospital was closed. I saw Moroi-san in town, but she was not with us when the last bus left."

I asked, "Tango-san, you didn't go to the Go club but went to F-Town?"

"Thanks to all of you, I couldn't go to the mineral springs inn."

Kocho looked doubtful and said, "What happened to Utsugi-san? Today, we gave lectures in this village's Young Men's Club and Young Women's Club. Hitomi lectured all morning in the theater club. In the afternoon, I put on make-up and performed. We left here around nine in the morning. Utsugi-san was working in her room. I thought she may be tired and napping. I went to see."

Kocho found the manuscript Akiko was working on in her room but Akiko was gone.

Soon after the meal ended, Detective Suspicious wandered in.

"Detective, there may be another case," said Kamiyama Toyo.

"What? Stop being a menace. You're a demon who stirs up suspicions."

"No one has seen Utsugi Akiko-san. A lost adult would be an amusing story any other place, but in this house, it's alarming."

"Of course. When was she last seen?"

"Around nine this morning, Kocho-san saw Akiko-san working in her room. That's the only report. The painter Doi, Dr. Kose, and I battled at billiards. Of the others, Kazuma-san and Tango-san went to F-Town; Miyake-san, Kyoko-san, and my wife went to N-Town. And Yashiro-san?"

"I went with Ayaka-san to the mineral springs inn. We left around nine."

"So everyone went somewhere. I guess our billiards group has nothing to offer. Dammit, when did she go out? And where?"

Tsubota Heikichi's wife, Teruyo, spoke up.

"Sometime between nine and ten, I saw Utsugi-sama go out."

"Where were you?"

"Here in the living room. Oh, yes, she had a drink of water in the kitchen. I asked if she was going out. She said, 'Yes, for a short walk.' She left through the dining hall wearing *zori* sandals."

"What time was lunch?"

"I don't remember, but I was preparing lunch. I thought, She'll be hungry when she returns. I wondered what she'd like to eat."

The next day, Utsugi-san's drowned body was discovered in the basin of a waterfall deep in Mount Miwa.

AUTHOR'S NOTE: This case is nearing the final act. The next time, everyone's abilities will be gradually revealed.

As promised in the previous notes, Dr. Kose leaked a portion of his observations on the properties of *The Case of the Nonserial Murders* to us. I must tell a story of grace and kindness.

Eureka and Four-Foot Nose-sensei of Kyushu thought the multiple murderers had different motives and were cunning, whoever they were. I didn't expect to be overwhelmed by kindness. Despite a tinge of embarrassment, I set out to write a detective novel with the least possible level of shame. I didn't notice this until this year the need for supreme enlightenment.

Embarrassing an adult is wicked; therefore, I will be gracious and lightly injure everyone.

Recently, a fellow tried to bribe people around me. I was annoyed and troubled. He offered them the prize divided into equal shares to be spies and collaborate on an answer. It's a collapse of morality and a loss of sportsmanship.

An editor of novels in Japan said to someone close to me, "You'll ask about the murderer and on the sly investigate his notes for half of the prize. I can buy a pair of shoes with that money."

The attempt to buy the motive is wretched. Although I must harden myself, I despair. After careful consideration, my fate is the inability to sincerely understand. I confess I have no room for sympathy.

Sakaguchi Ango

19

THE ALIBI GAME

A mountain stream flowed before Miwa Shrine. Its rushing waters grew and poured into Lake Miwa. Essentially different from a water source, the stream gathered springs in the back mountains. Water is abundant, creates a basin of the falls at the bottom of the valley that bends from Miwa Shrine, and forms a deep pool larger than 3,500 square feet. Rock cliffs shot straight up in all directions. The water surface was tranquil and turned green in the amazing stream of sunlight. Eddies lurking under the surface made swimming and fishing impossible.

Utsugi-san dressed in Japanese clothes was floating on the water surface and gently swirling back and forth in the eddies.

It looked like she had been pushed from the cliff. No evidence proved she hadn't committed suicide. Although the sun shined on the flat land, rain often falls during the morning and evening in the mountains. On the evening of August 3 and early dawn on the fourth considerable rain fell and washed away footprints. Finding signs of struggle would be difficult.

Utsugi-san's body was discovered in early dawn the next day, the fourth. The police doctor came out and finished the autopsy in Sourin Temple by evening. From her stomach contents, he determined she was killed three to three and a half hours after her last meal.

Lately, many of us often went out and ate our meals in the dining hall at irregular times. Even the men's legs that boarded the first bus had to leave the Utagawa house at 7:30, so they ate wherever they were going.

However, we remembered Akiko ate breakfast with Kyoko, the Kamiyamas, and me around 7:30 yesterday, the third. That day, Kamiyama forgot to glance at his treasured watch and didn't know the exact time. The crime was discovered between 10:30 and 11:00.

After dinner on the fourth, Detective Suspicious gathered us and Dr. Ebitsuka, Nurse Moroi, and Shizue in the living room. He greeted us with, "I want to kill myself, too. I can imagine how much this troubles everyone. Please bear with me. Was Utsugi-san murdered or did she kill herself? There is no clear evidence. I believe it's natural for some to see murder right away.

"As a rule, a person who commits suicide doesn't immediately leap to her death but instead performs several actions beforehand. For example, she will take off footwear or place her belongings on the ground. Sometimes, a woman will bind both legs over her clothes to prevent an untidy hem. But this is not absolute. Although Utsugi-san jumped in wearing her footwear and carrying her handbag, there is no reason to conclude this was murder. I think it's natural that after several unsolved murders, we will investigate another murder."

More politely, he said, "I deeply appreciate your statements. In the investigation, I must hear your alibis for yesterday. I appreciate your exceptional consideration all previous times and now as well."

His greengrocer-like affability emerged. He knows how to handle us quite well.

"I will begin by questioning Miyake-san. Yesterday, you went to N-Town and spent the whole day?"

Mokubei nodded.

"Yesterday, I asked Teruyo-san to prepare an early breakfast and left before seven-thirty. I went on the first bus and returned on the last."

"Did you notice anything strange about your wife yesterday?"

"To me, that woman was always strange. We came to this house together, but we lived in separate rooms. We lived apart. She was silently killing me. Everyone was aware of her casual situation with Wani. That woman could not go three days without the flesh of a man. I'll leave the rest to your imaginations. I had no reason to verify the truth other than in my imagination. Mine was not a true marriage. An obvious truth was the woman slept with other men."

"You're not with your wife from day to day."

"That's right. She was more than a stranger. Since this was a battle, more than a stranger, she was the enemy."

"Of course. No, I find it hard to forget someone with dangerous international connections. Forgive me for saying, but the will for peace comes from both sides."

"It doesn't. Unlike international connections, this is fate. The nation may be eternal, but humans live fifty years, and making peace with horrible people is unnecessary. In short, we were divorced."

Unable to hold back, Pikaichi said, "If that's the case, aren't your regrets cowardly?

"A man with regrets may indicate cowardice. One

more thing comes with your regrets, a stupid man with the swagger of vanity and thinks of his wife as a maid or an object. Women writers are justified in starting a revolt. Jealousy is fine, but aren't you a little raunchy for saying in public your wife couldn't go three days without being with a man? More than Utsugi-san, your character is contemptible and shameful."

Unable to find words for a counterattack, Mokubei paled and shot back an angry look. Detective Suspicious aptly intervened.

"Miyake-san, what plans had your wife made for the day? You were aware of those details."

"I absolutely was not."

"Miyake-san, do you have friends in N-Town?"

"No, I was tired of being bored and went out with no particular aim. I looked in the window of a book shop. My shopping consisted of buying a magazine. If they don't remember my face there, I don't have an alibi."

"Did you leave early on the first bus? Does everyone here usually go to N-Town on the first bus?"

No one answered. Kisona spoke up.

"Yesterday, I went to N-Town but on the second bus. We ladies have to get ready, walk slower than the gentlemen, and take the second bus. I went with Kyoko-sama and met Nurse Moroi at the bus stop. We got off at Taisho-dori in N-Town. I left Kyoko-sama to go shopping. We met again to wait for the last bus where Miyake-sama joined us."

"Yashiro-san, did you go shopping?"

"No, I visited a friend. I lived in this area a few years ago and befriended the wife of Honma, a dry goods dealer. I spent the entire day there."

Detective Suspicious nodded and turned to Nurse Moroi.

"I'm at a disadvantage when questioning you. You can push aside police and patients alike and not answer. Where did you go?"

"Yesterday was Sunday, my day off. I went to purchase medications."

"I don't believe it took you all day to accomplish your errand. Please fill in as many details as you can."

"After that, I strolled around. Anyone who leaves this place deep in the mountains and goes to town walks around."

"That's reasonable. What you say is always reasonable. Thank you."

Detective Suspicious probed the N-Town alibi of each person who responded with caution. In the end, only Kyoko had a clear alibi. Kisona-san shopped for various items and window shopped. But with no acquaintances, if no one there remembered her, what could be done?

Nurse Moroi arrived in N-Town on the second bus at 12:30, bought medicine at the pharmacy across from the terminal bus stop, and returned by the bus that left at 2:30. She got off the bus and went directly to the pharmacy to place her order. Then she wandered around town. She collected the package of medicine, boarded the bus, and returned home. During those two hours, she strolled around town and had no alibi.

Mokubei had the worst alibi. He left on the first bus and arrived at N-Town at 10:30. He wandered around town until the last bus at 5:00.

"But Miyake-san, is there not one person at one place over six and a half hours who would recall your face from a brief exchange?"

"That's obvious. Because people have an abundance of inclinations, there is no set way to move forward. An unfamiliar land is simply remembered as similar roads, houses, forests, and temples. What direction is this? Where does this road lead? Your entire consciousness is not a unified panoramic picture.

"I simply enjoyed walking here and there with no plan in mind. During that time, I interacted with no one. There's nothing I can do about that now. I have no reason to live my life worrying about alibis. If I knew this sort of incident was about to transpire, I would have concocted the perfect alibi."

Detective Suspicious nodded and asked, "Miyake-san, did you know anyone on the first bus?"

"No, I'm not acquainted with the villagers. And I pay little attention to faces."

"Were you with Ebitsuka-san?"

"No, we weren't together," said Mokubei.

"So Kyoko, Yashiro-san's wife; Kisona, Kamiyama Toyo-san's wife; and Moroi-san were on the second bus. And you, Ebitsuka-san?"

Ebitsuka's expression stayed blank. He said, "I rode the third bus."

"What time was that?"

Ebitsuka didn't answer. The detective took out a bus schedule.

Depart F-Town	→ Arrive N-Village	→ Arrive N-Town
7:00	8:40	10:30
9:00	10:40	12:30
11:00	12:40	2:30
1:30	3:10	5:00
5:00	6:40	8:30

Depart N-Town	→ Arrive N-Village	→ Arrive F-Town
7:30	9:20	11:00
9:00	10:50	12:30
10:30	12:20	2:00
2:30	4:20	6:00
5:00	6:20	8:30

Figure 3.

"Ebitsuka-san departed at 12:40 and arrived at N-Town at 2:30 in the afternoon. Of course."

Detective Suspicious had a realization, ended his questioning of the warped doctor, and turned to Kazuma.

"Utagawa-san, you went to F-Town."

"Yes. I visited relatives in the mountains about two and a half miles outside of F-Town. I left on the first bus and returned on the last. I also had to walk to my relatives' home around half past noon. I left there soon after three."

"Naturally. On the way back, because both of you left on the first bus, you did not see Miyake-san until you returned to the bus stop in the village?"

"We weren't together because the first bus to F-Town was nearly thirty minutes late. When we travel to F-Town, we don't go to N-Village but to the bus stop in T-Hamlet. The distance is almost the same. At my walking pace, it takes me about an hour and fifteen minutes from this house to both places, but I'm walking downhill."

"Which direction is T-Hamlet in?"

"You pass the beech forest and the mineral springs inn and descend the winding road to the bus stop in T-Hamlet. The inn is a little over a mile from here and not even two miles from the inn to T-Hamlet. The whole trip lasts close to three miles."

"So that's another route."

Detective Suspicious looked amazed. He turned to Tango.

"Tango-san, you walked in the opposite direction to attend the postmaster's Go meeting. In fact, Bookworm and I went to the postmaster's Go meeting and enjoyed the games. You probably didn't hurry to F-Town. Again I have to ask, which bus did you take?"

Unfazed, Tango took out a cigarette and looked around. The detective noticed and lit his lighter.

"Ah, thank you," said Tango, bowing his head. "Around nine o'clock, I parted company with Yashiro Shunpei-san and Ayaka-san at the beech forest. I walked down the winding mountain road; the bus comes along at random times. When a bus came around the corner, I raised my hand, stopped, and boarded. Please, show me the schedule. Let me see. This may have been the bus that leaves N-Village at 10:50 for F-Town. If I walked the entire way to F-Town and discovered a fish trap, I'd find an opportunity to eat sweetfish. I'd eat, take a nap, and go home."

"I understand. That's for your health more than the Go meeting. Ma'am, were you at the mineral springs inn the whole time?"

"No. I stayed forty or fifty minutes then came right back. I enjoyed the bath for around thirty minutes. To save fuel, the water was lukewarm. I like warm baths and enjoyed it."

"How was the water quality?"

"I don't know, but the water was cloudy and muddy."

I went there every day, too, but didn't know what kind of hot springs it was. I heard it works on wounds but haven't seen particularly ill people appear for a hot spring cure. The smell is slightly offensive and peculiar, but it's not overwhelming. The area near the springs is famous for being free of mosquitoes. That is something.

Finally, Detective Suspicious turned to me to ask about my movements yesterday. Earlier, I explained my day. I left the house with Ayaka-san around 9:00, arrived at the mineral springs inn around 9:30, and was unable to work. I dropped a fishing line, relaxed in the springs, took a nap, wrote down a few things, and returned in the evening.

However, none of the inn staff came to my sanctuary. Thus, the feats of fishing, going to Mount Miwa, and killing Akiko would not have been impossible. Detective Suspicious missed nothing. He should have remembered that. He closely examined the bus schedule and honed in on a few issues. For example, in Mokubei's case, how he went by the first bus was unclear. He went by the first bus but turned back to return to the town where Akiko-san was being killed. Perhaps he returned on the five o'clock bus.

Kocho-san and Hitomi Koroku were eliminated as suspects. From ten to three in the afternoon, they attended lectures and training during the meetings of the young men's and young women's societies. Kamiyama and Pikaichi made bets on the billiard games played with Dr. Kose. All three were excluded.

"However, Ebitsuka-san ..."

Again, Detective Suspicious stared at Ebitsuka.

"You went to N-Town on the 12:40 bus. I'd like to hear what you were doing between nine and twelve-forty."

As usual, Ebitsuka glared and did not answer.

"Very well. Ebitsuka-san, until today, I respected your human rights and tolerated a lot from you. All right, Ebitsuka-san? My tolerance meant I respected your human rights, and in return you show your contempt. Today, I've had enough. If you don't explain, I will. Do you mind?"

Ebitsuka's burning eyes rolled once as he fought his rage, displayed his contempt, and looked away.

Detective Suspicious sliced away the threads of his bag of patience.

"Allow me to describe your movements. Yesterday, you went around to the back gate of Utagawa's house sometime between 9:40 and 9:50. At that time, you should have met Utsugi-san as you began your walk. You went around to the kitchen of Utagawa's house and asked the maid Yae to call Nurse Moroi. As she told us earlier, she left for town on the second bus. Hearing this, you blushed and had an immediate change of heart. Because you were in the fishing hut, you told the maid to tell Shizue-san to go there."

Ebitsuka paled and trembled.

"You rude bastard! That's a lie!" he screamed. Unmoved, Detective Suspicious stared daggers at him and never looked away. Already given the order, Eight-Foot Nose and Bookworm closed in on him from the left and right sides.

"Given the message by Yae-san, Shizue-san wondered what was happening and rushed to the fishing hut. You were waiting there with your stethoscope dangling and told her you were certain she suffered from a disease of the chest. 'Today I will diagnose your health,' and took her hand. Shizue-san, frightened by your behavior, said, 'No, I'm not ill. Excuse me, I must go.' You tightened your grip and said, 'No, you're not.... You'll be naked even if I have to strip you.' Then you tried to kiss her."

"Nonsense! You bastard! The insolence!"

He shouted with menace and seemed ready to leap. The two officers beside him grabbed his arms.

Detective Suspicious's cold eyes stared down Ebitsuka.

"The shocked Shizue-san resisted and tried to escape. She shook you off. You sprang. She freed herself. You sprang again and finally grabbed hold of her. Shizue-san shrieked. Fortunately, Yura-sama was strolling around the lake at that time and heard her screams. She peeked into the fishing hut. Your plan was foiled. Shizue-san was able to explain her peril. Well? Shizue-san is also here. If this is not enough, shall I ask Yura-sama? Frustrated, you dashed like a madman to the house. That happened around ten o'clock or 10:10. Now, Ebitsuka-san, where were you until the bus came? This 12:40 bus was twenty minutes late and arrived at N-Village around one in the afternoon. What were you doing until one o'clock?"

Ebitsuka glowered at Detective Suspicious.

"You idiot! You're insane!" he shouted, swung both arms, leaped up, turned, and flew out of the room.

Ebitsuka stopped in the hallway and turned around.

"God will punish all of you! Kill all of you! Lunatics! Fools!"

He swung his arms like a gorilla, turned, and disappeared.

"Why didn't you arrest him?" asked Kamiyama.

"Why?" said Detective Suspicious coolly, "I have no proof."

20

THE PRIME SUSPECT

The detective's interrogation ended. When we were about to retire to our rooms, Kazuma and Ayaka returned. Their faces were blanched. They found a piece of paper on the desk in the room they left locked.

Identical to the previous incident, these words were written in pen on Utagawa's writing pad.

August 9, the Day of Destiny.

That evening was topsy-turvy because Akiko's body was being sent to the cremation site. All of us headed to Sourin Temple. The area from the autopsy room to the main temple seemed to be partly transformed by disorder. While listening to the chanting of sutras, they saw off Akiko carried on a cart then returned to eat. Kazuma and Ayaka were kept busy. With no time to go back to our rooms, we stayed at the dining table and went to our rooms after being questioned by Detective Suspicious.

Kazuma, Ayaka, and I knocked on Dr. Kose's door.

The doctor was rummaging through a trunk. He listened to our story but was unmoved.

"Oh, really?"

His rummaging became frantic. What was he looking for? Finally, relief swept over his face. His prize was a solitary sock.

"What? A sock? What kind of evidence is that?" I asked with disgust. He smiled and said with good humor, "It's not. I'm going on a trip tomorrow then on to Tokyo. My ulterior motive is to visit her. She appreciates cleanliness. What is a sock? I always take note of her orders."

"Have you been defeated?"

"No, this is the road to victory," he said and caught his breath.

"I have no honor. I was engrossed in gambling on billiards and failed. But the murderer will not escape. What did it say? August 9, the Day of Destiny. August 9 is coming. Again I implore you, Utagawa-sensei, and your wife, please be careful. It's best to wind up the cord of the room key and attach it to something. Please be cautious about food, too. During the day, refrain from walking alone, you must live in groups. Vigilance is key. If you see someone, assume it's the murderer."

Dr. Kose took out a new necktie and smiled reflexively.

I asked, "Why are you going on a trip?"

"I'm looking for physical proof."

"The proof isn't here?"

"No, it's not. The murderer exposes his dilemma in the relationship between time and space. Psychology, however, lacks physical proof. My search lay there."

"Do you know who the murderer is?"

"Yes, it must be that person. I'm certain. However, it's a calculation of space and time. What I have can't be brought to court as proof. If, in the end, proof never surfaces, I will bring proof to court in the form of a time-space calculation. This is desperation. It'll be awful if I fail."

He dropped his head into his hands.

"Where are you going?"

"Everywhere. The whole world. Anywhere I must. With willpower and desperation, I will even dive into the water."

A little embarrassed, he grinned.

The breakfast table the following morning received Akiko's remains. Everyone assembled at the table. Wani, Tamao, Chigusa, Utsumi, and Akiko had been killed. Ebitsuka was far away. Twelve remained. Dr. Kose was going on a trip. Eleven people surrounded the table.

Kamiyama Toyo said, "Kose-san, you're off on a trip to look for physical evidence. How? Can you leak a hint of your inference? I believe the peak incident occurred on July 26, Kayoko-san's murder. When the work of the killing demon targeted the painter Doi, Kayoko-san's murder was the objective. The motive for the murder may be simple and obvious."

Dr. Kose did not give a simpering reply.

Pikaichi said, "So I'm the target of the killing demon? I'm sorry I likened him to a hopeless wooden doll. If Kayoko-san's murder was the target, how is the resolution simple and obvious? Who is the murderer? Uh, our very own corrupt lawyer!"

"I don't know that. I said the motive was simple and obvious."

"Well, what about Akiko-san or Wani or Utsumi?" asked a sneering Tango.

"They're different," said the lawyer Kamiyama, deftly handling his question. His rival, a literary man, was a pain.

Tango asked, "What's different?"

Kamiyama said, "I'll leave that judgment to the detective. The seven murders can be broadly divided into two groups. In the first, all of us could be the murderer. In the three murders of Wani, Tamao, and Tamon, anyone could have poisoned Tamon and put the morphine in the sugar pot. In the second, particular people could have murdered Chigusa, Utsumi, Kayoko, and Utsugi. No one else could have committed these murders. What happens if we eliminate each person who could not be the murderer? If dissatisfied with the person who could not possibly escape being a suspect, why don't we listen to the explanation, become the jury, and hand down a decision?"

No one responded. Kamiyama Toyo coolly said, "Let's begin with Chigusa's murder. She returned alone on the road back from the cremation site. No one escapes being a suspect. Of the people who returned in groups of two or three, Kazuma-san returned and went to Sourin Temple for thirty minutes. He doesn't have an alibi and can't escape suspicion. In the end, the people who returned home in groups and above suspicion were Kose-san and Hitomi-san; and Kazuma-san, the priest, and I. The painter Doi arrived first. The five men of Utsumi-san who came next, Kazuma-san, Miyake-san, Tango-san, and Yashiro-san have no alibi."

Nobody spoke, so Kamiyama Kisona said, "Well, Doi-san and Utsumi-san, the first and second to arrive, don't need alibis. Of course, the walk took time."

Kamiyama nodded at our understanding.

"Also, Utsumi-san went out to Miwa Shrine to rendezvous with Chigusa-san. He didn't see her and returned home. However, he may have gone out at that time to kill Chigusa-san. A typical scenario would be to blindfold Chigusa-san with a *furoshiki* cloth and use it to strangle her.

"As intimate friends, I could imagine her allowing him to playfully blindfold her. When she least expected it, he strangled her. I believe Utsumi-san can't escape being a suspect. During this time, the painter Doi returned ahead of Utsumi-san, so Doi-san may be the only person who's not a suspect.

"I, like Doi, was alone; therefore, I can't escape being a suspect. I'm quite familiar with this village's geography and ascended from the cremation site to the cliffs. From there, you can come down 800 to 1,000 feet without being seen. A back road there crosses the valley and comes out at Miwa Shrine. Lumberjacks rarely walk that road. The grass over there is tread on, short, and grows little.

"In ten to fifteen minutes, you can walk this back road to Mount Miwa, go around the mountain to the back gate of the Utagawa house, and down the obvious road to the house. This secret path prevents anyone alone from being eliminated as a suspect.

"The painter Doi returned before Utsumi-san. This should put him beyond suspicion, but that's not possible. Everyone can run the secret path. But there's one more problem."

Kamiyama donned a haughty expression.

"My fundamental belief is to avoid talking about people who aren't here, but a problem is a problem, and I must bring this up. Nurse Moroi stated Chigusa-san left for her rendezvous at 6:00. However, no one else saw Chigusa-san leave at 6:00. In short, until what time did Chigusa-san remain in the house? Although others saw her up to 5:00, the next hour is unclear. Nurse Moroi has an alibi between 6:00 and 8:00, but Chigusa-san had been killed by 6:00."

The group's previously indifferent faces could no longer mask their strain. Kamiyama Toyo looked smug, not worried.

"Even in the crimes of sons and mothers in the countryside, there are things like foreshadowing, false evidence that cannot be accepted at face value, pressing knowledge, and surprises."

He had sparked their interest and dove into the topic.

"Next, in Utsumi's murder, the murderer waited for the painter Doi positioned to see down the second-floor hallway to look away and passed through. Therefore, the popular view is the murderer was not on the second floor. However, the painter Doi was drunk. That must be taken into consideration. Kazuma-san, Kose-san, and others close to the position in the hall where Doi-san planted himself would be scolded by him if they showed their faces. People further away than Tango-san wandered to the bathroom but Doi-san didn't try to pick a fight. The bathroom is located opposite the position where Doi-san enshrined himself."

He looked amused as he surveyed the group.

"Hitomi-san and his wife's room is across from Tango-san. I'm next to Tango-san. Next, Miyake-san and Utsugi-san were opposite Yashiro-san, who was next to an empty room. He could pretend to go to the bathroom on the second floor but go downstairs. From his entrenched location, the drunk painter Doi would not be able to discern his movements."

The group became agitated. This, however, was nothing more than clever talk. Spasms ran through me because truth does not come from a void.

"I hear what you're saying, but haven't I always maintained the murderer went downstairs and killed Utsumi? The more important problems are: did I go to the bathroom, and did Pikaichi see me?"

"Calm down, Yashiro-san, we're merely discussing simple possibilities. Unfortunately, the painter Doi was drunk and doesn't recall that moment. I presume that is so and am outlining the limits of these simple possibilities."

"Since we accept Pikaichi was drunk, the long distance from Tango's room does not have to be a problem. Kazuma and Dr. Kose should have been able to go to the bathroom. Wasn't Ayaka-san the only one confined to her room?"

"Exactly. My reasoning about this was mistaken. Limiting my target to Tango-san was unusual. Kazuma-san and Kose-san should have been able to go to the bathroom. Here's my conjecture from the night's circumstances. When Kazuma-san or Kose-san opened a nearby door, Doi-san screamed as if he could bite. Doi-san was drunk and the next day may not have remembered, but from the other rooms, we could assess the situation from the painter Doi's yelling. From far down the hallway, Doi-san was certainly shouting."

This time, the group seemed persuaded by his truth. Kamiyama hurriedly said, "Now, on to Kayoko's murder. Her poisoning and Tamon's murder occurred at the same time, but their characteristics differed. In Tamon's murder, no one was in the kitchen from 1:30 to 3:00. Any one of us had the opportunity to put morphine in the sugar pot. Kayoko-san was reading in the living room and might have seen the murderer. Being seen by Kayoko was no problem because she had to die, too."

Kamiyama briefly diverged from the theory of Kayoko being murdered accidentally instead of Pikaichi. Pikaichi's expression said, "Shut up," but he showed no sign of wanting to complain.

"Kayoko's murder is a problem. In this case, there was no time for the poison to be slipped in over several minutes. The people able to spike the sugar begin with those in the kitchen: Tsubota-san's wife, Kisona-san, Yae-san, and Ebitsuka-san; those who went to the bathroom: Ayaka-san, Kyoko-san, Kazuma-san, Yashiro-san, Kose-san, Miyake-san, and me. In addition, the one with the least ability to escape suspicion is Doi-san who switched coffee cups with Kayoko-san. Naturally, Doi-san stands in the position of heightened suspicion."

Pikaichi showed no interest in Kamiyama's random musings.

"The problem is the chipped coffee cup. Usually, Teruyo, Yae, and Kisona were in charge of the coffee cups and could distinguish between them. The rest of us also knew Doi-san's cup was chipped but not its pattern. The greater problem was Doi-san destroyed Utagawa's coffee cup by acting like Susanoo Omikoto, the chaotic god of storms and the sea.

"As the number of guests grew, the painter Doi-sama's fate was to be assigned the chipped coffee cup. If the murderer did not know this, this murder could not have happened.

"I see Kayoko's murder as the murderer's original aim and don't accept it as a failed assassination of the painter Doi. If Kayoko's murder was the objective, the prime suspect is the painter Doi who switched coffee cups. He can't escape being the prime suspect. If the murderer was not Doi-san, he deduced his coffee cup was spiked with poison. The murderer knew Kayoko-san's coffee cup was chipped.

"However, one case is the two cups could not be distinguished. The other is the murder expected the cup with fewer chips, that is, the painter Doi's coffee cup, to be handed to Kayoko-san that day. The server Yae inadvertently handed it to Doi-san as usual.

"Alternately, the murderer knew Kayoko-san's coffee cup was chipped but had no chance to examine each coffee cup. I believe the rush to drop the poison into any chipped cup caused the mistake.

"As explained earlier, Kayoko-san was familiar with the situation in this house's kitchen. Reasonably, she knew the chipped coffee cup might be used in the dining hall. In addition to planning Kayoko's murder, this killer was well acquainted with this household."

I could no longer put up with this and said, "In Kamiyama-kun's version of the situation, the murderer settled the inheritance problem in the Utagawa family. What about the cases of Wani, Utsumi, and Utsugi-san? If the inheritance problem of the Utagawa family was the motive for murder, several murders may happen to the eleven people. Hasn't little been determined in that regard?"

"Did one murderer kill them all, or did a different murderer kill each victim? We can't decide on the spot whether one murderer or multiple murderers committed these crimes. Depending on the circumstances and the number of murderers, the cases take on distinct forms. We'll postpone thinking about that problem and look at Utsugi's murder next?"

Kamiyama sounded calm like he saw through to the murderer.

"The list of people having an alibi from the end of breakfast to evening three days ago must begin unluckily with the three-man billiards squad, Doi-san, Kose-san, and me. We three locked horns and delayed trips to the bathroom.

"Next, Kyoko-san, Nurse Moroi, and Kisona, who took the 10:40 bus, the second bus, to N-Town, had to leave this house an hour earlier. They rode that bus from 10:40 to 12:30 and have an alibi because the estimated time of the murder falls between 10:30 to 11:00. Next, Kazuma-san visited relatives in F-Town, and almost no suspicion surrounds his alibi. Now to the remaining five."

Kamiyama grinned awkwardly.

"That's a surprise. I, too, am a suspect," said Tango Yumihiko. His sleepy eyes suddenly shifted to Kamiyama. "You wandered out of the beech forest when I went out to the road to catch the 10:15 bus."

"Excuse me, Tango-sensei, but your wandering shows you have no sense of time. You don't carry a watch. Have you lived the past ten to fifteen years without owning a watch? Your target may have been 10:50 for the 12:20 bus.

"But there is proof. Villagers rode the 12:20 bus with you, Sensei. As you said, you waved down the bus in the middle of the road. That was corroborated.

"Detective Suspicious knew this from the beginning. When the detective came to question us, he asked more questions but came to study our expressions. He's a proper scoundrel."

Tango said nothing.

"The people able to kill Utsugi are now Tango-san and the mineral springs contingent, Yashiro-sensei and Ayaka-san. Both traveled the usual roads and possibly killed Utsugi-san in an expectedly short time. Now, on to Miyake-san.

"Right now, there's no proof Miyake boarded the first bus on the third. He might have boarded from N-Town, but the situation changed. He came back, committed a crime, and he went home. At 5:00 in the evening, he boarded the bus with an aloof expression and came home. That is not impossible. Finally, Ebitsuka-sensei and the above five cannot escape being suspects in this case."

The grinning Kamiyama took a notebook from his pocket.

"The truth is I'm a busybody. I take precise notes. Once again, I'll list the suspects in the four murders.

"Chigusa's murder: the painter Doi, Utsumi-sensei, Kazuma-sensei, Yashiro-sensei, Miyake-sensei, Tango-sensei. However, Nurse Moroi's evidence may be false.

"Utsumi's murder: Tango-sensei, Hitomi-san and Kocho, Kamiyama-san and Kisona, Utsugi-sensei, Miyake-sensei, Yashiro-san and Kyoko, and the residents of the main house.

"Kayoko's murder: the painter Doi, Tsubota Heikichi-san and Teruyo, Kamiyama-san and Kisona, Miyake-sensei, Kazuma-san and Ayaka, Yashiro-san and Kyoko, Dr. Kose, and Ebitsuka-sensei

"Utsugi's murder: Tango-sensei, Ayaka-san, Yashiro-sensei, Miyake-sensei, and Ebitsuka-sensei

"Looking them over, one of the two people connected with each case is Yashiro-sensei. Kyoko has an alibi for Utsugi's murder. The other is Miyake-sensei. Only these two could have committed all four murders. Ebitsuka-sensei and Tango-sensei could have committed three murders. Everyone agrees this is a strange tale. Of the seven murders, Tamon's, Tamao's and Kayoko's have a coherent motive. Compared to the other four with assorted motives, these three murders are the principal crimes. Looking at the common suspects in the above four cases, the person linked to the primary motive does not appear among the suspects."

His explanations left a deep impression on the group and gave them a lot to mull over.

"But there are problems," said Kamiyama and casually read their faces. "What on earth does this mean? The first problem is the variety of motives for the seven murders. Were the crimes committed by different murderers? Were the murders part of a coherent plan devised by the same murderer? In the former case, common sense says that's impossible.

"Even in the queer world of artists, multiple, unrelated murders are almost impossible. Literary people are mostly master criminals. In the style of so-called detective novels, the great detective is said to be a master criminal inside out, but that's not so.

"Literary people who write novels are master criminals inside out. Detectives are different. The detective does not create but discovers. According to Yashiro-sensei's theory, Dr. Kose cannot write a novel, and that may be the character of a great detective. That's the truth.

"The opposite is true for literary people such as yourselves. That means you have the character of a master criminal as do lawyers. I can't compare to you because my business creates human connections. However, compared to ordinary people like us, the sensei is a genius. We, ordinary people, have a gift for detective work and being criminals. Genius sensei have absolutely no ability at detective work and have the character of master criminals."

Kamiyama's face wore a smile that succeeded in being both weak and mocking.

"If the seven cases looked like murders planned by the same murderer, the problem becomes why did the murderer devise separate, unrelated murders? The murderer did this on purpose to hide the true motive. Which murder or several murders were the murderer's true objectives? The purpose of the other murders was to deceive. Why was this trick needed? Well, if the motive were known, we would know the murderer."

Kamiyama Toyo said the same thing as Dr. Kose.

"What is the motive?" I asked.

"The motive is the problem," he said with a queer chuckle.

"The world's great criminals are gathered under one roof and, like me, have no way to uncover the motive. The most obvious motive is not necessarily the murderer's true motive. The motive with the most obvious gain is not always the murderer's true objective. Dr. Kose, what do you think?"

Dr. Kose did not answer. Tango did.

"Kamiyama-kun gave us the suspects common to four murders and told us only Yashiro and Miyake were common to all the murders. However, he did not give the possible suspects for the murders related to Utagawa's fortune, which can be seen as the key crime. There's an accomplice. Was this crime committed by one person or two or more people? In the short time of almost half a month, seven people were killed one after the other while under strict police vigilance. This would have been impossible without an accomplice."

"You're right," said a nodding Kamiyama.

"The dilemma with the Utagawa murders is killing Utsumi was impossible even with two murderers, for instance, if Kazuma-san and his wife were the accomplices. Could there be a third accomplice?"

An indignant Kazuma said, "I realize I'm a prime suspect. I can do nothing about that. I don't care at all because I have no interest in suspicions and suspects. What concerns me is August 9. Who is planning what? If I'm killed next on August 9, what will happen?"

As he spoke, the anger drained from his face, and his voice weakened. Anxiety and terror distorted his face.

Dr. Kose checked his watch and stood.

"The time has come. Excuse me. I intend to return by August 9. Take care of yourselves. I'm captivated by Kamiyama-san's grand reasoning, but the time is late," he said in a panic and rushed out.

21

A RENDEZVOUS, A TORTURE SESSION, AND AN ARREST

After breakfast, I went to the mineral springs inn. The proprietor seemed out of sorts.

"Yesterday was awful."

"You know?"

"Yesterday, the police came twice to conduct interviews."

"It was terrible."

I asked what happened. He said Detective Suspicious's group showed up first. Later, a man close to six-feet tall came. He looked like an amateur sumo wrestler who earned the highest rank of *yokozuna*. That was Kamiyama Toyo. He climbed out the window in the cottage to the mountain stream and checked his watch as he exited. Also, Dr. Kose panicked and left like a man in pursuit this morning. He surely went to investigate Mokubei's alibi in N-Town. He's a busybody. But he's a villain with a critical eye.

The proprietor, who was ignorant of the nature of the murders, had the unsettling thought I looked like a criminal because the detectives came to investigate. I also fell into a strange fantasy, like I unknowingly killed someone during an epileptic seizure. This is not talk for the workplace. My thoughts wandered to the identity of the murderer and couldn't write one character.

Kamiyama Toyo did not return home that day or by dinner the following day. When we gathered around the table for our evening meal, out of nowhere, Dr. Ebitsuka's pale face and gleaming eyes appeared.

His slow hobbling footsteps echoed as he walked halfway around the table and turned in front of me toward Mokubei.

"You're a hypocrite! Miyake Mokubei!" shouted Dr. Ebitsuka. He thrust out his right arm and pointed at the side of Mokubei's face. His exaggerated gesture was like a baseball umpire's. Spirit filled his whole body, and he stood like an expert spearman. He pointed his hand like a spear and pressed his finger below Mokubei's ear.

He shouted again, "You're a hypocrite, Miyake Mokubei!"

"On Sunday, August 3, you, Miyake Mokubei, had a secret rendezvous with Moroi Kotoji in N-Town. The other day, you cursed me. What did you scream? While you wore the mask of justice and cursed your wife's infidelity, weren't you committing adultery with Moroi Kotoji? Damn you! You hypocrite, Miyake Mokubei! What do you have to say? Dammit! You hypocrite! Miyake Mokubei!"

Kamiyama Toyo didn't go around the main house but opened the door from the outside to the dining hall and entered. He looked astonished but was amused and laughed.

"Miyake Mokubei, a hypocrite. Aah, ha, ha. A masterpiece! Your best work! What next? Ebitsuka-sensei, do you want me to tell you next complaint? A pitiful mistake of adultery. The fact is you're a jilted man. Ah, ha, ha."

For an instant, Ebitsuka was stunned by the impertinence of the arrogant Kamiyama Toyo. When Kamiyama stopped talking, oblivious to the details, his arm shot out again, and he glared at Miyake.

"What do you have to say? You hypocrite, Miyake Mokubei!"

Strangely, they heard police sirens echoing down the hall. The approach of Detective Suspicious's team and the officers raised a racket.

The sight of the police officers aroused Ebitsuka. He pointed at Miyake and said, "All of you! Look! The hypocrite Miyake Mokubei! He wears a mask of righteousness, curses me, and curses his wife's infidelity. He's a hypocrite and committed adultery with Moroi Kotoji."

Filled with a fierce soul, he pointed at the hypocrite. Officers sidled up to him from the left and right and grabbed his arms.

"What are you doing? Dammit! This is outrageous! The hypocrite is over there, wearing the mask of justice."

Eight-Foot Nose and Officer Minamigawa Yuichiro held tight to an arm and pressed like they were about to lift the diminutive Ebitsuka.

From a corner, Detective Suspicious said, "Ebitsuka-san. This is wretched, and we must go now."

The feet of the seized Ebitsuka flapped on the floor.

"Are you half asleep? He, Miyake Mokubei, is a hypocrite who lies to the world. You impertinent fools. All of you!"

"Ebitsuka-san. The police can't do a thing about hypocrites. That's in the realm of Buddha-sama or Christ," said Detective Suspicious and smiled.

"It's wretched, but we'll put aside the hypocrite. First, we must arrest a criminal who injured another. The criminal was caught in the act of torturing Nurse Moroi Kotoji.

Her body was covered with burns and stab wounds, and she was near death. Ebitsuka Koji, you are under arrest."

Two detectives took Ebitsuka away.

"Please, excuse our intrusion," said Detective Suspicious and turned to leave.

"What the hell happened?"

"It's insane. When the hospital closed this evening, the doctor locked up the hospital, tied up a naked Nurse Moroi, and began to horrendously torture her using red-hot metal tongs and surgical scissors. Her confession uncovered the hypocrite Miyake Mokubei. That brought us here. Neighbors reported they heard screams. We rushed to Ebitsuka's hospital and discovered the insanity. We could barely look at the horrific scene. The lawless doctor burned her flesh, spilled a pool of blood, and yanked out her hair. It was not a medical treatment. Fortunately, Bookworm was an army medic with medical knowledge and experience in the storm of war. Perhaps not saving her life might have been better."

I asked, "Was he the murderer in all the murders?"

"If I don't investigate, I won't know," said Detective Suspicious and left.

Kamiyama Toyo eventually sat down.

"Well, that was a surprise. When they came to the dining hall, I thought it was for the hypocrite, you, Miyake Mokubei. I'm red-faced. From yesterday until today, I walked to N-Town to investigate the cheat Miyake Mokubei. In fact, the confession of Nurse Moroi Kotoji was a bit wrong.

"On August 3, Nurse Moroi had a rendezvous with a sugar daddy, newly rich off the black market. Miyake-sensei and Dr. Ebitsuka waited impatiently for Nurse Moroi at their respective inn as men jilted in tragic affairs. During the gruesome torture with red-hot tongs, she lied and gave the name of Miyake-sensei. Moroi-san is a scoundrel with a surprisingly cold intellect. She certainly has the temperament of a major criminal."

Mokubei did not speak. But how long had he exhibited this unexpected hatred of Ebitsuka? He was convinced Nurse Moroi saw this. He's also a coward and a jealous, deeply suspicious, warped man.

I asked Kamiyama Toyo, "Why did you go to the mineral springs inn to investigate me. Were you running around investigating everyone's alibi?"

"Yes, I was. At my core, I'm a lawyer and love this sort of thing. My investigation took me to F-Town. Kazuma-san had an alibi. Tango-sensei's out. He boarded the 12:20 bus, seemed to wander the streets, and waved his hands like he was swimming. Both the conductor and driver remembered this well. But Miyake-sensei, Nurse Moroi was on the first bus, but you weren't."

Kamiyama stared at Mokubei, who didn't engage or answer.

"Dr. Ebitsuka suspected Nurse Moroi and Miyake-sensei. He had grounds for suspicion. Because Miyake-sensei was not on the first bus and took the 12:40 bus to N-Town, the same bus as Dr. Ebitsuka. In other words, Miyake-sensei left the house before 7:30, but where in the village was he until 12:40?"

Mokubei didn't answer or try to. His expression remained the same. Nothing changed. Face pale and distorted, he looked down in shame, like he couldn't bear to listen to the others.

Tango's words dripped with sarcasm.

"Kamiyama-kun, no one recruited you, but being a police informer must have been interesting."

An unconcerned Kamiyama Toyo said, "Ah, ha, ha. While living in the midst of a quick succession of murders,

I would have been disturbed if my detective spirit hadn't been sparked."

When we retired that evening, Eight-Foot Nose and Officer Minamigawa Yuichiro were on watch duty on both sides of the exit downstairs. They were following the order Detective Suspicious gave them last night.

Kazuma said to Eight-Foot Nose, "Thank you for doing this. But aren't we fine, now?"

"How?"

"Well, is Ebitsuka-san in custody?"

"Yes, he is."

"In that case, this level of caution is unnecessary."

"Yes, but headquarters ordered us to stand guard until August 9."

Kazuma felt safe with the arrest of Ebitsuka.

22

AUGUST 9, THE DAY OF DESTINY

Dr. Kose did not return by the evening of August 8. Late that night, the anticipated August 9 began. Eureka's eyes shined as she sat all day in the dining hall where everyone gathered. Eight-Foot Nose and Bookworm kept strict guard in the hallway of empty rooms.

Detective Suspicious joined us for dinner.

"August 8, eight pm? It's all eights. During the war, the superstition was the war would spread. That would have been awful for police like us. Without a doubt, this case expanded, and our reputation plummeted."

A phone call came from headquarters. Detective Suspicious took the call. When he returned, he said, "Well, it appears Ebitsuka-san is giving a grand speech in the holding cell at headquarters. Tonight, a kill-off will unfold in this house. This is Kamiyama's opinion. Tonight, Ebitsuka-san's soul will come to this house. It may be squeezed into a corner somewhere nearby right now.

"Also, Moroi Kotoji-san was admitted to the prefectural hospital and is in serious condition, or it may be hopeless. Her death would be a problem for the authorities. We deeply apologize and are providing treatment. That woman is surprisingly strong-willed, a rarity in this world. That strong will works even while she is unconscious. For the most part, she's delirious and talking nonsense."

This case may not be over after all. I looked at Kazuma's face; he seemed ill at ease again.

Today is the twenty-seventh day since the deaths of Tamon and Kayoko. Tomorrow presents a problem, the first anniversary of Kajiko's death. In an ordinary year, a magnificent memorial service would be held. This succession of murders and the problematic day created feelings of dread among the attendees. Therefore, the memorial service was rescheduled for next year. Only a priest will chant sutras this year.

Kamiyama turned to Detective Suspicious and said, "Yes, that nurse acted as a master criminal. It was creepy when she stared at you with the whites on the bottom of her eyes always showing. At any rate, will something happen on August 9?"

"If I knew that, I would be finished here. It's too bad we don't have the mythical powers or minds like Ebitsuka-sensei's. Kamiyama-san, you conducted a meticulous investigation, but how is your mind's eye? Please, I'd like to hear your thoughts."

"I have a question for you, Dectective. It concerns the estimated times of the murders from the autopsies. Were they absolute?"

"Well, I believe they're fairly reliable but not absolute. Fortunately, in these seven cases, the bodies were quickly discovered. The longest delay was the discovery of Utsugi-san twenty hours after she was killed. Therefore, the estimated times are almost certain, but we're not absolutely sure."

"How was Chigusa-san blindfolded?"

"With the dark blue *furoshiki* wrap she used as a tote. It was folded in half to make a triangle, wrapped around her head, and tied in the back. The triangle covered her face and dangled to her chest. The murderer lowered a rope around her neck and strangled her."

"What does that mean? The murderer was a close and trusted friend and, I imagine, proposed a game of hide-and-seek, blindfolded her, and killed her. That's one possibility."

"That's your theory. We agree she may have blind-folded herself."

Pikaichi's gravelly voice shouted from the side, "What are you saying? During the game of hide-and-seek, a true demon came and strangled her."

Kamiyama blew out air.

"You and a woman of her age go to Mount Miwa to play hide-and-seek."

"No, I couldn't. That's not it."

"The dumb, homely woman, Chigusa, and the hunch-back poet would not do that sort of thing. A hug or a kiss is natural. They could do something so trite. Compared to that, however, a game of hide-and-seek would be impossible. Utsumi-sensei devised a plot and hid somewhere. The true demon went there and killed. What do you think? This is one fantasy, an artistic reality. If this explains all that happened, the murder should be appreciated for its artistry."

Detective Suspicious smiled.

"That's the puzzle. The intuition and imagination of artists sometimes exhibit divine power. That may be true. In borrowing all of your artistic divine powers, there's one thing I wish to tell you. In the first incident, Mochizuki Wani-san's case, the bell from Ayaka-san's shoe rolled under the bed holding the corpse. What do your divine powers say about this?"

"That's it. It's definitely you. Detective, it's her. It has to be. Isn't it obvious?" shouted Pikaichi, with eyes shining.

Ayaka sunk into the depths of terror. Her wide-open eyes stared at the officer."

"Since I came to this house, I never stepped one foot into Mochizuki-san's room."

"As expected, this fox is extraordinary."

Without thinking, Pikaichi nodded.

"The excuse so far is a surprise. Why are you babbling about never stepping one foot in there since coming to this house? This is not a Turkish or Indian harem. The house is filled with ten people in two buildings, isn't it? Upstarts do not know the wider world and say ridiculous things. This sort of tiny house is a harem and napping room for the kitchen staff. During the night, a sensible mosquito walks around and sucks blood in each room and makes fools of the people."

Ayaka's stunning eyes filled with anger and drilled into Pikaichi.

A nodding Detective Suspicious intervened.

"It is as you say, Madam. You definitely did not drop the bell in his room. The reason is Mochizuki-san's Western-style jacket was used to clean under the bed. Also, only one bell fell off."

This time, Kamiyama Toyo nodded.

"That is a curious puzzle. Did the murderer place Ayaka-san's bell there on purpose?"

"Maybe. A bell is a bell, but why was the floor under the bed wiped clean. Everyone, use your divine powers."

No one answered. Detective Suspicious pushed, but no one spoke up.

"One more thing, this is not divine power. I'm open to

everyone's advice, excuse me for saying, but of all the cases, this one is critical. I hope all of you will cooperate. As you know, the ploy of a secret rendezvous was repeated in this case. That is its unique characteristic. The fundamental guess is Utsugi Akiko-san also went to Mount Miwa but not for a rendezvous. If she went for a rendezvous, who was her companion? It's fine to name someone who's not here. I'd like to hear what you think?"

Pikaichi said, "Well, that may be the case. She did not walk aimlessly in the mountains or forests. I'm not being rude, but the police do not recognize the sublime truth of humanity. Utsugi-san was a woman of virtue, deep sexual passion, and should have been loved and respected. An odious murderer killed such a woman with a life full of tears and regrets. Her rendezvous companion could not have killed her because of her custom to move on to the next man in a short time. He may have been obsessive, persistent, and had traces of excessive love for a bad woman, but it was superficial. In fact, she wasn't an obstacle."

Kamiyama could not hold back.

"Ah, ha, ha, ha."

"The painter Doi is a wonder. Only your state of mind is fully explained. However, do not limit a man killing a woman to the meaning of the excessive love of a bad woman and an obsessed man. Although the man falls in love, the woman escapes. The painter Doi said that. As time passes, she moves on to the next man. In other words, wouldn't that grave condition kill her again? A person being killed for that reason is commonplace in this world. Doi-sensei is a horrible man. I don't understand his mental state at all."

"No, what? I'm saying the rendezvous partner did not kill her."

"Then Doi-sensei may have been the rendezvous partner," said Kamiyama Toyo, in between guffaws of laughter.

"But it's fine if she went out to a forest in the mountains for a rendezvous or visited the man's room."

"So she goes to his room under the recent tight security, including detectives on watch. You can't say that. It's a crime. But did she go out to a rendezvous? Is that foundation certain?" asked Detective Suspicious, with uncharacteristic shyness.

"Actually, several items for use in a rendezvous were found in Utsugi-san's handbag. Does a woman like Utsugi-san carry those items all year long?"

"She was a modest gentlewoman. If you're speaking of long ago, … If you cross that line, you'll face seven enemies. This vital modesty is found nowhere in this world. The police can only understand people through lust."

"Oh, I'm terribly sorry," said Detective Suspicious without anger. He smiled and bowed his head once toward Pikaichi.

Dinner ended and the group retreated to the living room.

A sheet of paper was stuck to the center pillar there.

"What is this?" said Tango, the first to discover and examine it.

"Oh no. It has come. August 9, the Day of Destiny. This has become a popular poster lately."

Tango did not look worried, but the rest of us were alarmed.

Kazuma stared at the paper and stood paralyzed. His expression tensed. That made sense. After Ebitsuka's arrest, Kazuma's inner spirit should have been at peace. How could the demon Ebitsuka roll into a fireball, stick up the paper, and hold his breath in some corner?

I noticed Detective Suspicious was scrutinizing each face like his sharp eyes would start a fire.

~

AUTHOR'S NOTE: To date, I've been swamped by solutions from many readers.

As explained each time, Dr. Kose has not deduced the murderer from facts unknown to all. None of you know about the conclusive proof he discovered at his trip destination. However, the doctor deduced this from the facts known to all. The grounds for deducing the murderer include all of Dr. Kose's knowledge that all of you possess.

As for the solution, providing the murderer's name alone is not good enough. The reasoning must enable us to take the case to a court of law and prosecute. The length of the deduction doesn't matter, but please, if possible, do your best to be brief. It doesn't have to be on manuscript paper. Letter-writing paper is fine, but we'd greatly appreciate characters written in clear, standard script.

Address your entry to *Nippon Shosetsu-sha*. On the envelope please write *Detective Novel Solution*.

I apologize for the boasting in these notes. The author's intent is to offer intellectual amusement to all of you. In a damn uninteresting world, an enjoyable game for leisure is a gift at any time, on any day. I simply appreciate washing away the wrinkles from grimacing faces.

Feel free to answer without fear of embarrassment by the heartless publication of convoluted solutions and absurd reasoning.

Dividing the prize would be formidable; therefore, the person having the best solution will receive the prize. On the other hand, if not one solution pinpoints the murderer, I promise the entire prize will be given to the best solution.

If someone's deduction exactly matches Dr. Kose's, that will be a great defeat for the author. Discovery demands far more ability than creation. Without a doubt, the person who writes a clear and correct solution will be Japan's most famous detective. I'm just flattering you. This may prove that no genius like that exists. Ha, ha, ha.

The author's performance is over. Your enthusiastic performance will gain thunderous ovations far and wide.

Deadline: April 15, 1948.

Sakaguchi Ango

23

THE FINAL TRAGEDY

The guards stayed on high alert that night.

I went upstairs in the Western building to see Detective Bookworm standing in front of my room, and a patient Eight-Foot Nose stationed in front of Kazuma and Ayaka's room. Both watched the doors of the rooms from opposite ends of the hall.

Detective Suspicious and Officer Minamigawa were prepared downstairs, including an emergency ladder at the ready, and assessed the situation on the grounds.

Eureka lingered in the upstairs hall, pounced on any of us who went to the bathroom, and became our escort for safety's sake. She took the water for sobering up brought for us by the maid and tasted it for poison.

A grumpy Eight-Foot Nose angrily snatched the cup from her.

"You call me for this."

"To do what?"

"I taste for poisons," he said and held the water in his mouth.

"Oh, all right."

The surprised Eureka-san stared at Eight-Foot Nose with a look that betrayed deep emotion.

"You are so kind. You think that much of me. I should be happy. If that's true, I'll marry you."

Eight-Foot Nose's eyes flashed displeasure.

"Don't be ridiculous. I have a wife."

"What? What difference does that make? I will become your wife anyway. I hate the idea of a mistress. Can't there be two wives? I will adore half of you, but don't get too full of yourself."

"Does that happen?"

"You're so stupid. It's convenient to adore half. I will adore Four-Foot Nose."

"Oh, really?"

"It'll make you happy. Just a bit," said Eureka to a grinning Eight-Foot Nose who pinched her cheek. She pressed forward with confidence.

"Isn't tonight lovely? I'll give you a wedding ceremony this fall in a Tokyo fugu restaurant. You have savings."

"It's nothing to be ashamed of."

"Then it will be fugu. I'll feed you," she said.

An amateur thinks mysterious love affairs and a mixed bag of ghosts and demons of the murdered shyly come out at this time. At four in the morning, a piercing scream sounded on the other side of the door of a love affair. The room belonged to Kazuma and Ayaka.

The sounds came from a desperate fight. Next came the sounds of exhaustion and collapse followed by silence.

Eight-Foot Nose pushed the door. It was locked.

"You two stay here."

He ran downstairs, raised the ladder, and smashed in the window from the outside. He climbed in; Detective Suspicious followed.

The lamp was out. Their flashlights lit the room.

A person lay on the floor. From her bare breasts, obviously, it was Ayaka lying on her back. Face down and doubled over on her was Kazuma.

"Don't disturb the scene. Look for the switch and turn on the light," said Detective Suspicious.

Eight-Foot Nose found and switched on the light.

He tried to sit Kazuma up, but he already died an agonizing death. A cup still containing water was on the desk. A white powder had been sprinkled in the water. It looked like potassium cyanide.

Blood trickled from Ayaka's mouth. As he moved Kazuma to the side to lift Ayaka, her eyes opened.

Eight-Foot Nose asked, "What happened?"

She weakly opened her eyes but did not answer. A memory suddenly seemed to return, and sorrow filled her eyes. She turned her head. When they helped her up, both noticed the blood flowing from her mouth and shivered in despair and fear. They had her gargle and offered first aid, but she had bitten her tongue. The wound was not serious.

Ayaka came to her senses and straightened her collar. She let out a small, hopeless cry when she became aware of Kazuma's dead body beside her.

"What happened? Please try to remember," said Detective Suspicious. He stared hard at her while waiting for her answer. For a moment, she returned the same hard stare.

She asked, "How long have you two been here?"

"We just came in. We heard a racket coming from here, set up the ladder outside, broke the window, unlocked it, and jumped in. What happened?"

Ayaka raised Kazuma's body to his knees, but there was no response. She looked up at the two men as if in prayer. Detective Suspicious shook his head from side to side. Emptiness returned to her eyes. Kazuma's corpse slumped off his knees. She set her hand on the bed to stand and stood thinking for a short time. She walked from the bed and leaned on the desk and the chair to the window. A cool wind blew in through the broken glass. She seemed to calm down naturally.

Dawn came. Ayaka left the window and sat on the bed.

"Was the light on?"

"No, after jumping in, we turned it on."

She nodded.

"My husband stayed up late. When I opened my eyes, the light was on. He was facing the desk absorbed in something. I woke with a start. It was dark, and someone was pressing on my neck. I was shocked and tried to get up. My husband said, 'It's me,' and let go. The force wasn't strong, like he was trying to kill me. I don't know what it felt like but was surprised and managed to sit up halfway. My husband was gentle and hugged me. He said, 'I will die. Please die with me. I'm no good.'"

Detective Suspicious nodded to encourage her.

"I was appalled and asked in what way. Instead of answering, he moaned, 'Uh.'" All of a sudden, I thought he was going to hug me tightly, but he pressed on my neck. I resisted as if in a dream but tumbled over and remember nothing more."

Detective Suspicious nodded.

"Please, think a little harder. Did your husband say anything else?"

Ayaka thought but shook her head.

"Of course. 'Please die with me. I'm no good.' I see. He said it like it had all gone wrong and the police were closing in."

"No, it wasn't like that," Ayaka said. "He didn't say it like that. He said it was already no good. Last evening, my husband came to my bedroom. He was pitifully haggard. Impatient and unable to bear being here another moment, he was frightened. I understood the reason because he saw the threatening paper posted on the pillar in the hallway. My husband believed Ebitsuka-san was the murderer and was relieved when he was arrested. That's why the posted paper was a terrible shock. Anxious and frightened, I felt helpless and went to bed early. Whenever I opened my eyes, my husband was turned to the desk and absorbed in thought."

Detective Suspicious nodded. He began to examine Kazuma's body. The wounds on his face and hands were scratches made by Ayaka when she fought back. His pajamas were torn, and the shirt buttons were ripped off.

Detective Suspicious ended his examination and said, "You were in danger."

"It's better you lost consciousness. If you continued fighting back, you probably wouldn't have come around. Your husband thought you were dead and prepared to kill himself."

"Why?"

"It's distressing, but your husband was the murderer in all of the tragedies so far. We know that but had no physical evidence. Therefore, we could not arrest him."

"You're wrong," screamed Ayaka. "I know it wasn't him. Last evening, when we went to the dining hall, the posted paper was not on the pillar. I am sure because I remember glancing over there. I entered the dining hall with my husband who never left or took one step away until the meal ended."

"That makes sense," said Detective Suspicious and nodded. He looked embarrassed and seemed troubled. "The truth is we posted that paper. August 9, the Day of Destiny. In other words, the day of destiny for the murderer. This cynicism would be known to just the murderer."

Detective Suspicious looked askance at Ayaka, now unnerved, and betrayed a little pride.

The forensics team from headquarters hurried by car and arrived around 10:30. A little after eleven, Dr. Kose returned.

Given the extraordinary event of the extinction of the Utagawa family, I was in a daze in the living room. Dr. Kose flew in from the dining room entry.

"I was overtaken by police cars on the road. After they passed, I recklessly sprinted, but I'm out of shape," he said, panting. Detective Suspicious's police team came downstairs to the dining hall.

"Kose-san, you're back but too late. While you were away, the tragedy ended."

"It's over? Was Utagawa-sensei killed?"

"No, Utagawa Kazuma committed suicide."

Dr. Kose's expression changed to agony. He looked about to collapse from disappointment.

"Damn, I'm too late! I'm an idiot. No sleep. No rest. The failure of a lifetime!"

He was cut by the pain of hopeless regret.

Detective Suspicious smiled and said, "You were quite busy. No sleep? No rest? How sad. But we didn't sleep last night, either. At any rate, you'll come to terms with it."

Dr. Kose's entire body surged with a dreadful rage.

"Dammit! I failed. That was my last chance! Well, it can't be helped. Now, I have no honor but will wipe that smile off his face."

"Wipe the smile off of whose face?"

"The murderer's."

"Utagawa Kazuma-san is dead. He killed himself, "Detective Suspicious calmly said, but Dr. Kose paid no attention.

"Utagawa-sensei was killed by poison?"

"Yes, potassium cyanide."

"Is there a suicide note?"

"No, but during the night, he wrote and erased, and wrote and erased something. It was vigorously erased and cannot be read. Perhaps he intended to write a suicide note. It's been passed to forensics."

Dr. Kose nodded.

"I believe a suicide note was written. I expected this murder. I predicted a suicide and knew preparations had been made. At the time of the first murder, Mochitsuki Wani's murder, Utagawa-sensei's murder had been set up to look like a suicide."

Detective Suspicious was astonished by Dr. Kose's assertion.

"We'll convene in the other room, and I'll explain the technique of the detestable murdering demon."

Dr. Kose urged Detective Suspicious and his team to come with him. The officers reluctantly followed.

24

WILL THE MURDERER EMERGE?

Dr. Kose and the police never appeared in the dining hall for lunch. Eureka appeared when lunch ended and ordered the group to remain there. When the utensils were put down, Nagumo Ichimatsu-san and Yura, Shizue-san, and even Tsubota Heikichi-san and Teruyo, everyone related to the case, streamed in and took a seat. The police and Dr. Kose followed. A dozen or so people dressed in official and personal clothes stood along the walls like they were encircling them. Dr. Kose sat in a chair placed at the head of the table.

Dr. Kose spoke quietly. Resigned sorrow tainted his expression.

"This murderer is a tea master who prefers style. I hoped against hope he would delay the final crime until my return. Because unlike murders committed out of desperation like Chigusa's and Utsumi's murders, the final touches for the final act were prepared before the first murder of Wani and ready to be carried out at any time. Even now, it's not over. I relied on the murderer's confidence. On

August 9, the Day of Destiny, the poster appeared. The murderer used this chance for a splendid finale."

Kamiyama Toyo interrupted.

"Our crowded party has been gossiping for a little while but mostly complaining. Was Kazuma-san murdered, or did he kill himself? Murder or suicide, pick one."

"Needless to say, it's murder."

"Ha, ha. This is bizarre. Who is the murderer?"

Dr. Kose did not answer. For a few moments, he stared at Kamiyama Toyo.

"Kamiyama-san, you are a keen observer. The other day, you deduced the murderer and estimated the probability. Please, repeat that for the fourth incident, Utsumi's killing."

"Like what? Like the night, the painter Doi shouted in front of Ayaka's door. Is the problem the probability after that?"

"No, before that, we were in the living room after eating. Was the time nine something? Yura-sama came with Nurse Moroi and said she couldn't find Chigusa. Then Nurse Moroi said something extraordinary. She said Chigusa-san went on a secret rendezvous. How did she know? Chigusa-san showed her the rendezvous note from a man. Ayaka-san was asked by the man to pass the note to Chigusa-san and read the man's name written on the note. When asked who was that man, she said she couldn't say. And after that ..."

Dr. Kose said no more and encouraged Kamiyama to tell the rest.

"Let me see. My notes should accurately record that," said Kamiyama while consulting his notes.

"Soon after, Ebitsuka-sensei suddenly shouted, 'You idiots,' and left. Then the mortal struggles of the painter Doi and Ayaka-san began."

"What caused that desperate struggle?"

"I'm not sure. There's nothing in my notes. Perhaps the trigger was a petty matter."

Dr. Kose nodded.

"That is crucial. No obvious reason exists because you wrote nothing in your notes. The quarrel was sparked by petty comments. It began with Dr. Ebitsuka shouting, 'You idiots,' and storming off. The painter Doi chuckled and said this house is a nest of abnormal erotic desires, a brothel. Hearing this, Ayaka became indignant and screamed at him, calling him a lowlife, and telling him to go back to Tokyo. This was the beginning of the fight. Then …"

The doctor nodded again at Kamiyama, who nodded back, and said, "That is true. Does the fault lie in the painter Doi's bad mood? Doi-sensei is a bit of a mean drunk. Ayaka-san sprung to her feet and began the mad dash. Her clothes were ripped and torn. Finally, we intervened and broke it up. The two continued screaming at each other as we separated them. I was shocked. Doi-sensei was already in a frenzy and chased Ayaka-san from the dining hall and out to the dark garden.

"We followed them and seized the painter Doi who was slapping Ayaka-san in the shadows of the pine trees. We separated them, but the expected pause did not happen. In the third attack, Ayaka-san fled at full speed into her room and locked the door. Grabbed by men nearby, Doi-sensei continued yelling in front of Ayaka's room until a little after twelve-thirty.

"Utsumi was killed during that time. Starting with the screaming Doi-sensei, alibis were established for the residents of the second floor. Doi-sensei's eyes were playing tricks, and he couldn't go down the stairs. However, Doi-sensei was drunk and didn't remember every detail.

Someone could have gone downstairs and killed Utsumi-san. This business is subtle."

"Who could have been the murderer?"

"Well, both Ayaka-san and the painter Doi."

Dr. Kose nodded. His eyes scanning the party overflowed with intensity.

"This murder may have been planned ten months ago. Perhaps one murderer traveled in disguise to this area. The murderer surveyed every back road going to Mount Miwa and devised a thorough plan. The fact is the murderer grew a beard temporarily during the summer. During that period, he may have traveled to this area and became intimately familiar with the local geography.

"Although the murder was planned in detail, unplanned murders must be committed because of unavoidable circumstances. That was the case for Chigusa and Utsumi. The murderer was scrupulous from the beginning, and anticipated and planned for emergencies. Chigusa's murder was a clean-up operation.

"The killer noticed an unexpected blunder. During that night, Utsumi-san had to be killed, too. Without a doubt, strategies to handle emergencies were planned for events expected from the beginning.

"As planned, the method was executed skillfully. A plan drawn up on a desk often has mistakes. This time, the murderer left a troubled psychological footprint. However, in the plan of a genius murderer, perhaps created with the help of Japan's best psychologists, artists like yourselves did not notice this footprint. I became aware of this footprint much later."

Dr. Kose seemed to breathe in regret.

"Maybe this psychological footprint is a unique footprint left by the murderer in this case. At the critical moment of life and death to the murderer, Utsumi's murder was a unique vulnerability that should be called the turning point. What was this unique footprint left by the murderer? This follows a criminal sequence. Its explanation is predictable. I will begin with the murderer's name."

Dr. Kose's easy calm immediately quieted the trembling of the tense group. He turned to Kamiyama and said, "I asked this before, but who are the most improbable murderers of Utsumi?"

"Ayaka-san and the painter Doi."

Dr. Kose nodded.

"The painter Doi is the most improbable. That was because he screamed constantly at the same spot. His position overlooked all the other doors and was the best place to observe the comings and goings. If a head poked out of a door, Doi-sensei honed in and started raving.

"This kept everyone in their bedrooms. During that time, someone else must have killed Utsumi-san. In other words, Doi-sensei created his own alibi and, at the same time, played a larger role as the watchman.

"While protected by Doi-sensei's clever lookout, Ayaka snuck out of her room and went downstairs, repeatedly stabbed Utsumi-san to death, and went back upstairs. Because she was protected by the lookout Doi-sensei, Ayaka was calm, washed the knife, washed bloodstains from her hands and legs, and quietly returned to her room. Out of fear of some unlikely event, the next morning, she went to Utsumi-san's room to wake him up and discovered the crime.

"In other words, any fingerprints left behind could be conveniently explained away. Before discovering the crime, Ayaka-san could have hidden bloodstained clothes anywhere outside of the rooms in the Western building, or may have worn just her panties to go to kill Utsumi-san, or may have gone out without a stitch of clothes on. At the risk of death, the couple's omniscience and adventurousness took a gamble here."

Pikaichi laughed mockingly.

"The great detective has presented the footprint of a troubled psychology. Hey, Great Sensei, what about the tiny problem of the murderers of eight people? It's different from a farce or *rakugo* performance. Isn't that a strange guess? There's no clear proof, is there?"

Dr. Kose neither blushed nor paled, and he gently nodded.

"I will explain the troubled footprints in order. I'll begin my explanation with the first murder. Perhaps Doi-sensei and Ayaka-san knew Utagawa Kazuma-san fell madly in love when he met Ayaka-san again. Also, the Utagawa family was a wealthy family, rare in this generation. Ayaka-san plotted to divorce and marry Kazuma. In other words, they planned to kill him before she married Kazuma-san. Doi-sensei was especially good at fighting with Ayaka-san and splitting up and persisted in extorting consolation money from her. Creating this seed of malicious discord was one of the most important tools needed to execute this plan."

"Utter nonsense. The great sensei takes charge and instantly not getting along with others becomes proof of complicity in a crime?"

Dr. Kose ignored him.

"Last fall, Ayaka-san married Kazuma-sensei. She explored and reported on the situation in the Utagawa family. She reported everything about the rumors surrounding the suspicious death of Kajiko-sama, Kayoko's mother; and Tamao-san's behavior; and sorted out the situation here. Doi-sensei disguised himself, visited this area to conduct a detailed survey of the geography, and conceived the plan.

"Ayaka-san expertly ensnared Tamao-san and achieved the first three invitations of the three literary sensei: Mochizuki Wani, Tango Yumihiko, and Utsumi Akira. Because these three responded to the invitations, she sent a slightly menacing letter to Kazuma-sensei that intimated Kajiko-sama was murdered. He invited Miyake-sensei and Yashiro-sensei and Kyoko-san. All of this went according to plan. The four uninvited guests, Doi-sensei, Kamiyama-san and Kisona, and me, joined them.

"The hated Kamiyama-san appeared to be as hated as Doi-sensei. That was to be expected given the surprise of uninvited guests. Summoning me, as the amateur detective, added a sense of criminality. This trick was formulated to make the appearance of the out-of-place Doi-sensei seem natural.

"Also, both Doi-sensei and Ayaka-san knew nothing about me. Ayaka-san may have learned of my existence from conversations during meals in the Utagawa home. The luring of an unknown amateur detective was another ingenious machination of the couple. On that same day, the first murder was carried out as planned."

I couldn't see Ayaka-san's face from my seat. However, her solemn expression I glimpsed as she listened to the serious talk reflected no meaning other than a virgin's innocence.

25

THE FATAL ERROR

Dr. Kose continued, "We can't forget the murders began on the day Doi-sensei arrived. This was the most advantageous situation to him, the sole newcomer to this house. Furthermore, only Doi-sensei refused to live on the same floor by declaring his hatred of Ayaka-san and was given the Japanese-style room on the first floor.

"This prerequisite was part of the exacting plan. First, Mochizuki-sensei was killed. He was slipped sleeping medicine and stabbed to death. Wani-sensei was a big man with physical strength, often had relations with Ayaka-san, and was put to sleep to prevent that. Fearing Ayaka-san would be the suspect if sleeping medicine killed him, they adopted an elaborate plan to stab him after drugging him.

"One mistake was putting the sleeping medicine in the geranium. This mistake became the fatal error. This made Chigusa's and Utsumi's murders inevitable and pushed those two into a fatal predicament."

Pikaichi took on the attitude that this had nothing to do with him.

"When the geranium was boiling, the soba noodles were being made in the kitchen. Tsubota Teruyo-san was there as were the observers: Utsugi Akiko-san, Chigusa-san, and Ayaka-san.

"Only Ayaka-san was away from the group preparing meat pies near the location where the geranium was being boiled. The others were in the opposite location a distance away.

"According to the plan, at that time, the painter Doi dangled a rat snake about six feet long, passed under the window of the dining hall, and destroyed the serpent that ate chickens. He cheerfully appeared and chatted about his empty stomach and the evening's side dishes. The plan would have succeeded if everyone stuck their heads out the window to look. The snake-lover Tsubota Heikichi-san jumped out the window to help. Ayaka-san took this opportunity to drop in the sleeping medicine. However, the demon Amanojaku, aka Chigusa-san, lives. The young lady appeared and ignored Doi-sensei's energetic performance; thus, the plan failed miserably. So the desperate murders of Chigusa and Utsumi were unavoidable."

"So Chigusa witnessed the scene where the sleeping medicine was dropped in?" asked Kamiyama Toyo, sounding disinterested.

"She didn't witness the scene. Chigusa-san thought the criminal was Tamao-san. She believed Tamao-san moved the boiled medicine into a flask and cooled it down, and knew it was poured into the boiled kettle, but Tamao-san was killed.

"Chigusa-san had a sudden realization. She ignored the painter Doi's snake charmer and was positioned facing Ayaka-san. Therefore, other than Tamao-san, Ayaka-san was the only other person who moved closer to the boiled medicine. Thus, when she found out Tamao-san was stran-gled, Chigusa-san, who believed without a doubt Tamao-san was the murderer, was shocked. She shouted, 'What? This is very strange. What's going on?' and had an epiphany. That moment made Chigusa-san's murder necessary."

Dr. Kose continued in a calm tone.

"I'll describe the murders in order and return later to Chigusa's murder. Now, I'll start with Wani's murder. Around one in the morning that night, when Utsugi-san visited Wani-san's bedroom, the door was locked. Utsugi-san held the key Wani-san gave her earlier and should have been placed in her room.

"Needless to say, at that time, the painter Doi was in Wani's bedroom. Perhaps Ayaka-san placed a stolen pass key in Doi's room and locked the door from the inside. Utsugi-san showed up when he was about to begin.

"Doi-san ducked under the bed in a panic when Utsugi-san returned. He stabbed Wani-san aiming for his heart to kill him. He may have wiped the knife clean of fingerprints using Wani-san's jacket under the bed out of fear his height or other characteristics could be determined from traces left in the dust.

"After wiping the knife clean, he deliberately left behind one bell from Ayaka's slipper. This was the cunning of a rare criminal. The preparation to make Utagawa Kazuma-sensei's murder look like suicide was embodied in the single bell left behind."

For the first time, the cool-headed Dr. Kose showed a hint of emotion on his face. Although the meaning was different, it resembled the emotion of a connoisseur of the arts.

"As we know, Ayaka-san was asleep in the same room

with Kazuma-sensei. Until around three in the morning, Kazuma-sensei faced the desk. His beloved wife was asleep before him for a long time. In other words, the only person with an alibi that night was Ayaka-san.

"This alibi was the testimony of a husband for his wife; therefore, the police might have doubts. Thus, this alibi did not necessarily hold. However, one person in the world, Kazuma-sensei alone, believed Ayaka-san's obvious alibi and was not suspicious.

"On the other hand, Ayaka-san's bell was in Wani-san's room and left at a place wiped clean. In that case, it was not there earlier but intentionally placed there by the murderer. Ayaka-san became a suspect, but it was impossible for her to be the murderer.

"Kazuma-sensei was not suspicious when he should have suspected everyone as the murderer. His absolute trust was ingeniously established in the first murder. This provided the final measure to kill Kazuma-sensei and make it appear to be a suicide.

"Therefore, in the end, Kazuma-sensei suspected everyone but trusted Ayaka-san. Perhaps he drank the entire drink offered by Ayaka-san with no misgivings. He believed the potassium cyanide recommended by Ayaka-san was sleeping medication and drank it. As I expected, Kazuma-sensei was poisoned."

Kamiyama Toyo asked, "Why didn't you warn Kazuma-san?"

Dr. Kose's face dropped and he said, "I am the stupidest man in the world. I expected Kazuma-sensei would not suspect his beloved Ayaka-san based on a warning from me. I overestimated the murderer. I believed the murderer would not carry out this crime until I returned. But the murderer saw the letter that said last night, August 9, was the Day of Destiny and may have believed I did that and was on my way back. Officer Hirano stuck that paper to the pillar. I'm not complaining. This is not Officer Hirano's oversight. It was all my great blunder."

For a short while, Dr. Kose lowered his miserable face.

26

THE LIFE-AND-DEATH STRUGGLE

Dr. Kose raised his head and resumed talking.

"On to the second murder, Tamao's killing. This was very simple. Tamao-san was dead drunk that day. She vomited terribly then fell sound asleep. From the beginning, the location of Tamao-san's room was perfect, like she was saying, 'Please, kill me.' Her murder was easy work. The painter Doi snuck in, strangled her with the cord of the iron in the room, turned off the light, and left.

"But why was morphine powder spilled? Look at the odd people here, like Ebitsuka and Nurse Moroi. Perhaps he left behind that mischief to broaden the range of suspects. But I can't guess the meaning with certainty.

"This has been straightforward so far. But when Tamao's killing was discovered, Chigusa-san was appalled and suspected Ayaka-san had something to do with the sleeping medicine. At that moment, Chigusa's murder had to be carried out without delay."

The doctor's face showed his enthusiasm. From this point on, the cases piled up. Pikaichi was calm and held his tongue. Like a guileless innocent, Ayaka-san listened carefully.

"As scheduled, Wani-san would be cremated that afternoon. The painter Doi and Ayaka-san met to plan how to kill Chigusa. First, Ayaka-san forged the rendezvous letter from Utsumi Akira-sensei and passed it to Chigusa-san as a message from Utsumi-san.

"To make it believable, when the coffin was sent off, Ayaka-san walked with Utsumi-san to the gate. She probably never imagined Chigusa-san would show the letter to anyone. A beautiful woman loves secrecy in love. However, the homely woman shows off love. The expert Ayaka-san was blinded by her own inclinations and forgot to unravel Chigusa-san's idiosyncrasies. She never dreamed Chigusa-san would show the rendezvous letter to anyone."

I doubted this was true, but somehow had to believe it. But I still didn't think Ayaka-san was a murderer. Dr. Kose must be playing a prank. I couldn't imagine another true murderer could be named. The doctor continued.

"The sutra reading ended at the cremation site, and the fire was lit. We started home around 6:06 in the evening. In the fake rendezvous letter, the meeting would take place between 6:30 and 7:00 behind Miwa Shrine.

"At that time, the painter Doi made various plans. He confirmed the return of the cart that brought the body and immediately incorporated it into his plan. The glib Utsumi-san rode on the cart. Doi-sensei pushed from behind with two youths pulling with great force. They quickly climbed up the valley and disappeared from view.

"When they climbed out of the valley, Doi-sensei stopped pushing the cart from behind. He waited for them to pass further down the road and flew down a side road. He ran at top speed, came out behind Miwa shrine, and chatted with Chigusa-san waiting there. Utsumi-sensei would stroll by later.

"Doi may have proposed a game of hide-and-seek, covered her face with a furoshiki wrapping cloth, and strangled her. He immediately rummaged through her handbag and stole the fake rendezvous letter. This all happened in less than five minutes. He ran, got ahead of the cart, and returned before Utsumi-sensei, who got off the cart before it started up the steep rocky hill. The hunchback's legs were unsteady. He repeatedly rested each leg then walked down a little and took a long time to travel the hill. Meanwhile, Doi-sensei easily got ahead and arrived first at the Utagawa home.

"Doi-sensei officially appeared first in this area but came to the Utagawa home on the third day. He was seen in unfamiliar areas, from back roads to locations usually avoided. This was certainly a part of his well-crafted plan.

"Chigusa's murder went smoothly. Both murderers should have escaped danger. Needless to say, they knew the surprising fact that Chigusa-san had shown the rendezvous letter to Nurse Moroi."

Dr. Kose's explanation of the incidents revealed more and more vulnerabilities. I looked at Pikaichi. He was not concerned about me and acted foolishly and selfishly like this was someone else's problem.

"That night, maybe a few minutes after nine, Auntie Yura and Nurse Moroi came to the living room. Chigusa-san had gone out to her rendezvous around six. Nurse Moroi had seen the letter and knew the man's name. When the painter Doi and Ayaka-san realized that, they were unnerved and had no time for calculations and measured deliberations.

"Unaware of Chigusa-san's murder, Nurse Moroi hesitated to reveal the man's name. However, if another murder were discovered, she would have no reason to remain silent. In that case, the forgery would be uncovered.

"Because Ayaka-san passed the fake letter to Chigusa-san, she would be exposed as the forger. Then the full story would be revealed. To prevent this, either Utsumi-sensei or Nurse Moroi had to be killed.

"All in all, Utsumi's murder was also easy. Although Nurse Moroi hesitated to state the man's name in the living room, she may have leaked it to someone in the main house or recorded it in a diary. In that case, the safest path was to kill Utsumi-sensei within the night. They could not delay and had no time for careful consideration.

"The immediate plan to kill Utsumi had to be arranged. Perhaps this thorough pair decided how to handle this crisis. The fighting, grappling, fistfight, and abuse ended with Ayaka-san fleeing outside. Doi-sensei chased her and was seized. Until the others caught up, they planned to act like they were fighting. In other words, more than the vicious fight we saw and felt, they were engaged in a life-and-death struggle."

Somehow, the majority of us were persuaded. Was Ayaka-san the true murderer? Is what Dr. Kose said so far a joke? It's possible he named the true murderers. Nevertheless, how hard was it to believe Ayaka-san was an actual murderer? Most of us seemed to share that state of mind.

With little regard for our opinions, Dr. Kose continued.

"The two devised and succeeded in a plan to murder Utsumi. They performed a fight as skillfully as in a play. Ayaka-san fled outside at lightning speed. Doi-san chased and cornered her until we caught up with them.

"As explained earlier, in this scheme, the painter Doi played the role of the lookout screaming in front of Ayaka-san's door and lashed out at any head poked out a door. Under his watch, Ayaka-san went downstairs, took a knife from the parlor, and killed Utsumi-sensei. It was an ingenious plan.

"We had no reason to know the two were not at each other's throats but had joined forces to place the murderer Ayaka-san beyond suspicion. Even by Kamiyama-san's reasoning, only she was eliminated as a possible murderer.

"The clever and scrupulous Ayaka-san already prepared for the unexpected incident that night. She convinced the others her habit was to leave her door unlocked on the inside and carefully set up her flight into her room during this crisis as nothing out of the ordinary. In other words, from the time Doi-san arrived, Ayaka-san lived in Kazuma-sensei's room. If she hadn't set this up, she wouldn't have been able to explain her escape to her room in this crisis.

"At first, I doubted her facile explanation for inserting the key on the inside of her door without fail. But when Yashiro-sensei and others asked, Ayaka-san said her carelessness led to her habit of leaving her room door unlocked on the inside. That sounded too glib. A murder with everything planned in minute detail becomes more believable. However, they prepared the murder in detail but had no time to ponder the day's crisis that was a bolt from the blue. Thus, the pair left behind footprints of defeated mental states."

27

THE PSYCHOLOGICAL FOOTPRINT

From the beginning, Dr. Kose talked persuasively about psychological footprints. Psychology is the business of literary types like us. Still, I had no idea what to think. Dr. Kose's response was to look at each of us.

"Perhaps everyone here is an expert who should be called Japan's best psychologist or critic. However, none of you was aware of this footprint. That is not your fault, perhaps the performances of the two murderers were too true to life and left little room for suspicion.

"If I may add another impertinent cause, the murderers reasoned everyone would blindly accept the events at face value. That is, you forgot to doubt and blindly accepted the truth of a conflict between Doi-san and Ayaka-san. This gave birth to the excuse for overlooking the psychological footprint."

The timid city dweller Dr. Kose, who hated pride, looked self-conscious and slightly embarrassed by his statements .

"Both of them expected problems to arise out of the blue and did not delay for a second. They started fighting, stepping on each other's words. The sudden fight was fierce. They slapped. He grabbed and swung her around and threw her down. Ayaka-san ran outside. Their performance was realistic.

"However, I'd like to sketch that night's events again in your minds. Specifically, Hitomi-san, Yashiro-san, Miyake-san, Kazuma-sensei, Kamiyama-san, and I were the men in this room. All of these men were Ayaka's friends and fought to protect her from Doi's violence.

"The night before, when the painter Doi was violent toward Ayaka-san, didn't Hitomi-san, Yashiro-san, and Kamiyama-san stand up to Doi and help her? They did so that evening, too. So much happened, and we expected none of it. Everything happened so fast. He was hitting her and tossing her around. We came to our senses, leaped, grabbed and pulled him away, and thought it was over.

"After being separated, they quarreled a little longer. We were shocked when Doi leaped again at Ayaka-san. She dodged him and fled outside at top speed. This is what I call the psychological footprint. Most of the people who happened to be there were Ayaka-san's good friends. There was nothing outside. There was no ally to help.

"She ran around outside and escaped to the main house. The men in the main house were a sickly old man and an elderly servant. The villagers' homes were over two miles away. The police box was also two miles away. If we met robbers while traveling late at night on these unfamiliar roads, we would probably blindly take off and escape into the darkness. But that night, was it reasonable for her to flee into the dark night where there was no one to help and not towards her many friends who happened to be there? Wasn't she about to be killed?

"She was tossed around before our eyes. She'd been beaten so much her clothes were torn, and blood flowed from her knees. She didn't run to her friends but ran outside into the dark. This is bizarre in human psychology. What compelled her to fly outside where there was no one to help? There must be a reason."

Dr. Kose stopped. Was he embarrassed by his earnestness? In the next moment, he said, "I also have expertise in acting. And that day, I sensed no unnaturalness on their parts. When Utsumi-san's cruel death was discovered the following morning, I finally could suspect Ayaka-san. Utagawa Tamon-sensei and Kayoko-san were poisoned on the same night a week later.

"The events of that day are probably clear in everybody's mind. When Officer Hirano questioned everyone, Ayaka-san accused Doi-san of being the murderer and called him a finger magician. The painter Doi remained calm and stacked Go stones on the side. He said, 'This is a love story of black-and-white fantasies. Behold,' then leisurely displayed his finger magic. When he finished, he argued and said he didn't know when he would be poisoned and didn't want to be in this house. He accused her of being the murderer. 'Who could have poisoned them besides you?' he yelled. I thought that was strange. I was concerned because she was not that sort of person at all.

"On the night of Utsumi's murder, that horrible fight was triggered by a trivial event. However, today the intensity of the animosity is absent from their words. The intensity of malice filling their words is gone, too. Despite the fight, Doi-san is calm and isn't leaping at Ayaka-san. I wondered, Why is this? The mystery of the violence of that fight was revived in my consciousness. My eyes finally sensed the unnaturalness of the impossibility of that psychological footprint when Ayaka-san flew outside into the darkness. Eventually, I saw through to the careful deception by the pair, but it came too late. Was the performance too perfect or the plan too clever?"

As usual, Pikaichi fell into a heavy silence. His silence was not necessarily unnatural. The psychological footprint was deficient somewhere in its decisive persuasive power. Our thoughts and Pikaichi's calm face were bizarrely in harmony and, in short, created a strange, foolish dementia.

Dr. Kose continued.

"Now, to the fifth murder, the poisonings of Tamon and Kayoko. In Tamon-sensei's case, Ayaka-san mixed morphine into Tamon's exclusive sugar pot and added morphine to the pudding. The addition of morphine into the pudding immediately put Ayaka-san under suspicion. First, she put morphine in Tamon's sugar pot and pretended to be unaware of it being put into the pudding. She was prepared. This job was simple and clear. Ayaka-san did not work particularly hard.

"The problem arises with Kayoko's murder. Fortunately, Doi-san's boisterous behavior over consecutive nights chipped more than a dozen coffee cups. A once adequate set of cups became inadequate. The plot was conceived with only one chipped cup mixed in the set. The plan was to kill Tamon-sensei at the same time as Kayoko-san on Kazuma-sensei's birthday.

"Kayoko-san usually did not come to the dining hall. Therefore, her coffee cup had more chips than Doi-san's. Apparently, Kayoko-san was treated like a maid and treated worse than the guests. Doi-san knew this fact and switched coffee cups. By the exquisite feat of finger magic, he put the poison in the cup and offered it to Kayoko-san.

"For this trick to succeed, they needed to create opportunities for the others to poison the coffee cups. This was Ayaka-san's role. Specifically, she chose the time and went to the bathroom with Yashiro's wife. As expected, she knew coffee would be served in the living room and returned upset to the dining hall to say she saw a mysterious figure in the garden from the bathroom window. She lured Kazuma-sensei, Yashiro-sensei, and me to return with her to the bathroom. Others quickly stood, and some joined us to go to the bathroom. A few had to go because dinner was over. Kamiyama-san and Miyake-san went to the bathroom.

"Five or six others had the opportunity to put poison in the cups of coffee set on the table in the living room. If the supporting performance was completed, there should not have been any glitches in the painter Doi's feat of dexterity.

"After nimbly slipping in the poison, he expertly switched his cup with Kayoko-san's. This performance was a grand success. Enraged, Doi-san glared at Ayaka-san and accused her of trying to kill him. Ayaska-san pointed at Doi-san and called him a liar and the murderer because he's a master of finger magic. The great performance of this exchange was also planned.

"Most of the prime targets for murder had been killed. The final target, the murder of Kazuma-sensei, remained, but the nonserial stone in the nonserial murders had to be thrown. Utsugi Akiko-san was selected to be sacrificed and dropped into the basin of the waterfalls to drown. As I said earlier, I verified the truth of the final incident after Tamon's and Kayoko's murders. By discovering the psychological footprint, I deduced the entire story of the incidents without physical proof.

"Thus, I believed I had no alternative but to wait for the next incident to catch the murderer in the act. We could follow Doi-san with the aim of gathering clues about the next murder. Fortunately, Kamiyama-san and Doi-san were passionate gamblers at billiards every day. I also bet on billiards and got in on the action. But I failed again.

"I didn't understand. Because Utsumi's murder was a major incident at an unforeseen critical juncture between life and death, it was a delicate affair and a brush with death. Ayaka-san grabbed a dagger and acted. This was an exception among exceptions. Looking at Kazuma's murder, the last murder, I believe that was Ayaka-san's turn in the nonserial murders.

"I shadowed Doi-san here and believed I understood the start of the next nonserial performance. My brash expectation was ably outwitted. Doi-san secretly promised a rendezvous with Utsugi-san at the waterfall basin at Mount Miwa .

"That day, however, Ayaka-san went to the mineral springs inn. On her way home, she took the back road Doi-san ran down when Chigusa-san was murdered and came out at the waterfall basin. Utsugi-san was waiting impatiently for Doi-san. As Ayaka-san nonchalantly strolled up to Utsugi-san near the basin, she sent Utsugi-san plummeting over the falls.

"Then Ayaka-san ran down the same back road and reappeared on the original road. She immediately returned from the mineral springs as if nothing happened in the beech forest."

28

THE DILEMMA OF PHYSICAL PROOF

His reasoning was striking. He explained the entire story of the nonserial murders and exposed the truth. However, I needed more persuasion. No trace of impudence appeared on Pikaichi's calm, apathetic face, and Ayaka listened intently with a detached look, like an innocent. While Dr. Kose's reasoning persuaded us, we were also persuaded by the murderous couple's blamelessness.

The two persuasive powers maintained a fine equilibrium. In either case, the final persuasive power was missing. Needless to say, the final piece Dr. Kose lacked was the dilemma of no physical proof.

Dr. Kose easily balanced the equilibrium of these persuasive powers and continued speaking matter-of-factly.

"Now, I will move to the final murder. If the outrage between Dr. Ebitsuka and Nurse Moroi had not occurred, the murderer would have expertly used them. Both Ebitsuka-san and Moroi-san even surprised the methodical murderer. That was inevitable.

"If Kazuma-sensei, the owner of this home, cruelly

murdered his father, Tamon-san, he did so without knowing Ebitsuka-san was Tamon-sensei's grandson as we heard from the elderly Katakura-san. The murderer didn't know, too. The unforeseen appearance of this man had great value. If not for Ebitsuka-san's outbreak of madness, he would have played the role of the prime suspect in Kazuma's murder.

"Luckily or unluckily, Ebitsuka-san went mad, attacked Nurse Moroi, and was arrested, so the final act had to return to the first plan. That is, Kazuma's murder made to look like suicide would be carried out as planned. I still haven't examined the scene of Kazuma's poisoning and only know what the police told me. However, I expected this murder more than ten days ago. Just as the deduction has been correct so far, the following deduction will provide the correct solution.

"Perhaps Kazuma-sensei was worried and did not sleep well until this morning. His intense anxiety came from his belief the murderer had to be Ebitsuka after seeing the letter stuck to the pillar in the living room the previous night. He was relieved by Ebitsuka-san's arrest but overwhelmed by the panic engulfing him.

"A sense of doom kept him from sleeping. As dawn approached, Ayaka-san might have suggested he take sleeping medication. Then Kazuma-sensei drank the potassium cyanide and died. That should have looked like suicide. Without proof he killed himself because he was the true murderer, Ayaka-san dressed like she fought his attempts to force her to kill herself and die with him. To reveal Kazuma-sensei's confession of 'I'm no good' to the world, she bit her tongue and acted dazed for a moment. Thus, the murder planned ten months earlier ended with an artful finishing touch."

The composed Pikaichi did not ask one question and

didn't mock his companions as idiots. Dr. Kose's finishing touch had to be challenged and attacked. His unwavering, matter-of-fact tone raised the last challenge.

"I went to Tokyo. After she married, Ayaka-san had the habit of going to Tokyo once or twice a month. She always went with Kazuma-sensei to Tokyo but didn't go around Tokyo with him. The inherent danger kept Doi-sensei and Ayaka-san from exchanging letters. They always met face to face somewhere.

"In order to carry out a meticulously planned murder, being well-informed about everything in advance and creating a detailed schedule were necessary. Consequently, when Ayaka-san went to Tokyo, the two had to meet somewhere.

"I heard obliquely from Tsubota Teruyo-san that Kazuma-sensei and Ayaka-san stayed in their home while in Tokyo. Even if Ayaka-san went out alone, she always returned within the night. She never went out alone and stayed overnight. Seeing that, the meeting place had to be in Tokyo or a nearby city.

"I took photographs of Doi-san and Ayaka-san, returned to Tokyo, and made many prints. I enlisted the cooperation of thirty friends. They went around Tokyo, of course, and as far as Yokohama, Urawa, Omiya, Chiba, and Hachioji to comb the geisha restaurants, cafes, and inns. As a result, the pair's nest was detected in a burned-out geisha restaurant not far from the city center.

"They always met once or twice a month and enjoyed a quiet half day together. The proprietress of the geisha restaurant, a maid, and a colleague of mine, acting as their escort, left Tokyo on the first train this morning. They should arrive here at five o'clock this evening."

Dr. Kose took a piece of paper from his pocket.

"A few minutes ago, I received this telegram from my friend. He notified me of their departure this morning."

Dr. Kose opened the telegram, placed it on the desk, and quietly began to read.

"As planned, the proprietress and maid of Semimaru departed on the first train."

Dr. Kose muttered, "Semimaru. Semimaru. That's the name of the restaurant."

Pikaichi remained calm and did not flush.

A commotion erupted near one wall. Several detectives scrambled to the front. Ayaka-san's chair fell over. She stood and tore at her chest, swayed, and swooned. The detective's arms were too late. She crumpled to the ground and crawled like she was clutching at two or three floor planks. Finally, she collapse and lay motionless.

A doctor mixed in among the detectives came forward to examine her. He attempted artificial respiration on her several times but eventually stopped and stood.

I suddenly remembered and looked at Pikaichi. Five detectives close beside and behind him firmly held and pulled him to his feet. He stared at Ayaka-san's prone figure on the table but, perhaps, could see a part of her.

Pikaichi's fierce glare drilled into Detective Suspicious.

"Take me to her. To Ayaka."

Detective Suspicious had trouble deciding, averted his eyes, and said nothing.

"Detective, do you understand? I want to go to Ayaka. I'm her archenemy. Can't you see? Now I will publicly confirm that Ayaka and I were the murderers."

Detective Suspicious consented with a nod.

"First, let go of my arms. Give me my last taste of freedom."

Pikaichi shook free of the detectives' holds and slowly walked around the table. When he passed behind Dr. Kose at the head of the table, he lightly stroked the doctor's head and gave his parting shot.

"You've done well. The Boy Detective. You have earned a reward."

He kneeled before Ayaka's corpse.

Pikaichi took her hand and stared at her face in death for several minutes. He raised his head and said to no one in particular, "It was stupid. You didn't have to die. There's no reason for the proprietress and maid from the restaurant to come, is there? That evidence will blow away. It was wonderful you had the wisdom to believe in me. But you were too rash. Now, I can do nothing. Your suicide is your confession. I'm a murderer. Very well. From the friendship for a loved one, your husband, Pikaichi, confesses his love. Amen."

Pikaichi held Ayaka's hand with reverence and kissed it for a long time. It was too long. Although a vicious man, Pikaichi's figure conveyed sorrow that pierced the others' hearts.

He released her hand, staggered a few steps, and fell forward. The end had come for Pikaichi.

WINNERS OF THE SEARCH FOR THE MURDERER

Winners for the Correct Solution

First Prize
10,000 yen for the Solution (95 points)
Kataoka Teruo, 5-2559, Kamimeguro, Meguro-ku, Tokyo

Second Prize
5,000 yen for the Solution (90 points)
Akimoto Shusaku, Wakatsuki-mura, Kamiminochi-gun,
Nagano Prefecture
Shoji Kimihiko, Nakamura-cho, Manden-gun, Kochi
Prefecture
Sakai Jun, 1-1, Kawara-machi, Tou-ku, Osaka

Third Prize
2,000 yen for a Close Solution (70 points)
Tanaka Mitsuru, 1-795, Nogata, Nakano-ku, Tokyo

Fourth Prize
1,000 yen for a Partially Correct Solution (50 points)
Murata Motoko, 1-369, Shimoochiai, Shinjuku-ku, Tokyo
Arai Tamotsu, 4-758, Totsuka-machi, Shinjuku-ku, Tokyo
Ooi Hirosuke, 1463, Senzoku, Meguro-ku, Tokyo

MY POST-SELECTION THOUGHTS

Eight letters deduced the correct solution of Pikaichi and Ayaka acting as accomplices in murder. Of these, the deductions of Kataoka-san, Akimoto-san, Shoji-san, and Sakai-san equaled that of Dr. Kose. All were partly right about the method of each murderer and why Chigusa and Utsumi had to be killed. They deduced the full reason for the fight before Utsumi's murder. As for deficiencies, the unnatural events of the shoe bell in preparation for murdering Kazuma and Ayaka fleeing into the darkness outside were overlooked.

In particular, Kataoka-san gave extremely detailed descriptions for all other instances, and one part was flawless. His solution surpassed the other three and took first place. The other three were hard to tell apart.

I promised a prize to the top winner, but four solutions were right. I couldn't bear to throw away the other three. As the author's defeat penalty, I paid 5,000 yen each to the other three. However, the author was delighted to pay this defeat penalty. I was truly happy they figured out intricate points.

The third-place winner, Tanaka-san, gave an accurate account of the need to kill Utsumi-san, but the method of each murder could not be said to be correct. One part was far off the mark. Compared to the other four, it failed. The examination of the details was inadequate. However, he deserved to be paid something for defeating the author.

The fourth-place winners, Murata-san and Arai-san, and Detective Ooi Hirosuke, who was Four-Foot Nose and my sole challenger, named the correct murderers but were far off target on the details. The author did not feel this prize reflects my defeat but my deep respect for their unearthing the murderers.

Like Detective Ooi Hirosuke, the discovery from the conceptual argument of the inheritance problem as the sole motive for the murders was only used in a formulaic interpretation for one type of detective novel and not deduced from the specific facts. Therefore, the interpretation of the details was chaotic, and the sole merit was naming the murderers.

In my opinion, perfect reasoning by four people over each detail identical to the reasoning of Dr. Kose was not a proud moment for me. They were able to get it right. The conventional formula of a detective novel is not a problem. A detective novel must be rational.

Human nature is warped unreasonably and irrationally and causes unimaginable behaviors. That makes it unreasonable to speak of a rational solution. Not only in Japan, I believe ninety-nine percent, no, about ninety-nine percent of detective novels in the world are irrational.

Many solutions that named the wrong murderer used the process of elimination. Different from a true crime, if thirty people appear in a detective novel, the murderer must be one of them. Therefore, the process of elimination is believed to be the most convenient and effective technique. When limited to the process of elimination, the murderer is not necessarily found.

In other words, the trick in a detective novel is to use the process of elimination and design for its failure when it is the sole device to deduce the solution. According to the process of elimination, the person with the perfect alibi is no longer the murderer but is the true murderer. That's the trick. The detective novel is exquisite. But most conventional detective novels find this trick impossible. Therefore, human nature is warped. Irrational behaviors and mental states are forcibly fabricated. Both the authors and the readers swallow detective novel tricks with zero skepticism.

When I was a junior high school student, I was impressed by a short detective novel I read by Sato Haruo. The title escapes me. Some fellow lost the book. A friend who was knowledgeable about psychology was looking for the book. When the fellow who lost it first took the book and left, he needed to make a trip to the bathroom. As he descended the stairs from the second floor, he placed it in a dark place like a beam in the wall, then he went to urinate. People often forget what they were about to do when they go to the bathroom. He remembered sometime later but never found the book.

My rationale for criminal psychology is an accurate sketch of human nature. I love reading detective novels. Each time human nature and rationality are betrayed. A dazzling serious murder case unfolds, and deducing the murderer becomes complicated. I thought I'd like to write a completely rational and human detective novel. The human rationality of the detective novel was taught to me by the novellas of Sato Haruo-san.

In that sense, I think four people sending in perfect solutions is proof I achieved my objective, and I am happy.

Who could have guessed the first letter I pulled from

the mountain of solutions would be the correct solution by Akimoto-san of Nagano? Because the correct solution was immediate, I was shocked. This was no good. Then I looked at three more letters. The third letter was the correct solution by Shoji-san of Kouchi. This was bad and got worse. I thought fifty or sixty people may have guessed right. Unluckily, one-third of the first ones I read were correct. I was a little shocked by each one.

The author of the best solution was the actor Kida Michio of Morikawa Shin's troupe. The author felt kicked in the shin by the unthinkable point of view of contemporary detective novels from an unprecedented way of thinking.

It began with the position that Shizue was Utagawa's servant, a rare beautiful woman, the princess Shizue, served in the Utagawa's house. While she became the maid to the old man Tamon and attended to him, when bored, she read a novel selected from the detective novels from all ages and places on Tamon's bookshelf. Poisonous blood in the innately murdering demon was aroused. She thought about the tragedy of blood night and day. This is the origin of the nonserial murders. The circumstances to carry this out are built into an old-style elegant story.

This wonderful work caught me by surprise. I deeply thank all who presented enthusiastic solutions and who read with pleasure.

Sakaguchi Ango

ABOUT THE AUTHOR

Sakaguchi Ango was a novelist, essayist, and critic on topics of farce, *koun ryusui* in Zen Buddhism, divine enlightenment, absolute loneliness, rakugo performers, and visiting great historical sites.

He was a dissolute writer of the *Buraiha* (Decadent School) of post-war Japan. His debut work was the novella *Kogarashi no Sakagura kara* published in 1931. His notable works include *Kaze Hakase, Nihon Bunka Shikan, Darakuron, Hakuchi, Sakura no Mori no Mankai no Shita, Niryuu no Hito,* and *Furenzoku Satsujin Jiken.* He received the 1948 Nihon Suiri Sakka Kurabu-sho, an award for mystery writers, and the 1950 Bungei Shunju Dokusha-sho, an award from the readers of the magazine *Bungei Shunju.*

He was born Sakaguchi Heigo on October 20, 1906 in Niigata, Niigata Prefecture, Japan, and died February 17, 1955 in Kiryu, Gunma Prefecture, Japan.

CREDITS

Japanese source text:
Aozora Bunko. Sakaguchi, Ango. "Furenzoku Satsujin Jiken," *Japanese Novels*, Vol. 1, No. 3 - Vol. 2, No. 7, August 1, 1947 - August 1, 1948 (in Japanese). Accessed September 9, 2016.
Input by: kompass
Revised by: Asato Tsutomu
https://www.aozora.gr.jp/cards/001095/card42626.html